Through Her Eyes

Beth Kery

An Ellora's Cave Publication

www.ellorascave.com

Through Her Eyes

ISBN 9781419966873
ALL RIGHTS RESERVED.
Through Her Eyes Copyright © 2009 Beth Kery
Edited by Ann Leveille.
Photography and cover art by Les Byerley.

Electronic book publication April 2009
Trade paperback publication 2012

With the exception of quotes used in reviews, this book may not be reproduced or used in whole or in part by any means existing without written permission from the publisher, Ellora's Cave Publishing, Inc.® 1056 Home Avenue, Akron OH 44310-3502.

Warning: The unauthorized reproduction or distribution of this copyrighted work is illegal. Criminal copyright infringement, including infringement without monetary gain, is investigated by the FBI and is punishable by up to 5 years in federal prison and a fine of $250,000. (http://www.fbi.gov/ipr/)

This book is a work of fiction and any resemblance to persons, living or dead, or places, events or locales is purely coincidental. The characters are productions of the author's imagination and used fictitiously.

The publisher and author(s) acknowledge the trademark status and trademark ownership of all trademarks, service marks and word marks mentioned in this book.

The publisher does not have any control over and does not assume any responsibility for author or third-party Web sites or their content.

THROUGH HER EYES
ɞ

Author Note

Dear Reader,

Through Her Eyes was the first book I ever submitted for publication. It's been interesting for me to revise this edition for Ellora's Cave. *Through Her Eyes* contains many of the plot elements that I've come to use and love—the atmospheric, haunted nineteenth-century mansion contrasting with the modern, urban setting of my hometown, Chicago; suspense with a touch of paranormal light; and of course, two lovers who are destined for one another. Not to mention flat on their butts in love and lust. I hope you enjoy!

Chapter One

Claire settled into bed and stared at the book dubiously — *Dreams, Prophecy and the Future* by Sebastian Fortescue. She'd found it in Aunt Isabelle's extensive library earlier this evening, wrapped in one of Isabelle's expensive, luridly pink, Estée Lauder-scented scarves to highlight it on the shelves. A note tucked inside the cover read:

Dearest Claire,

This is the book you're looking for. Good luck, my skeptical little seeress. When you finally accept what you are you'll know what it is to exist on the knife's edge of desire and doubt. Choose desire, darling — even if it seems to threaten not only your life but your very sense of self. Perhaps if you do, more than one of us will be redeemed.

Claire's eyes stung. Isabelle had only been dead for six weeks. Seeing her handwriting and smelling her scent made her feel as if her aunt stood beside her. Knowing she'd never see her again sliced deep.

The message admittedly freaked Claire out a little. It also totally confused her. That was Isabelle for you, always the walking, talking fortune cookie. But given the intensity and disturbing nature of her dreams recently, Claire didn't feel like she had a choice but to go forward with her plan.

Besides, Isabelle's death had created a profound attitudinal shift in her. For the first time in her life her psychic abilities didn't feel like a curse. They felt like a heritage, part of Isabelle's legacy to her.

It was time to stop running from the truth. Her dreams had escalated from being merely disturbing to downright terrifying ever since she'd inherited Isabelle's Hyde Park mansion. Claire'd had enough bizarre, suffocating dreams with allusions to a sexual voyeur and hints of even worse...disturbing things. She'd always had random moments of psychic knowledge but her true forte was the precognitive dream. Her special dreams almost always came true.

Almost always. That was what she needed to remember.

Claire certainly didn't want *any* part of her most recent dreams to come true and she was determined to make sure they didn't. Yes, she was a novice at this paranormal nonsense, but maybe if she became more proactive in seeing a vision...maybe there was a chance she could do something to change the future?

She had to try. Her excuses about being a scientist and not believing in psychic phenomena wouldn't hold up in this instance. She had to take some responsibility, didn't she?

Why did I have to wait until after you were gone to finally listen to you, Aunt Isabelle?

She opened the book and began reading intently.

An important delineation must be made between psychic awareness that is intentional and psychic awareness that is random. Intentional psychic knowledge is attained when the psychic holds a certain purpose in her conscious mind and then opens a channel to the unconscious or universal mind via a trance state. In some cases psychics are able to gain knowledge through lucid dreams. The psychic consciously asks a question or focuses on a certain topic, then utilizes a dream state to acquire knowledge. It should be noted, however, that the dream state is more intense and unpredictable than most trance states, as it is closer to the unconscious, universal mind. As a result, some have suggested that dream states are more difficult to control than the trance state.

During random psychic incidents, circumstances such as the emotional intensity of the event, personal relationships and the strength of the psychic's ability combine to force knowledge upon the psychic even when it does not seem to be her conscious will. There are various exercises and visualizations that the psychic may complete that will assist in blocking unwanted information, thus protecting the psychic from unpleasant, harmful or malignant influence.

Claire rolled her eyes impatiently when she read the part about malignant influences. What was that supposed to mean—ghosts, demons, monsters in dark closets?

She went on to read the exercises that were included, both for protection from undesired stimuli and for the induction of trance, and was forced to give Sebastian Fortescue a begrudging nod of respect. The suggestions weren't that different from the relaxation, stress management and visualization exercises she used in her private practice as a psychiatrist to help people with issues like chronic pain, a desire to stop smoking or just highly stressful lifestyles.

She lay back in bed and began to focus on her breathing, just as Mr. Fortescue recommended. The book had suggested that she hold a specific purpose in her mind. Claire mentally floundered, wondering what her focus should be. She just wanted to experiment to see if it was at all possible to control any of her psychic ability. She didn't think she was ready to find out why she kept dreaming that she was side by side with a man who she had a sickening suspicion was worse than just a sociopathic sex deviant.

A relatively safe compromise occurred to her.

Let me see whatever it is I most need to see.

She wasn't aware of crossing the line between meditation and sleeping vision but suddenly she found herself walking down a darkened hallway. She glanced down and saw her bare feet on top of the oriental carpet she knew ran down Isabelle's—now her own—downstairs hallway. Her hands swept over her waist and hips. She was wearing a short satin nightgown.

The nightgown I was wearing when I went to sleep.

The realization made her reach up and touch her face and then her arms. She felt solid and warm. She must be awake. Somehow she'd left her bed, come downstairs without remembering.

Her fingers brushed across the delicate filigreed silver and turquoise bracelet that Isabelle had given her right before she died. The metal felt cool when she pressed it to her wrist. She vividly recalled taking it off and setting it on her bedside table before getting into bed. The realization that she was sleeping caused the world around her to shimmer and then solidify abruptly.

She gasped. It was as if she'd just seen reality form and lock into place before her very eyes.

Keep going. Don't be afraid. This is the power of conscious dreaming.

"Aunt Isabelle?"

The dense, gravid silence seemed to swallow up her shaky query. Despite those reassuring words a prickle of fear raised the hair on her arms. The huge old house seemed alive around her, full of secrets...menacing. She looked back uncertainly toward the grand staircase.

Something was wrong.

The air around her pulsed with energy. Her senses were sharper than they ever had been in a precogitive dream. She realized that her eyesight, even here in the shadowed hallway, was preternaturally acute. And her hearing...

Even as she thought it she became aware of the sounds of people in the house. Panic swelled in her breast before she reminded herself that she was dreaming. Voices and laughter emanated from behind the doorway to the left of her. The entrance led to the game room in the basement. Claire heard the faint click of a cue striking a billiard ball and rock music.

Her brow furrowed in confusion. She lived alone.

Was this what she was supposed to see? She reached for the door. Her hand fell to her side as courage failed her.

She had no knowledge of the rules of this lucid dream world. She didn't want to take the chance she'd be marching into some future party wearing nothing but a short, clinging nightgown. She sent a stern mental command to her sleeping self to remember to wear less revealing nightwear to bed.

Before she knew what she intended she stood at the library door. Perhaps it made sense that she would go to her favorite room in the house to console and soothe her mounting fear and anxiety.

Let me see whatever it is I most need to see, she repeated the mantra in her mind.

When she opened her eyes she was inside the library. Her desire was apparently her mode of transportation in this strange world instead of her feet. Maybe Aunt Isabelle was trying to show her a different book that she should read?

A slight rustling noise reached her sensitized ears. She wasn't alone in the room. She exhaled shakily, a strained substitute for a scream. A fire leapt in the hearth. She glanced out of the two large bay windows. Snow blanketed the ground and shrubbery.

So. It was winter in this future world.

He sat in one of the armchairs that flanked the fireplace. His elbows rested on his long legs, his head rested in his hands. His posture communicated a sense of profound fatigue.

Or sadness?

Claire couldn't be sure. She moved forward. Could he see her? She leaned against the corner of the leather couch, watching him with growing fascination. He seemed vaguely familiar to her but she couldn't pinpoint where or when she'd seen him. His dark hair looked thick and silky where it fell across his hands. If she reached out to touch it, would she actually feel the soft texture?

Her fingers itched with a desire to try.

She started when he abruptly sat back. Her eyes widened in alarm, thinking that he would see her. But he showed no awareness of her despite the fact that his eyes were trained somewhere just to the left of her location. She swallowed thickly.

She didn't know him after all. But God, she wanted to…in every conceivable way. She blinked in vague surprise at the thought and the accompanying strong sexual response of her body. What an erotic dream, to be able to view this beautiful man at her own leisure without him even being aware of her.

Her nipples pulled into tight painful points, even the soft fabric of her nightgown abrading them. She vividly pictured him pinching the sensitive crests while he studied her face for a reaction. The image carried the familiarity of a memory and yet was excitingly new to her. Her thighs clamped together to alleviate the sudden pinch of pleasure at her pussy.

All of that—just from looking at him and imagining him touching her.

"Who are you?" she whispered raggedly. But of course he didn't respond. Claire understood she was an observer to this future event, a mere ghost.

He wore only a pair of faded jeans. Her gaze trailed with slow fascination over well-defined shoulder and arm muscles covered in smooth, dusky skin. The sight of his rounded pectoral muscles gave her an almost uncontrollable craving to sink her teeth gently into their denseness at the same time that she scraped her long fingernails over one of his dark brown, erect nipples. The way his torso slanted to a trim waist and ridged, hard abdomen was pure art.

Her gaze lingered at the top of his jeans. She imagined sliding the tip of her tongue just beneath the denim and tasting his smooth skin. Her eyes widened when she examined the fullness at his crotch and left thigh.

Impressive. And he didn't even appear to be aroused.

Heat suffused her face, belly and pussy. God, she was suddenly one hundred percent wanton because she even felt her ass tingle with sexual energy. Sebastian Fortescue had failed to mention the effect of the lucid dream on her libido, apparently.

No reason to be concerned. It was a dream, not reality.

Not reality yet anyway.

But through her growing sexual tension there still existed an unformed, poisonous sense of unease. Something definitely was wrong. Something was going to happen.

She needed to warn this man. That's what she'd come there to do. The realization galvanized her into action.

She moved quickly around the couch and stood in front of him.

"*Hey!*"

She waved her hand in front of his face frantically. "Hello, is anybody home?" she called loudly. But he just stared past her, oblivious, cocooned in a shell that she couldn't penetrate.

Claire studied him with a growing sense of both awe and dismay. Now that she stood closer she clearly sensed his desolation. She almost saw a blackness surrounding him…not an aura of evil or malignant intent but instead the barrier of suffering. She'd seen the veil before with her patients but never so clearly.

His loneliness and despair reached out to her even across the barrier of time.

She studied him more acutely, still plagued by a sense of familiarity. His hair looked black in the darkened room. His skin was olive-toned and smooth—incredibly erotic-looking in the flickering light of the fire. He was a big man. The armchair didn't seem to quite contain him. His facial features were masculine and bold yet finely drawn. A well-trimmed, dark goatee framed full, sensual lips that were pressed into a grim line.

Claire felt compelled to touch him, to reach him. Her need to do so grew until it was mandatory. It was not an acceptable option for him to remain cut off from her. She had to reach him. She *must* forge a connection. She had to penetrate his prison of solitude. She needed to form a conduit between them.

But how?

Maybe her unusually potent sexual attraction to him held the key? Why not use it to facilitate the psychic connection between them?

A log popped loudly in the hearth, making the man's gaze shift to the fire. Claire concentrated deeply, weaving reality with the threads of her desire. Before she could doubt herself she reached out and touched him.

Her fingertips made contact with his lower lip. Her breathing halted. Her fingers trembled, bringing her into further contact with the alternating roughness and softness of his flesh. His heat.

She watched, her eyes wide in trepidation. He'd gone completely still. His gaze moved slowly from the fire and locked directly on her face. Claire struggled to inhale but to no avail.

Maybe forging a connection with him hadn't been such a great idea after all.

God, why hadn't she noticed his eyes before? They were obviously his most striking feature—the eyes of a predator, a beautiful, sinuous animal but a hunter nonetheless. The fact that they were unexpectedly moist with emotion left her feeling even more overwhelmed by their impact.

She felt pinned by that scorching gaze.

She stood so close she felt like she could reach down into him. His light eyes were a bold contrast to his dark hair and skin. They glowed like silvery crescents in the fire-lit room. She watched, mesmerized, as the long, dark lashes blinked once. Twice. Amazement overcame her.

He could *see* her. And he obviously didn't trust what he was seeing.

He suddenly grasped her upper arm in a vise-like grip. A small sound of anxiety leaked past Claire's lips. He squeezed, as if experimenting at the unexpected sensation of soft, female flesh in his hand. A thrill went through her at his touch.

"It's okay. Please, it's okay. I can't believe you can see me."

She wasn't sure that he'd even heard her though. He stood to his full height, his body gliding slowly against the length of her. When he finally straightened he towered over her. His hands reached for her clumsily and Claire realized he was unsteady.

"*Claire?*"

She mentally reeled in confusion at the fact that he knew her name. His voice had sounded shaky with disbelief.

Her senses were pitched so exquisitely that her being itself seemed to reside not in her head but just beneath where his hands touched her upper arm and lower back. Consciousness no longer meant rational thought, only sensation. She felt the electrifying glide of his fingertips and opened palm, the rasp of the fabric of her gown as he stroked her. He pressed her hip, drawing her closer.

A painful need suffused her as she watched his mouth lower.

He took her like he was a starved man and her mouth was an unexpected succulence that had magically appeared before him just as he was about to concede death. It was consumption as much as a kiss.

Claire's nostrils flared like an animal's inhaling the scent of its mate. A strange sensation came over her, like she was falling, but not into space. Into *him*...into the essence of desire.

Her mouth and tongue became as wild and hungry as his. She grasped a handful of silky hair at the back of his head and increased the pressure of their already intensely carnal kiss.

Her action seemed to awaken something primal in him. A low growl emanated from his throat. He bent her over his arm, forcing her to arch her back, crushing her breasts into his chest. The big hand that held her at the hip stretched, his fingers curving into her ass. With a tensing of his biceps and a flick of his wrist he brought her fully to him, grinding his thick arousal into her soft, harboring cleft. Their groans of pleasure entwined. His lips moved over her, devouring her, his mouth hot and demanding on her lips, throat, ears and neck.

"You won't leave, Claire," he muttered angrily into her neck between hot open-mouthed kisses, scraping his teeth against her sensitive skin. "You're mine. You will *not* leave me."

Claire cried out, confused by his words but aroused at the sensation of both of his hands palming the backs of her thighs and sliding upward, bringing her nightgown with them. He firmly grasped both cheeks of her ass and flexed his fingers possessively, molding her flesh to his palms in a bold, proprietary manner that made liquid heat surge from her core.

With an abrupt motion he hooked his thumbs into her silk panties and drew them down to her thighs. His hands were back on her bared ass in a second, massaging both buttocks almost roughly before running a finger down the crevice.

"I want your promise."

He raised his head and stared down at her, compelling her to meet his gaze. She gulped back her desire. He was a complete and utter stranger to her but he was making tiny, erotic circular motions over her asshole.

She'd never let a man touch her like that. The effect was electric. She felt moisture trickle from her pussy to her clenched thighs. He stared hawk-like, apparently waiting for a reply. She wanted to answer but what could she say? She wasn't *his*. She didn't even know him. She would leave him the second that her brainwaves altered and she slid out of the dream—kicking and screaming in protest all the way, no doubt.

"I-I would not willingly leave you," she finally whispered truthfully.

His gaze grew fiercer. A cry slid past Claire's lips when she felt his other hand move down her cleft and a long finger slid into her wet slit.

"Oh God," she moaned at the pleasure as he stroked her higher, then inserted a second finger and flexed his biceps, powering into her until her vision blurred.

"That's not good enough, Claire. I want your promise."

Claire began to rock on him in mindless arousal, grinding her clit against his dense erection, circling her hips instinctively to both map the shape of his cock and pleasure herself. The slurping sound of his fingers driving into her wet pussy reached her ears, making her more frantic. "I don't even…I'll try not to leave you. But how can I promise that?"

"Desire it with all of your being. Make it a desire so great it can't be denied," he replied with a small, grim smile. "Wish it, Claire. Want it." He watched her steadily as her facial muscles tightened with arousal and he continued to finger-fuck her high and hard, rubbing a place that caused her eyes to roll back in her head.

"Say it. Promise me."

"Oh!" Her breathing came faster and with increasing irregularity as he built the friction in her to the point of eruption. She bucked her hips wildly against his fingers and the steely pillar of his cock that was becoming more and more delineated as it strained against his jeans.

He stopped moving his fingers abruptly. Claire cried out in protest.

"You haven't said it."

He stilled her bucking hips with one strong hand and moved back slightly, depriving her of the pressure of his cock against her clit. Claire thought she saw his jaw harden at the abrupt cessation of her rubbing against him like a cat in heat but his hand remained steady and his eyes resolute.

She stared at him, more in bemusement and dazed arousal than actual protest of what he wanted. Her eyes widened when she felt him remove his fingers from her pussy, slide along her perineum and press to her rectum. She'd soaked him with her juices but Claire wasn't accustomed to being touched there. She stiffened in his arms.

"Take it." His voice sounded rough with arousal, insistent but also strangely soothing. "You belong to me. All of you. You know that. Don't resist me."

Claire moaned deep in her throat and shut her eyes at the surge of desire that crashed through her. She bit her lip hard, stopping herself from coming at just the stimulus of his words. So possessive. So demanding. Claire wasn't into submitting to men. She wanted equality and respect in her relationships.

And...safety.

The thought made her eyes spring open wide, because she did feel safe with this man. Safer than she ever had in her life, despite the fact that the feelings he was evoking in her were so incendiary that they might destroy the very concept of who she thought she was.

He held her gaze as he pushed down on her hip. Claire took the hint and pressed against his finger. He penetrated her slowly to the knuckle. A puff of air burst out of her lips. He said nothing but she read the stark need in his preternaturally light eyes.

"I promise that I won't leave you," she whispered as he proceeded to slide in and out of her ass. Her soul felt like it was laid out bare before him, utterly vulnerable but pulsing with a life force she'd never before experienced. Her heart skipped one then two beats when he smiled.

Lord have mercy on her he was beautiful—his smile a brilliant light that she would never have expected could have radiated from such a dark, desolate spirit. A deep dimple dented his right cheek. He palmed the side of her neck and held her steady for both his piercing stare and penetrating finger.

"That's what I wanted to hear. Unclench your ass cheeks, baby. You're making this harder on yourself. Relax. Let me in."

Claire breathed out slowly and relaxed. As she succeeded, the nerves all along her sacrum, nerves that she hadn't even known existed before, delicate branches of sensation that ran from her anus to her pussy to her clit, began to tingle with newly awakened energy as he continued to stimulate her. Her lips fell open and she groaned softly. His smile was gentle and cherishing even as he began to finger-fuck her asshole more deeply, all the while watching her like he found the sight fascinating.

"There. That's better," he murmured, almost as though he was talking to himself. His thumb tenderly brushed her jaw. "I can feel you letting go. Your cheeks are getting pink. If I bared your breasts right now they would be blushing too, wouldn't they? Your nipples would be hard, sweet, ripe berries just begging to be eaten. Your lips are getting red. You know I love that about you—you can never hide your desire. So tempting."

He lowered his head and caressed her lips with his own. He paused there for a second, both of their mouths open, sharing their breath, not kissing really, just scraping and rubbing their lips together. Claire groaned into his mouth, aroused by the erotic contrast of his lips savoring her flesh with featherlight caresses while he pounded his fingers into her ass with increasing force, his palm making erotic slapping noises against her buttocks when he penetrated fully.

Her hips had begun to move in counterbalance to his strokes as a primitive, powerful friction grew in her. She cried out as her pleasure mounted.

"You tell me where the blood flows thickest and hottest while I finger-fuck your little ass, baby," he coaxed in a whisper against her seeking lips. After a few seconds of hearing only her gasping breath he smiled against her mouth and rubbed his fingertips against the side of her neck.

"Answer me, Claire, or I'll punish you. It wasn't a rhetorical question."

She tried to ignore the spurt of warm liquid that flooded her pussy at his sensual threat. Even though she knew the answer to his question she hesitated. She wasn't used to speaking of such things out loud. She felt her heartbeat in just that part of her anatomy, each pulse causing an exquisite pinching sensation of pleasure that verged on pain at being left unattended.

If it wasn't assuaged soon she would go mad.

"My clit," she finally whispered.

His nostrils flared with arousal. "It'd be erect and dripping if I dropped to my knees right now, wouldn't it?"

Claire's eyes rolled back in her head. He couldn't continue to do this to her. She had been riding the crest of orgasm for the past few minutes now while he teased her with his deep voice and the highly intimate penetration of her body. He seemed to know just how to keep her skimming along the wave without lessening her pleasure or tipping her over into the depths of relief. It was torture and it was killing her but she'd likely beg on her knees at some other time and place for him to do it to her again.

"Claire?"

"Yes, God, *yes*, I'd probably explode if you just breathed on me," she admitted. She felt him pause for a second at her honesty. He began to finger-fuck her ass with a new, slightly upward motion.

"Oh!" She cried out at the slight discomfort of the new angle.

"Down." He pressed on the back of her head until her cheek rested on his hard biceps, forcing her to bend over. He moved to the side of her body and resumed his deliberate penetration of her ass. The new angle was divine. Claire keened with pleasure.

"Would you rather I dropped to my knees and serviced your clit until you exploded in my arms, or would you like it if I bent you over that couch right now and fucked your sweet little pussy? You decide."

"I would rather you fucked me," she moaned against his hard biceps.

"Are you sure?" he asked, his tone sounding amused, almost casual to Claire's ear. He enjoyed teasing her. The knowledge strangely aroused her even more. "It will delay your orgasm, perhaps. You may cool slightly in the interim."

"I need to feel your cock inside me."

She thought of how he had felt when she'd been rubbing against him awhile ago. She'd never felt a cock like his—so deliciously thick and long. All of that tumescent male flesh, just for her. She gasped when he withdrew his plundering fingers.

"I need to taste you even more. Raise your gown and spread your pussy lips."

She panted raggedly and her thighs quivered as she stood up and did what he'd demanded. He dropped to his knees without looking at her face. His hands slid up her thighs and onto her hips and ass, holding her steady.

He paused, his mouth just inches from her clit, and studied her. Then she saw him inhale slowly and knew he luxuriated in her scent. A sharp pain of need twanged through her clit.

Claire began to tremble uncontrollably at the sensation of his whispering breath. But she screamed full throttle when he placed his whole mouth over her clit and ran his tongue over her clit with hard, relentless strokes. Her hands gripped mindlessly at his head for balance as her world dipped and rolled and shattered anew with each fresh jolt of pleasure.

He refused to pause in his actions even though her knees almost collapsed from under her. He palmed her ass, his arms accepted her weight as he suckled firmly and lashed her clit with his tongue. He was so strong, and his control over her was so absolute, that he pressed her body rhythmically against his mouth as she came, playing her like he was a skilled musician and she his beloved instrument. He kept her there, not allowing her to move until he had patiently milked every last shudder of orgasm out of her.

Claire slowly began to regain control of her body again but still he continued to rake his tongue along her clit and slide up and down over her swollen labia. She could almost sense his anticipation when he lowered his mouth, pressing his entire lower face to her pussy. He dipped into her thickly creaming slit for the first time.

"Christ you're sweet," he muttered before he plunged deeply and moaned, vibrating her with his waggling tongue. He began to tongue-fuck her, slowly and deliberately. On his downstrokes he suckled and swallowed before he plunged into her soaking channel again.

She scrunched her eyes shut as emotion flooded her. He seemed genuinely starved for her. His need pierced straight through her—her flesh, her heart, her soul.

Although the orgasm that she had just had was the most powerful of her life, she was on the brink of coming again. She felt the climax, seemingly more powerful than the first, loom almost threateningly as he continued his sweet torture.

Oh God, let her never wake up from this dream.

Sharp, erratic whimpers of pleasure began to leak from her lips. Even the soles of her feet tingled with sexual heat. The muscles of her ass tightened to increase the heavenly friction.

Suddenly he pulled back.

Claire gasped and her hips thrust forward desperately for relief, finding none. "Oh please, please! I'll do anything...just—"

He gave her a small smile as he stood. Claire saw that his mouth, his chin, the dark hair of his smooth goatee, even his nose glistened with her cum. God, he'd practically drowned himself in her pussy. One hand began to tear at the buttons of his jeans roughly. Claire watched, spellbound.

"Your orgasm is going to be a powerful one. I'm selfish. I want to be buried in it when you blow. Come here," he said as he reached out and palmed the back of her neck, bringing her against him hard.

"I could die a happy man with my face buried in your pussy. Lick it off. Taste how sweet you are to me," he ordered between jaws clenched tight with what appeared to be barely restrained lust.

She craned her neck up as he lowered his head. His face remained expressionless but his eyes burned as she lapped her tongue over his chin, pausing to run her teeth over the edge. She experienced her sweet, musky, slightly salty essence for the first time in her life. But then she tasted him mingled with her—his sweat, his skin, her cum. She licked greedily then, along the furrow beneath his nose, across his cheeks, over every inch of his trim goatee, abrading her tongue as she slid up, soothing it as she stroked down.

She saved his immobile, sensual mouth for last, biting gently on his full lower lip, bringing him into the privacy of her mouth to suck him utterly clean.

"Enough," he whispered. Claire glanced up and recognized desire near the breaking point in his glittering, magnificent eyes. "Take off your gown."

She whipped it over her head and kicked away the underwear that had tangled around her ankles. Her heart beat almost alarmingly fast at her neck as he lowered his jeans and boxer briefs at once and his cock sprang free.

She placed her hand over her chest in a vain attempt to calm herself. His cock jutted forth from his body, the head so heavy that it weighed down the thick shaft despite his stark arousal. He was so large that he would likely split her in half. And he was so beautiful that she longed to take all of him anyway…even if she was left with a cleaved, broken existence.

"What are you thinking?" he asked quietly when he'd straightened and stood before her nude.

Her tongue flicked over her lower lip nervously.

"Once I have you I'll always be empty in your absence," she whispered.

Chapter Two
℘

She stifled a cry of surprise when he reached for her, lightning quick, and pushed her over the armrest of the leather couch. She caught herself just in time, her hair spilling forward on her face. Her breath stung her throat when he deliberately parted her ass cheeks and sandwiched the thick shaft of his cock in the cleft of her ass, spreading her even wider so that the thick head ran along her spine and the shaft pressed against her asshole, his testicles applying a steady pressure against her slick perineum.

She moaned uncontrollably. He felt like a hot, velvety smooth column of steel. The sheer weight of his cock stunned her.

"Do you often say things like that?" he rasped, flexing his hips slightly so that he stimulated her hungry tissues.

"Things like what?"

He leaned down and spoke quietly near her ear. "Things that make a man lose control. Things like that you'll feel forever empty when I'm not buried in your little pussy." He stroked one ass cheek tenderly with his fingertips before he held her hip steady with his hand and withdrew his cock. Claire pictured him holding that beautiful cock, preparing to plunge it into her body.

"Do you want to be taken hard?"

Her eyes clenched shut but two tears squeezed past her eyelids anyway. He would hurt her if he took her hard. She would *die* if he didn't. "Yes, take me anyway you want. I'm yours," she moaned desperately.

She felt him pause. Several more tears leaked out of her tightly pressed eyelids. It was humiliating to say it, even in a dream. But her body wanted him so much that she would have said and done much worse at that moment to get him to fuck her. She made a small sound of surprise when he leaned forward and pressed his lips gently to her hip.

"You're not afraid, are you? I don't want that, Claire." His breath feathered across her, roughening her flesh despite the fact that a wildfire leapt inside of her, ready to flash into a consuming inferno at any moment.

She shook her head adamantly. She had no idea what was wrong with her, why she couldn't even speak she was so overwhelmed with emotion. He didn't move for a moment but she sensed his intense focus, as though he sifted through her mental state, testing the surging waters of her emotions.

"All right then," he finally said. "Spread your thighs more and bend down farther until just the tips of your nipples skim the armrest."

Claire did as he instructed. She bit her lip but a full-throated groan escaped her anyway at the sensation of him presenting the broad head of his cock to her slit. He pressed down slightly on her hip. "Arch your back a little, Claire. There, that's so beautiful."

A drop of the sweat that had gathered between her breasts ran frantically down her heaving belly as she waited with unbearable anticipation. He pressed forward with his hips with a firm, relentless pressure but his fingers were gentle as he spread the delicate tissues of her pussy, easing himself in with maddening slowness, his hand holding her firmly in place for his conquering cock. Claire bit her lower lip even harder to stop herself from crying out at the sensation.

"Christ, you're small." He rocked in her gently and Claire instinctively reciprocated.

"Oh!" she cried out with delight when the rim of his full, plum-sized head pushed farther into her narrow channel. She tilted up against him to get pressure on her clit.

"That's right. Come back on my cock. Take it. Show me how much you want it while I watch."

Every muscle in her body clenched with agonized desire as she pushed back, taking him inch by inch into her pussy. Her lips pulled back over her teeth at the effort and at the sensation of him filling her. His girth stretched her, causing a delicious friction on her clit.

"I want you. I've never wanted anything as much as I want you."

She'd believed she was only thinking the words in her mind as her hungry, burning pussy ate him up slowly but she must have said it out loud because he suddenly stilled her hip with his hand.

"Are you being honest?"

"Oh yes." She rocked back and forth on the first several inches of his cock but he stopped her again, this time more firmly.

"If you truly want me that much then you'll take me now. The body always follows the orders of the mind."

He grabbed both of her hips and impaled her.

Claire's eyelids sprang open wide with shock. Her lungs refused to function. Even as she struggled desperately to breathe she became acutely aware of the erotic sensation of his full, round testicles pressed against the sensitive skin at the opening of her pussy. She rubbed up against him desperately.

"Ahh *God*," she sobbed. She shuddered and inhaled raggedly.

Apparently a shattering orgasm was the ideal cure for restoring air to the lungs.

She dimly heard his growl of arousal. Then there was no room for rational thought as he began to fuck her, long and hard, and sensation ruled her universe. He powered into her ruthlessly, his pelvis, thighs and balls slapping her pussy and ass in a frenzied fury. Her breasts bounced against the padded leather armrest as he pounded into her, her nipples hardening into painfully tight bullets of sensitive flesh.

It was too much. Too much pleasure, too much pressure, too much sensation. She'd never known anything like it. Her brain would short-circuit, she just knew it. Yet she pushed back on the couch frantically, eager to claim that small death of blistering climax. She dimly heard a voice calling, "Harder, fuck me harder. Use me. Take what's yours."

But surely that wasn't her, was it? Claire Allen would never say things like that.

Then he reached forward and pinched one of her aching nipples between his thumb and forefinger and she was exploding again, not even knowing who Claire Allen *was* anymore. There was only the two of them becoming one through the fusion of pure desire and the feeling of him stretching impossibly longer.

Even the sensation of him leaning forward and fastening his teeth on the muscle between her neck and shoulder didn't make her remember herself, nor did his harsh roar of completion so near to her ear or the feeling of his cock jerking and throbbing as he emptied himself endlessly into her. His loud shout segued into a moan of desperate need, an entirely intimate, personal sound that would be emblazoned forever on her memory, his teeth marking her as his own in the most primitive way.

A minute later her eyes opened wide in dawning wonderment.

She had just given herself so completely, so utterly, she would never be able forget this man. And he was only made of the ephemeral stuff of dreams.

The jarring memory of where she was, who she was...of how she came to be there caused a dark veil to slide down over Claire's consciousness.

She awoke, chilled and disoriented, lying alone on a couch. She'd been dreaming about the man in the library. No...it *couldn't* have been a dream. She wouldn't accept that.

She sat up abruptly and realized she was still in the library. Her gaze darted around frantically. The fire in the hearth had cooled. Only a few embers continued to glow with heat. Snow still covered the trees and shrubbery outside the window.

She was still in the dream.

Pain sliced through her as if she'd been dealt a blow when she saw him. He wore his jeans again and sat in the chair by the hearth. He leaned with his head in his hands, holding the same desolate pose she'd first seen him in when she came in the library.

He was alone again, distant from her...untouchable.

At least he was still there, she consoled herself. Claire paused when she considered what had just happened between her and this man—this complete stranger. But then she recalled the reason why she had wanted so desperately to reach out to him.

She had wanted to warn him. She reached out with her psychic awareness.

Yes, it was still there. Some threat, some danger as yet unformed but taking shape even at this moment. She stood, knowing she had to reach him again in order to alert him. This was *his* world. He had power in it while she was a mere ghost.

She went to him, her cheeks heating as she recalled what had occurred between them.

Fuck me harder. Use me. Take what's yours.

Her eyes clenched tight. Everything had spun so incredibly out of control. But at least she'd gotten his attention, she thought with a wry twist to her mouth. He'd seen her, touched her. Now she needed to warn him within the realm of the dream, get his help to stop whatever tragedy was about to take place here, in his time.

Claire glanced down, saw her nightgown intact, as if he had never touched her. Why had he covered her? Why had he dressed himself? She knew she should be glad that he had but instead she only experienced a sense of hollowness.

Once I have you I'll always be empty in your absence.

No, no, she couldn't consider that now. The sense of danger swelled, as though the threat existed simultaneously both in the house and within her own breast. She moved over to him, touching his shoulder.

"You have to come with me," she whispered urgently.

Claire didn't know what she'd expected from him but it wasn't the haggard, tormented expression that she saw on his features when he leaned back in the chair and considered her dully. Tears pricked behind her eyelids. Where was the heat, the focused, intense desire that she'd seen in his silver eyes before?

"Please come with me before it's too late."

She didn't trust herself to touch him again. Apparently her verbal plea was sufficient. He stood and followed her without speaking. Claire was too anxious about the unfolding danger to notice the way he trailed after her resignedly up the grand staircase, like a man being led to the gallows after years of torture and imprisonment.

She didn't hesitate when they reached the top of the grand staircase, heading directly for the master bedroom—Aunt Isabelle's old room.

Enough illumination from the moon and streetlights came in through the windows for Claire to sufficiently see the large, elegantly decorated bedroom. Her brow crinkled in confusion. The bedding on her aunt's four-poster bed looked mussed, as though someone had just been lying on it. Otherwise the room seemed empty and eerily still. Even so, Claire sensed a watching menace. The claustrophobic sensation that she'd felt in her recent nightmares crept into her awareness. A sure knowledge passed through her, cold and sharp.

They weren't alone.

She walked across the room to the wood-paneled door that began at waist level. The door stood open, blocking her view into the space behind it. It was the entrance to the dumbwaiter—situated ideally so that the original owners of the nineteenth-century mansion could have trays or other items sent directly to their room from the kitchen staff.

Her skin pebbled with a deep, primal fear. She hesitated but the man behind her didn't. He seemed galvanized into action. He pushed her aside, his movements now forceful and determined. He opened the dumbwaiter door wide, exposing the interior to Claire's gaze.

She flinched.

Despite her desire to look away her gaze remained glued to the grisly spectacle. A body hung in the dumbwaiter shaft limply, the head falling at an unnatural, sickening angle. The woman's neck was broken. Long, fair hair spilled forward over her face. A silent scream rose in Claire's throat as the man reached forward. The body swayed at his touch. A rope had been tied around the corpse's neck.

He lifted, slackening the cruel hold on the woman's slender throat. A pale, lifeless arm fell forward through the dumbwaiter opening. The silver of the bracelet on her wrist glowed with a life of its own in the faint moonlight while the turquoise seemed dense and black, mottling the corpse's fair skin.

Claire stumbled back, escape her sole primitive directive. A dark figure stood in front of her, aggressively blocking her path to the door. Isabelle's face looked as stern as a judge's and deadly pale. She held up her hand but Claire couldn't determine in her rising terror if Isabelle was bidding her to attend to what was behind her or if she was angrily ordering her away.

Claire awoke to the sound and sensation of terrified, trapped cries in her throat. She sat up, gasping wildly for air. The sheets were damp with her sweat, the bedside lamp still on. She panted while her gaze flew anxiously across the everyday items of her room...seeking comfort, craving sanity.

She saw the skirt she'd set out for work tomorrow laid across the back of the upholstered chair beside her closet. There was the book, just as she'd left it on the bedside table—*Dreams, Prophecy and the Future.*

She shuddered.

"It wasn't real," she assured herself.

The vision of the dead woman hanging in the dumbwaiter, then her aunt's white face and wrathful gaze, flashed graphically into her mind's eye. She shoved aside the book. The silver and turquoise bracelet still lay on her bedside table. The same bracelet she had seen on the corpse's wrist—

"It'll never happen," she mouthed soundlessly.

She inspected her body with her eyes and hands, assuring herself that she was intact. Alive. Her final thought caused her to shake her head irritably. Her imagination had more than likely been stirred up by the book. Nothing more.

She stilled.

Logic implied *all* of it had been a figment of her imagination, of course.

Even the part about the man.

She rose on shaky legs and made her way to the bathroom. The cold water on her face helped a little, clearing her head. She buried her face in a towel, letting the mundane sensation sink into her awareness.

The nightmare portion of her dream had already begun to fade in intensity. But as Claire experimentally probed portions of her memory with cautious mental feelers she realized the first part of her dream—the dream of the man—still remained locked in breathtaking detail in her consciousness. Experimentally, she reached beneath her panties.

A whimper escaped her throat when she felt the abundant juices lubricating her pussy.

She stared at her reflection in the mirror, her dark blue eyes looking enormous in her face. Somehow she already knew what she would see when she shoved aside the strap of her nightgown.

The bruise looked dark and livid against her pale skin. His mark of passion remained.

Chapter Three

Des Alvarez's heartbeat escalated when Claire finally pulled into the driveway of the Hyde Park mansion. He told himself that his reaction was sheer relief at seeing Claire Allen alive and well. At least if she was safe right now, at this very second, he could do everything in his power to make sure that she stayed that way.

But he knew that part of his reaction was a remnant of the crush he'd had on her years ago, if crush was what one politely called his response to that picture of her in a bikini that Isabelle used to have propped out for the world to enjoy. Des had enjoyed it all right, even more than those two other college kids from Loyola who he'd supervised while doing the renovation work in Isabelle's library.

At the time Des hadn't believed he'd had the nerve to enter the Preskill mansion again. He was glad now that he'd taken Isabelle up on her offer. He'd needed to face his demons. His familiarity with that old house should come in handy now.

Not that his nightmares didn't provide him with more than enough familiarity with the Preskill mansion.

He watched as Claire placed one leather high-heeled pump on the driveway. Pale, silky-looking hosiery encased a long, shapely stretch of leg. The ivory linen skirt that she wore had ridden up around her thighs while she drove. Des experienced a healthy jolt of pure masculine arousal arrow straight to his crotch when he saw the flash of a white garter.

"If only real life could have instant replay," he mumbled wryly. He'd always been a sucker for a woman wearing stockings.

She opened the rear door of her sedate sedan, sticking her ass into the air while she reached into the backseat. He exhaled slowly. Claire Allen didn't require garters and stockings. She could wear granny pants and a girdle and still make his cock turn into a ponderous steel pipe in his jeans.

A host of ideas regarding what he'd like to do with her pretty ass paraded lewdly across his mind before he shook his head to clear it. *Dios!* This was his reaction after seeing her for all of two seconds while he was parked in his car nearly a hundred feet away? He scowled as he carefully shifted his cock into a less constraining position down his thigh.

He frowned. He didn't relish the idea of having so little control over his sexual urges.

Especially when it came to Claire. Maybe he'd never officially met her but Des had suspected for a long time now that Claire Allen would play a very significant role in his future.

It took him back twelve years to when he'd been working on his master's degree at Loyola and doing occasional renovation work to make extra money. It had all started because of that picture of Claire in Hawaii. She'd been wearing nothing but three tiny triangles of fabric and a smile that could light up a man's universe. What had Isabelle Preskill been thinking, displaying a photo of her eighteen-year-old niece like that, on top of the baby grand in her elegant music room with three horny young men running around? Claire could have put a handpicked Hugh Hefner centerfold to shame and she might as well have been stark naked for all the good that bikini did her.

That ill-placed photo had once been the fuel for some seriously pornographic masturbatory fantasies. Des grinned when he remembered some of his more creative ones.

As if.

A twenty-three-year-old male could really whip up the sexual gymnastics in his brain, thanks to all those rampant hormones.

He'd kept up on some of the details of Claire's life over the past few years. Isabelle could be irritatingly stingy about elaborating directly to him but she would gossip freely with Carl Alvarez, Des' dad. For reasons better left unexamined, his father was always all too eager to pass on information to Des about Claire.

He'd learned that she didn't date that much and that she was totally devoted to her career, a fact that her parents bemoaned and Isabelle supported wholeheartedly.

He also knew that Claire belonged to a prestigious private practice located on Michigan Avenue. From what he'd learned about psychiatrists in his work at the FBI they were a pretty uptight bunch. That's what a lot of people thought about FBI agents too, Des admitted, although people on the inside often had different opinions about his bunch in the Violent Crimes Unit.

He was going to have to seriously rein in his lust when it came to Claire if he was going to protect her, he mused. The weird thing about it was that he planned to seduce her in order to do it. The sooner he got her into bed, the quicker he would be in a position to ensure her safety. He was going to have to be a bit heavy-handed to accomplish his goal but surely Claire would forgive him once she understood his motives.

Plotting to become intimate with Claire was a little detail that would cost him his job if Andre Malkovic ever caught wind of it. His co-worker had been watching Des like a hawk ever since he'd overheard Des talking to Special Agent Dawson of the San Francisco office. Des' boss had flat-out forbid him to continue investigating the Preskill angle. If Malkovic caught wind of this situation with Claire he'd probably go right for the jugular, giving Section Chief McNairy of the Office of Professional Responsibility all the nails he needed to pin up Des' hide for public display.

It wasn't as if Des wasn't giving the asshole ample opportunity. To an outsider it would look like Des was planning to become intimate with Claire in order to investigate her cousin. Definitely not something the Office of Professional Responsibility would be thrilled to learn.

But what else could he do? He wouldn't leave Claire in harm's way just because Des and his colleagues hadn't yet turned up the proverbial smoking gun. He was in a unique position to know things about this case because of his past, things that admittedly weren't the smoking gun either but still...things that made him warier than his peers.

None of those other agents or detectives out in San Francisco had ever shared a high school locker room with the likes of Kevin Preskill.

None of those other agents experienced his need to keep Claire safe.

He watched Claire's round, tempting ass as she sashayed up the steps with what looked like a bag of potting soil cradled in each arm.

Isabelle had once made an oblique reference to the fact that her niece had inherited her psychic abilities, even though Claire refused to acknowledge them. Des loved Claire's elegant, brainy looks but she hardly fit the image of a psychic. Isabelle's colorful, dramatic clothing and flamboyant personality had made her look much more the part. He studied the glasses perched on Claire's adorable nose when she turned in profile.

He sighed. If she ever did have a vision, Claire Allen would likely start herself on a seriously aggressive regimen of anti-psychotic medication. *Abuela* Anita would have a kitten if she ever found out, Des thought with a smirk.

He was likely the biggest fool in existence for doing it but he really didn't have any other choice. He needed to get inside that house.

He was determined to get inside Claire as well but that was a much more personal matter altogether, and one that fate had determined long ago. He'd cared deeply for Isabelle

Preskill and he'd kept clear of Claire for as long as he had out of respect for Isabelle's wishes.

Isabelle had been the genuine article—a true psychic. Des had no doubt of it. She'd helped him out on more than a few cases when the trail had veered off into the nether regions of frustration and meaninglessness.

And Isabelle Preskill had insisted Claire and Des weren't meant for each other.

Des watched through narrowed eyelids as Claire pushed in the front door with a cock-twitching bump of her ass. Christ, that woman couldn't be more right for him if she tried.

Isabelle may have been a powerful psychic but she'd been dead wrong when it came to her prediction about Claire and him.

A busy day at work the following day temporarily stifled Claire's chaotic emotional state. Not one of her six patients cancelled and afterward she worked with intense focus in order to make a deadline for an article that she and a colleague were coauthoring for a journal. Still, she finished in time to get out of the office by six-thirty. She made an unplanned stop at a local nursery when she realized how early it still was.

But she couldn't avoid home forever.

In fact, the nightmare of the night before had faded so much by the morning that Claire had forced herself to go into the master bedroom and inspect the dumbwaiter before she left for work. She'd gotten a hammer and determinedly removed the nails that sealed it shut. It hadn't been pleasant, but she was glad she'd eventually looked into the empty space of the shaft, seen the harmless-looking ropes and pulleys. True, she hadn't quite worked up the courage to stick her face into the darkness, to peer down into the depths of the house or up in search of a protrusion from where the rope that held the nightmare-woman's body might have been hooked.

She told herself that it hadn't been necessary, because a body would never hang there. It had just been a nightmare.

She'd even defiantly fastened the bracelet around her wrist when she was getting ready for work that morning. It had been a gift from Aunt Isabelle. Claire had worn it every day since her aunt had given it to her and she wasn't going to stop now because of an idiotic dream.

Despite her show of bravery, she had avoided the library. She didn't allow herself to think of why.

She listened to her phone messages while she glanced through her mail when she got home. Her mother had called. Claire knew from experience and from the casual sound of her voice that she just wanted to chat. Nothing serious.

Claire paused in her actions of heating up some soup for dinner to take a message from an Emile Peterson, who was looking for Kevin, Isabelle's adopted son. Apparently it was in regard to an emergency involving one of Kevin's San Francisco gallery employees. Peterson had been trying to reach Kevin repeatedly in Boston but Claire knew that Kevin had been out of the country on a hunting trip in Africa.

Lisa Modello, whom she'd hired to do housework one day a week, called to say that she would be there on Saturday morning to prepare Kevin's room for his arrival. Mark Shelley's friendly voice resonated from the machine, calling to confirm their luncheon engagement for Saturday. The smile she wore from hearing Mark's voice faded when she heard the final caller.

It was Kevin himself.

"Claire, it's me. I'm back in the States. Looking forward to seeing you this weekend. You must be getting lonely in that monstrous house. Can't imagine why you decided to live there instead of selling it. Anyway, my plane gets in at around noon on Saturday. Maybe we can find some kind of action in that lame city of yours." The tone of his voice lowered, becoming more intimate. "I assume the house will be as open to me as it ever was. *Ciao.*"

Claire grimaced, disliking the smugness and presumption in his clipped East Coast accent. Kevin's favorite emotion to "do" was boredom. No one and nothing ever supplied him with enough excitement.

Irritation flashed through her awareness. It was never far from the surface when she had to deal with Kevin Preskill. In all fairness, she had told him he could come to the house to get his things, settle whatever he needed to in his mother's home.

Her home, she amended grimly.

His words echoed in her mind, *I assume the house will be as open to me as it ever was.* She was probably imagining the suggestive tone but she doubted it. Kevin could make the most innocuous comment or the most casual glance seem indecent.

She busied herself preparing her simple meal. She was a grown woman and she'd handled Kevin Preskill for her entire life.

Always while Aunt Isabelle has been there, a living presence...a solid deterrent?

The thought made her pause but only briefly. She'd get through Kevin's visit and then maybe begin the process of severing her ties with her cousin. It was about time that she came to terms with the fact that she had no real relationship with Isabelle's son. The only thing that had made her tolerate him was consideration of her aunt's feelings. Kevin had always seemed to resent her close relationship with Isabelle.

She liked to think her distance from Kevin had begun because of their age difference. Although as adults it didn't seem like much, it had made a world of difference when Kevin and Aunt Isabelle had moved to Chicago from Boston when Claire was ten years old, soon after Uncle Larry's death. Isabelle had accepted a professorship at the University of Chicago and a sulky, angry Kevin had been forced to join her.

Having no siblings of her own and being at the age where teenagers possessed a certain glamour, Claire had been ready to worship her cousin. Kevin had initially lived up to her expectations of an exciting teenager. She remembered following him around like a hopeful puppy when she visited her aunt's house, longing for a morsel of affection from him. Kevin had been good-looking and aloof in a way that made people want to draw closer to him, even then.

Claire would always recall the afternoon she'd discovered his favorite hiding place beneath a large oak in the densely treed acreage at the back of the mansion. Kevin used to go there to smoke cigarettes illicitly. Claire had thought his secret smoking forbidden and exciting.

He'd been furious when he discovered her intrusion but his anger had been so calm and cold that it had confused Claire at first. He'd reached out almost casually and twined her braids in his hands, his hands twisting viciously until Claire cried out. She'd come up on her toes, desperate to escape the pain.

"I'll cut these fat braids right off your head if I ever catch you following me around or spying on me again. I don't care if you *are* my mother's favorite. Do you understand me?" he'd asked as he'd shaken her head violently with his hold and tears had scattered down her cheeks.

Her ten-year-old self had believed him wholeheartedly. She'd nodded her head frantically, whimpering in relief when he'd finally released her and dashing off toward the house.

As they grew older Kevin's attitude toward Claire continued to alternate between contemptuous irritability and tolerance. When Claire had entered adolescence Kevin had begun to look at her in a new way that she found even more disquieting than his former contempt had been.

On the surface Kevin had qualities that she knew many people would find appealing and desirable. Women seemed to find him attractive. He was the picture of urbane sophistication.

Although Kevin was the heir of a wealthy estate from his father, who had been the founder of a pharmaceutical company, he had made his own mark on the world. As the owner of several prestigious art galleries in the New York, Boston and San Francisco areas, he had taken what he had learned from Isabelle's innate taste and discrimination for style and art and honed it into an entrepreneurial resource.

Claire shoved aside her uneasy thoughts of Kevin, knowing she would never come to any worthwhile conclusions. Family was family. Sometimes you just had to put up with them.

She finished her light meal and went upstairs to change clothes, mechanically putting on a pair of frayed jean shorts and an old t-shirt, determined to tackle some of the maintenance and replanting required in the orangery. There were several horticultural books she wanted to consult in regard to some of Isabelle's more exotic plants and trees. The realization hit her—that would require entering the library.

She froze for a few seconds before she unfastened the clip at the back of her head and her thick, wavy hair fell down her shoulders and back.

Maybe it would suffice to merely trim back some of the overgrowth, use some of the soil she had bought today to replant one or two of the larger trees. She didn't feel like looking for books right now.

Or going into the library, seeing the chair where he'd sat, the couch she'd leaned over while he fucked not just her pussy but her mind, imprinting himself on her more surely than if he'd branded her.

Her eyes clenched shut briefly before she marched almost militantly out of her room.

The secret, she'd found, was to keep her mind totally focused on one task before moving on to another—sort of like in mountain climbing, when you couldn't consider hand and footholds two or three steps down the sequence. If you did your mind betrayed you and you became overwhelmed by the knowledge of the mind-numbing distance opening beneath you.

Sometime soon she would have to face what she remembered, try to make sense of what she dreamed. But not now, when it was still so fresh for her, so real and so damned exciting that her pussy had been enflamed and wet all day long.

She searched around in the kitchen cabinets for gardening tools, banging drawers and clattering utensils, feeling restless and irritable. A chill prickled her neck.

She glanced over her shoulder and scanned the empty kitchen nervously. Her eyes lingered on the kitchen opening for the dumbwaiter. It had been nailed shut in a haphazard manner, just like the one upstairs. But by whom?

Claire recovered after a moment and started rifling through the drawers again. The feeling of being watched had been occurring with alarming regularity ever since she moved into Isabelle's house.

The doorbell rang just as she finally located a small spade and slipped a gardening glove over her left hand. She distractedly swung open the heavy front door a few seconds later, half expecting to see some kid standing on the front porch asking for a donation for their summer soccer league or something.

Instead she stared up into the face of the man from her dream.

Her sense of self momentarily crumbled, the formerly solid barriers between dream and reality becoming indistinct…unsubstantial. The moment stretched as their gazes locked. He reached out and wrapped his hand around her upper arm, just like he had when he first saw her last night.

Claire cried out brokenly and stepped away from him as if she'd been burned.

He quickly withdrew.

"I'm sorry. You looked like you were going to faint. You're very pale." His light eyes searched her face with obvious concern. His voice was quiet, husky, the tone different from the harsh, desire-bitten intensity she recalled from the dream. But it was the same voice nonetheless. She would recognize it anywhere.

"What are you doing here?"

Puzzlement skimmed across his handsome features at her blunt question. He cleared his throat.

"I'm sorry. I should have called first but my father lives down the street and I was visiting. I'm Des Alvarez. I was friends with your aunt. I'm sorry that I didn't attend the funeral but I was out of the country with my father when she passed away."

She stared at him with so much focus that it took her a moment to realize that he studied her with equal intensity.

"I didn't know nature made eyes that color."

Her mouth gaped open. Had he really just said that or had she hallucinated the words, not to mention that low, intimate tone? Much to her surprise his cheeks colored beneath his dusky skin. He'd said it all right, and he appeared to be just as surprised that the words had popped out of his mouth as she was.

For some reason the knowledge that he floundered a little bit helped her regain some equilibrium.

"I could say the same about yours," she said with a small smile.

He cleared his throat. "Well, now that we've established that we're both freaks of nature, maybe we could move on to...what? The weather? Politics? The Cubs are sure having a shitty season, huh?"

Claire stared. Here was a side of him that she hadn't seen in the dream. Last night the sight of his smile had made her his slave. The lopsided, flirtatious grin curving his handsome mouth at the moment wasn't an ounce less powerful though.

He could take his pick—either one could bring her to her knees.

Her cheeks burned at the thought. She glanced away uncomfortably, feeling entirely too transparent.

"So you knew Aunt Isabelle?"

He nodded, crossing his arms over his chest and rocking back on his heels. Claire tried not to stare at the way his casual, entirely masculine pose swelled his pectoral muscles beneath his crisp, white t-shirt but she couldn't stop herself.

"Since I was fifteen years old or so. She and my dad worked together at the University of Chicago. I've done some renovation work on this house for Isabelle in the past. You're Claire, aren't you? Claire Allen?"

"How did you know that?"

He shifted uneasily on his feet at her sharp tone. "Your aunt spoke of you quite a bit. My father told me that you'd inherited her house."

Claire touched her flushed cheek, trying to hide her embarrassment. Of *course* that was how he knew her name. He must think she was an idiot, or extremely rude at the very least.

But what else could be expected? she wondered almost hysterically. She'd just had the most erotic, mind-blowing sex of her life with this man, and now she was standing here making small talk with him on her front porch. She'd just now heard his name spoken for the first time, despite the fact that last night he'd had his fingers high up in her ass and rammed his cock into places never before touched by a man.

Des. His name was Des. And he was real. Another wave of dizziness surged through her. She figured it was result of the strange combination of euphoria and dread that she experienced. Des must have noticed. His hand came out again as though he planned to steady her, but he seemed to think better of it after the way she'd reacted last time to his touch. He let it drop.

"Are you okay, Claire?"

A hysterical bubble of laughter burst out of her throat. "I'm sorry. You must think I'm acting very rudely."

"I don't think that," he replied quietly. "I shouldn't have just stopped by like this without calling first." He began to back away in preparation to leave.

"Don't go. I want you."

Claire's mouth hung open stupidly when she realized what she'd just said. "I mean...I want you to stay. I-I'd like to hear more about how you knew Isabelle. Please, forgive me. I don't think I ate enough for dinner. I get a little spacey when my blood sugar is low. Won't you come in?"

He hesitated. He probably was put off by her unstable mental condition.

"Really. I'd like to hear more about the work you've done on the house too," Claire added breathlessly. For a second she was positive that she'd scared away the man of her dreams.

"If you're sure..."

"I am." Even as she said it, she couldn't believe her own ears. She should be slamming the door in his face and telling him she would call the police if he ever set foot on her property again, not *encouraging* the potential outcome of that nightmare. And yet...

"*Please,* come in.

"So you work in construction?" she asked conversationally over her shoulder as she led him down the hallway.

She saw him nod once, his gaze averted.

Once they'd entered the sunlit kitchen Claire turned to face him, a bright smile plastered on her face. It faltered as she took in the reality of him standing there.

Maybe Aunt Isabelle was right. Her psychic ability must be strong. She'd gotten all of the details right. He was indeed tall, standing ten or eleven inches above her height of five-feet five-inches. The dark, silky hair wasn't black in the sunlight but the darkest shade of brown. The neat goatee was clipped so short that it might have been just a few days' stubble past a morning shave.

It highlighted his mouth.

Not that he needed something to emphasize his mouth. Claire's eyes would have been drawn to it automatically, sexy goatee or no. Her nipples puckered when she recalled what he'd done to her with that mouth. His phenomenal silvery eyes lowered as if he knew precisely what had just occurred beneath her t-shirt. Claire crossed her arms under her breasts defensively.

Damn. She wasn't even wearing a bra.

"Can I get you something to drink?" Claire asked, resorting to the safe social proprieties of convention. She'd seen the way his eyes had narrowed on her like a predator's, the way a fire had leapt into their grayish-silvery depths when he saw her erect nipples against her t-shirt. *That* was a look all too familiar to her from last night and the effect of it on her body was just as devastating today.

"Sit down." He nodded toward the barstools around the granite-covered kitchen island. "You said your blood sugar was low. I'll get something for you."

Her mouth fell open. She'd forgotten about her lie. "Err...I don't think—"

"Sit down, Claire." He waited until she complied before he turned to open her refrigerator.

"Looks like you're well stocked. What's your pleasure?"

He turned his head as he asked her, his manner casual and friendly. But his eyes seemed to lance right through to her secrets as if he already had full knowledge as to what would give her real pleasure.

But of course he didn't. That was just pure paranoia on her part.

"Maybe some fruit," she conceded slowly after a moment. "It's okay, Des. I can get it." Claire started forward as she saw him pull open her fruit drawer.

"Sit down." His voice was quiet but his tone was firm. Claire sat again slowly. "Apple? You've got some ripe, sweet-looking berries here too. What's wrong?"

She'd stood up abruptly as he held up the carton of strawberries.

"Nothing," she said hoarsely as she took in the way his dark brows knitted together in puzzlement. She sat down again, hard. Her legs had suddenly felt like they wouldn't support her weight.

Your nipples would be like hard, sweet, ripe berries just begging to be eaten.

The memory of him leaning over her and teasing her with his deep, raspy voice had suddenly leapt into her consciousness, seeming even more lifelike than her vision of him standing across the kitchen.

"The apple," Claire managed after a second. She tried to smile when she saw how his eyelids narrow suspiciously as he studied her. "Definitely the apple."

He nodded once, his face smoothing once again into total impassivity. He washed the fruit and pulled two paper towels off the roll, using one to dry off the apple and setting the other on the counter beneath her apple. Claire murmured a thank you.

"You might want to take off your glove," he deadpanned.

Claire looked down, surprised to see the gardening glove still on her hand. She laughed. "I'd just put it on when the doorbell rang. I'd forgotten."

His lips curved in amusement. Claire stared, entranced once again by the disarming flash of white teeth against his dark face, by that single, deep dimple. When she saw his smile stiffen she looked into his eyes, wondering why.

She recognized his familiar intensity. What did she expect? She couldn't go around gaping at the obvious bulge in the front of his jeans, stare covetously at his beautiful chest, gawk wide-eyed at his mouth without eliciting some kind of reaction out of him. He was obviously very masculine, likely very...*healthy* in his sexual appetites. What straight man wouldn't respond given the flagrantly wanton way she was reacting to him?

"I'm sorry. I'm a little out of it," she mumbled as she worked the stupid glove off her hand.

His eyes remained intent on her face but his voice sounded light and conversational. "No need to apologize. My sister gets low blood sugar sometimes. Makes her really cranky. I usually feed her then steer clear." He pushed the apple toward her. "Eat."

Claire picked up the fruit, not at all sure she was capable of swallowing. She bit and chewed mechanically.

He grinned at her compliance and started to turn away then froze abruptly.

Claire cried out when he grabbed her wrist, his fingers digging into the flesh painfully. Her apple thudded onto the granite countertop.

"Where the hell did you get this bracelet?"

Chapter Four

ઠુ

Claire's mouth hung open in shock. His gaze was fixed on the turquoise and silver bracelet on her wrist. The removal of her gardening glove must have just brought it to his attention.

"My...my Aunt Isabelle gave it to me."

He studied her intently. "*Isabelle* gave it to you? Where did she get it then? *When* did she get it?"

"I don't have any idea. Why are you asking me about this bracelet? What is it to you?"

He slowly unwound his hand from her wrist. He rolled his shoulders slightly as though trying to get rid of tension. Claire could almost feel his emotional withdrawal.

"My mother made that bracelet."

Claire saw pain flicker briefly across his features.

"Your mother?" Claire murmured, staring at the bracelet in amazement. "But...?"

Des shrugged in answer to her unasked question. "I didn't know Isabelle had one of my mother's pieces of jewelry. She never mentioned anything to me or my dad about it."

"Aunt Isabelle could have just bought it before she gave it to me."

He shook his head, looking as perplexed as Claire felt. "My mother's been dead for four years now. It's true that your aunt has bought some of my mother's artwork—some of her paintings. But my mother made jewelry as a hobby when I was young. She never sold any of it."

He glanced up at her. "Look, I'm sorry for jumping on you like that. It was just a shock, that's all." He picked up the apple from the countertop and tossed it into the garbage. He handed her a freshly cleaned one a few seconds later. "Can you tell me everything you know about that bracelet?"

"I don't know much, really. I'd been assuming it was an heirloom but I never actually saw her wearing it, come to think about it. She gave it to me the day before she died. It was odd. She told me that she'd figured out what the bracelet was for and then she put it on me." Claire laughed, trying to shake off the eeriness of the memory in light of the dream she'd had and Des' unexpected reaction when he saw it. Des went very still.

"She actually said that?"

Claire nodded. She set down the apple and unclasped the bracelet. "Here. I don't know how she got it but it obviously belongs to you...your family. Maybe Isabelle somehow knew that I would return it to you."

Des frowned distractedly before he gently pushed her hand back. "No, Claire. I wasn't trying to imply that it didn't belong to you. It looks nice on you. My mom would like you having it. My sister Angie has one that almost matches it, made with jade."

When she hesitated he took the bracelet from her and wordlessly put it back on her wrist, his dark head coming within inches of her face.

Claire didn't dare to look up at him as she inhaled the unique, familiar scent of him—soap mixing with barely a hint of this morning's applied aftershave and warm, clean male skin. For a moment she was paralyzed, as if every sensory receptor in her body flooded the circuits with electricity. She literally had to force herself, *force herself,* to picture that body hanging in the dumbwaiter so that she wouldn't reach out and touch him.

After he'd stepped back she continued to stare down at the bracelet, gliding her fingers across the smooth stones and metal in order to restore her calm. His words and actions had been so tender.

"Thank you." She sat back in her chair, blinking several times. "It's really strange, isn't it?

He nodded. "Strange things happened around your aunt sometimes."

Claire laughed and took a bite of her apple. "You *did* know her pretty well." She smiled, sensing some of the tension draining out of both of them. "I'd love to see the things you've done around the house. Do you want to show me?"

"Sure, if you want."

Claire trailed after him as she munched her apple, not even bothering to be polite and unglue her eyes from his ass as he sauntered down her hallway. She must have been banking her allotment of sexual energy for a lifetime, only to have cashed out the entire mother lode last night when she laid her first covetous gaze on Des Alvarez.

She forced her attention back to reality as Des led her into the formal dining room and proceeded to point out the renovations he'd supervised on the murals and paneling. At one point he smoothed his large hand knowingly across a panel to the right of the marble fireplace.

"See this panel right here? It's the only one that's not restored from the original wood."

"Was it damaged?"

Des shook his head as he considered the carved African mahogany panel. For a second he didn't speak, as if he were trying to solve an arithmetic problem in his head. "No, not really. See the design there on the wainscoting? It was chosen on purpose to camouflage something."

Claire peered at where he pointed. "What?"

"An oculus."

When he saw her blank expression, he explained, "Holes for viewing...for spying into the room. There was a compartment behind this panel, a little room where someone could watch and listen to what was going on in the dining room. You accessed it by a hidden door in the study."

Claire stared at him in amazement. "Wow. Just like in Scooby Doo?"

His lips curved into a grin. "Yeah, just like. The original owner of this house was a politician, politely put. He definitely lived up to Chicago's reputation for having some of the most crooked public servants in history. He probably entertained plenty of friends and enemies in this house and learned quite a few secrets using that oculus. Your house is full of secrets, Claire. Do you know of any other ones?"

Claire dropped her gaze. "I only know about the dumbwaiter, but I guess that's just unused, not a secret. Why did Aunt Isabelle have you change the panel?"

Des shrugged. "She didn't like the whole secret compartment idea. She had me replace the panel *sans* the oculus and seal off the compartment."

Claire shook her head in fascination as she slowly turned and inspected the ornate detailing and craftsmanship inherent to the beautiful room with new eyes. "How long have you been doing this kind of work?"

"I grew up in one of these historic Hyde Park homes. My dad likes doing woodworking and renovation in his free time so I learned it from him. I worked for a local renovation firm during high school and college breaks to make extra money."

She finished her survey of the room. "You're an artist—like your mother."

Claire got the distinct impression he wanted to change the subject when he shrugged. Had she embarrassed him with her compliment?

"Working with wood is sort of relaxing for me. It always has been. Maybe I do get it from my mom. She loved working with her hands. My dad is an artist too but he doesn't really work with his hands. Unless typing on a keyboard counts."

"He's a writer?"

He rocked back on his heels and crossed his arms over his chest in that casual stance that Claire found utterly masculine. Not to mention incredibly sexy.

"Yep. And a professor at the U. of C. That's how he and Isabelle knew each other. What about you?"

"What do you mean? Am I an artist?"

"No, Isabelle told me that you're a psychiatrist. I meant, did you get any particular gifts from your parents that you use in your work?"

"Well, my mom's a great listener," Claire mused thoughtfully. "She *really* listens, you know? She's not just thinking about her own agenda and nodding her head while you're talking. My dad's a businessman but he's a scientist too. He patented several industrial chemical compounds and that's how he started his own company."

"Your Aunt Isabelle was always intuitive about people. Maybe you're more like her," he said, his slow smile creating a meltdown between her thighs.

"What did Isabelle ever say to you that was so intuitive?"

Des shrugged and glanced away. "I used to have trouble sleeping. Bad dreams. Your aunt always seemed to know about it when it happened."

Bad dreams. Claire had problems with those as well. But Des wasn't talking about the kind of dreams she had. She knew instinctively that he was talking about the kind of bad dreams that come from personal tragedy or loss.

"Did Aunt Isabelle help…with the dreams, I mean?"

"Yeah, she helped," Des said eventually, his voice a low rumble. But Claire didn't think he sounded very convincing.

She bit into her apple, trying to sound casual. "You knew that she was a…" Claire couldn't bring herself to finish, too many early childhood memories of being regarded as a freak or worse impinging upon her.

"Psychic?" he finished for her.

"Uh, yeah. *Psychic,*" Claire emphasized with a shaky grin and a spooky wave of her hand. She took another bite of her apple, all the while hyperaware of Des' steady stare. What had he thought of Isabelle's claim? "And did you...believe her?"

"Sure." He must have noticed her incredulous look because he smiled and explained.

"In Colombia, where my father is from, people look at that kind of stuff differently than they do here. It's an accepted part of the culture. My grandmother is a real character. She sees spirits, holds conversations with the ghosts of my ancestors, asks their advice on everything from the location of her missing earring to what she should make for supper. Most of my family members have been named from the results of high-level summits between my grandmother and dead relatives. *Abuela* Anita believes that if the parents don't accept the name it's a sure sign of bad luck for the baby. Which definitely is true, because she harps on it so much to everyone that the kid inevitably feels cursed."

His smile widened when Claire laughed.

"My grandmother is the inspiration for several of the characters in my father's books. It's just a part of what she is...*who* she is. I don't think about whether or not I believe in her ability. I believe in *Abuela* Anita. She's a force of nature."

"Did you grow up in Columbia?"

"No, I was born here. My mother is from southern Indiana. I never even went to Columbia until the summer after my first year of college. My father felt it was too dangerous to take children there."

Something occurred to her and her eyes went wide. "*Wait.* Your father isn't Carlos Rivera Alvarez, is he?"

Des nodded.

She gasped. "He's one of my favorite authors. He's amazing. God, he's won several Pulitzer Prizes."

"Don't mention it to him when you meet him," Des said with a chuckle. "My father loves beautiful women, but a beautiful woman who likes his writing? He'll talk your ear off and before you know it you'll be neck deep in the old-world charm."

She didn't know about his father but *Des* certainly possessed an effortless ability to charm her. *When you meet him,* he'd said, as though it was inevitable that she would be introduced to his father.

And he'd called her beautiful.

Claire suddenly became aware of the proximity of their bodies as they stood there. Her eyes lingered on the sweep of his shoulders. She could see a steady pulse in his neck. She could perfectly picture herself putting her hands at the back of his head, encouraging him to lower, so that she could place her lips over that vein in his throat and feel his heartbeat against the tip of her tongue.

Her cheeks flamed at the graphic image and she looked down at her feet awkwardly. Her mind might be reeling with fear and confusion as to what to make of Des Alvarez but her body knew precisely what kind of sense he made.

"I didn't mean to presume," he said softly. "I just thought maybe you would like to meet him sometime. My father, I mean."

"You're right. I would like to meet him," she informed her toes.

"What about tomorrow night?"

Claire glanced up in surprise. "Boy, you don't mess around, do you?"

He gave a small shrug but he didn't apologize. "My sister Angie and I are making dinner for him tomorrow night. It's his birthday. He just lives down the street. I'd like you to join us."

"Oh...well, I'd like to but—"

"Say yes then."

Claire blinked, both surprised and aroused by his calm, steadfast manner.

"If you're sure it'll be okay with your family."

"It'll be fine. Do you want to see what else I've done in the house?" he asked with a hitch of his chin over his shoulder.

"Lead the way," Claire said as she held out her hand. She felt a little stunned. Had he really just asked her out? He'd seemed so casual about it, so blasé. For her part, her heart beat uncomfortably fast and her palms were embarrassingly sweaty.

"I wasn't exactly honest about something I said before, Claire," he said as they left the dining room.

"What do you mean?"

"Isabelle didn't really talk about you very much with me. In fact, she made a point of avoiding the topic of you when I was around."

Claire laughed as she followed him down the hallway. "Why would she do that?"

He smiled. "She had a very firm opinion about us."

Claire stopped. "*Us?*"

His eyebrows rose and his slow grin reminded her a little too poignantly of his dark smile last night. "What, Claire? The concept isn't all that reprehensible to you, is it?"

For a few seconds she just stared at him. God, where did she stand with him anyway? This moving back and forth between relating to him as a new acquaintance versus an intimate lover was causing her brain to have a serious meltdown. She bit her lower lip anxiously, finally deciding her best bet would be to just ignore his question altogether. "What sort of a firm opinion did she have?"

His slight smirk told her that he was aware that she'd dodged answering him. "That you and I weren't meant for each other."

Claire made an uneasy scoffing noise. "What do you mean? What did she say?"

"You want the exact words?" Claire nodded. "There was a picture she used to have of you on the piano years back. I used to have a certain...*interest* in it. Maybe lecherous fascination would be a better description."

"*Not* that picture of me in Hawaii." Her blush deepened when he just nodded, that deadly dimple in his right cheek clearly in evidence. Claire closed her eyes briefly in embarrassment. For the life of her she'd never figured out why Isabelle insisted on displaying that photo. She'd hidden it on innumerable visits to her aunt's house. Eventually she'd no longer noticed the offending picture so Claire had assumed Isabelle finally took the hint. She'd been mortified to think of Kevin seeing it.

"So anyway, one time Isabelle caught me admiring it. She whipped it out of my hand and put it face down on the piano, and in that queen of the realm voice she used to use once in a while says, 'She isn't for you. Now, I know it seems odd, Desi, that I would say it with such confidence, but you'll have to take my word on it.'"

Claire stared at him, speechless. What in the world could Aunt Isabelle have meant by it?

"Did she know something about you that would have made her want to keep you away from me?" The graphic image of the woman in the dumbwaiter flashed before her eyes. Nevertheless, she almost laughed out loud at Des' irritated scowl.

"Of course not. You're looking at a prime example of manhood here. Protective parents and relatives love me. Usually, that is," he added. He grinned widely when her laughter broke free. "Hell, I don't know why she said it. Maybe she thought you were too young and innocent for me at the time, which, let's face it, you were. I was in my master's program at Loyola and you had just graduated from high school. I didn't agree with everything Isabelle said, psychic or no. My father is always telling me I should respect my elders' opinions. I respected your aunt but..." He trailed off. His silvery eyes seemed to glow in his dark face as he watched her intently. "I have a very strong feeling she couldn't have been more wrong in this particular case."

Claire's amusement faded. Her cheeks burned with heat. "You thought it would make a difference to me, that maybe I wouldn't agree to go out with you tomorrow night if I knew."

It wasn't a question. She knew it was true. Des didn't bother to answer.

"It was Isabelle's opinion. Why she held it, I can't fathom. As I'm sure you know, Isabelle could be…idiosyncratic at times," Claire murmured, highly aware of his nearness and penetrating stare. It felt as if all the oxygen had been sucked out of the room.

"I just thought you deserved to know. She must have been really important to you," he said.

Their gazes clung for a prolonged moment.

Then he was suddenly turning around and reaching for the library door.

"Des."

He faced her abruptly, obviously alarmed by the sound of her voice.

"What…what are you doing?" Claire demanded.

He glanced at the library door and back to her pale face.

"I thought you wanted to see the work I'd done on your house? I designed and built the shelving in the library." He surprised her by reaching up and palming the side of her neck. The pad of his thumb settled gently on her pulse. Claire was ensnared by his gaze, unable to move for several taut seconds.

"Do you want to tell me what's going on with you?" he eventually asked. "Why do you keep looking like you're going to pass out cold? You were lying when you said it was because you were hungry. Why?"

She gasped with both alarm and indignation at his suddenly pointed, intense manner. "How…how dare you?

Why would I lie? I didn't even know you existed until today." Her heartbeat thumped loudly in her ears as he carefully studied her.

"Maybe I was wrong about you lying before. But there's no doubt that you're lying right now. Come in here, Claire."

It wasn't really a request. His mouth had turned into a determined, hard line as he pulled her into the library behind him.

"What are you doing?" she asked again with rising panic when he plopped her down on the armrest of the couch where he'd fucked her until her ears rang last night. She tried to get up but he pressed down firmly on her shoulders. Instead of fighting him she just gave him a defiant glare. His eyes looked like icy shards. *Oh no.* The hunter was back. Only this time it was the truth that he seemed determined to plunder from her.

"Tell me what you're hiding. Is it about the bracelet?"

"I don't know what the hell you're talking about."

He put his big hand back on her neck. She immediately pulled away from his touch. He merely put his other hand on the opposite side of her neck, forcing her to stay in contact with him.

"What's wrong, Claire? You're a psychiatrist. You must know that a human's heart rate changes when they're lying. If you're being so honest what difference does it make if I feel your heartbeat? Just tell me why you're lying, baby."

Her eyes opened wide when she heard him call her that. It brought up way too many memories of last night. Being in exactly the same location and having the flesh and blood man standing right in front of her, his hands on her skin, didn't help to alleviate the turbulence of her emotions any either.

"That's insulting. I'm not your *baby*," she hissed. She wanted to smack him when a slow smile curved his lips.

"You're lying again, Claire."

He ignored her look of disgust.

"Why didn't you want to come into this room?"

"Maybe I don't like this room. What business is it of yours?"

He just shook his head. His focus on her was absolute. If Claire didn't know better she would have sworn he was capable of reaching inside of her with those piercing eyes and plucking the truth straight out of her soul.

Her heartbeat escalated beneath his fingers until it was like a panicked bird beating frantically against a cage. A muscle leapt in his cheek as his gaze lowered over her hot cheeks. "Nature didn't make you to be a good liar, Claire," he murmured intimately. Both of them went entirely still when his eyes dropped down to her chest. Her heartbeat escalated impossibly faster, like she'd just had a powerful stimulant mainlined into her blood.

He removed his hand from her neck slowly. Claire stared in mixed fascination and disbelief when he reached for her breast. He lightly pinched an erect nipple between his thumb and forefinger. He rolled the pebbled flesh between his fingertips.

She moaned shakily.

"Is *this* why you've been acting so strange?" he asked her softly when her head fell back.

"*Don't*," she pleaded.

"Why not? It's obvious you like it."

If he'd said it with any degree of smugness she would have found the strength to resist him. But he hadn't. Instead he seemed genuinely gratified, even awed by the evident truth of his statement. He continued to pluck at her nipple through her t-shirt, his gaze narrowing intently on her face.

Claire closed her eyes to shield herself from the pure, undiluted lust burning in his beautiful eyes. She squirmed on the armrest to get pressure on her throbbing pussy. What kind of a crazed, desperate nympho would she be to sleep with a man who her psychic power suggested was somehow connected with her own death? If she didn't tell him to stop rubbing, pinching and lightly tugging on her nipple she'd soon be utterly lost.

His hand swept over her other breast, cradling her softly. When he began to deftly stimulate both sensitive, tight nipples at once, Claire groaned, recalling all too perfectly why getting lost with Des was such a temptation.

The uneven sound that skipped across her lips and the bright bloom of color in Claire's cheeks were the telltale signs of a woman just a few strokes away from orgasm. Des stilled his fingers, stunned at the realization.

Christ. How the hell had he gotten so lucky?

She'd been acting so strangely ever since she'd answered the door that he'd been worried she knew something important, something she was keeping from him…something about the Morningside Murderer, especially after all that weirdness with the bracelet.

But apparently she'd just been as primed for hot, sweaty sex as he'd been ever since he saw her standing there in the doorway wearing tiny cut-off shorts, the most gorgeous mane of strawberry blonde hair imaginable falling around her shoulders, her dark eyes wide with shock.

He watched her face while he pulled up on the bottom edge of her t-shirt, not dropping his gaze until he'd lifted it above her breasts. His cock tightened in sharp anticipation when he filled a hand with her. Her eyes sprang open and he looked down into depthless, dark blue pools of desire.

"Is this why you've been acting so jumpy? Because you needed this?" he coaxed. He smiled and shook his head incredulously. "All you had to do was ask, baby."

He groaned when he cradled both her breasts in his hand, the sound twining with her soft whimpers. Ah Jesus, she was lovely. He watched breathlessly as he skimmed his thumb gently over a large, pointed nipple and it pulled impossibly more erect.

Her breathy, catchy sound of arousal was music to his ears. He shaped her to his palms, knowing with certainty then and there he would never get enough of her. Just the sight of her was more exciting than anything he could imagine. She was a D-cup if he didn't miss his guess, but a more firm and shapely breast he'd never had the privilege to hold.

Her nipples would cause even a saint to celebrate the pure joy of sin. He cupped her from beneath, forcing the rosy tips into even further pronouncement as he studied her. His cock lurched furiously in his jeans. Her nipples were so red they looked like they'd been rouged.

She trembled in his hands.

"Oh God, Des?"

"Shhh, it's okay," he soothed, hearing her confusion, her desperation. "I was just admiring you before I taste you."

He bent his head and inserted one of her delicate nipples between his lips, laving it with his tongue, relishing his first taste of her. He patiently mapped every tiny bump, learning her shape, testing what pressure she preferred, using the feedback of her whimpers and sighs. Her subtle flavor tugged at the edges of his unconscious mind, seeming both exciting and new and hauntingly familiar at once.

He took her into his mouth and suckled, eager to drown himself in her sweetness, His cheeks hollowed out as he drew on her hungrily. When he felt her back muscles tighten and she jerked her hips spasmodically on the armrest of the couch his eyelids flew open in surprise.

She stared at him fixedly. The rigidity of her beautiful features made him lift her breast in his hand, gently manipulating an erect nipple against his teeth while he held her gaze.

She gripped his shoulders and cried out brokenly as she came.

He kept her breasts in his hands but rose to nip at her lips while she quaked in climax, eager to swallow her sexy whimpers and cries.

"Claire?" he queried when she'd quieted but her eyelids remained sealed shut.

She opened her eyes and regarded him warily.

Des was stunned. She'd just fucking *come*. She'd just had what looked like a grade-A orgasm from having him suck on a nipple for a minute or two. He knew women could climax from nipple stimulation sometimes but it was damned rare — usually occurring when lovers were exceptionally attuned to each other, their brains and bodies already templated together like a lock and key for the ecstasy they knew they'd find in the other's arms.

Amazement dawned slowly as he studied the wide-eyed beauty in his arms.

"You're *already* mine."

Des' feral, focused stare made Claire slide off the couch and slip beneath his arm in rising panic. Much to her surprise he didn't try to stop her. She pulled down her t-shirt and backed several feet away from him, needing space from her chaotic, completely irrational emotions.

She wasn't afraid of him, exactly. Well, perhaps she *was* but not afraid that he would hurt her. Her eyes flickered over to the library doors.

"Don't even think about it, Claire," he said, his tone ominously soft.

They just stood in a stand-off for a moment. His intense, perplexed expression as he studied her made her panic escalate for some reason.

"Take off your t-shirt," he said suddenly.

"No," Claire spat as she backed farther away from him. She couldn't believe what had just happened, that it was possible that he'd created such an inferno of need in her by just touching her breast, tasting her. Heat flooded through her all over again at the memory. It was as if his hot mouth and hungry suction had awakened a stranger in her. Now she didn't have the excuse of a dream for her complete, uninhibited response to him.

"Take off that shirt," he repeated as he took a step toward her.

"Why? You just saw me," she replied petulantly, knowing her response was nonsensical but unable to think of anything good in her confusion.

"Take off that shirt or I'm going to come over there and rip it off you."

Her eyes widened in disbelief at his quietly issued challenge. She thought about arguing with him but what was the point? Lord knew she'd been hankering to have him fuck her again since the moment she woke up from that cursed dream. She shrugged as if the matter was beneath her notice, throwing him a defiant look.

She started to remove the t-shirt, calling him a caveman and a bully under her breath as she did so. She froze when the t-shirt was gathered around her right shoulder.

Oh shit. The bruise of passion given to her by the dream Des.

His eyelids narrowed as he slowly ate up the distance between them. "Take it all the way off, Claire."

"But—"

His jaw clenched with irritation as he grabbed the shirt himself and lifted it over her head, tossing it carelessly to the floor. Her hair spilled around her shoulders but she couldn't be sure she was hidden from his lancing gaze. When she immediately covered the livid bruise with her hand he didn't say a word.

He just peeled her hand away.

For the life of her, Claire couldn't read his expression as he examined her shoulder through narrowed eyelids.

"It's not what you think, Des."

"What is it that you imagine I'm thinking, exactly?" he asked quietly after a moment. His eyes bore into her like drills, belying the casual tone of his question.

Claire swallowed heavily. How could she answer? She knew that the mark looked exactly like what it was—a bruise from a moment of mindless passion. God, you could still see the imprint of teeth. No wonder he looked so odd. He probably imagined she'd recently been with another man, that she had another lover even though she'd just shuddered in orgasm while he—a complete stranger—suckled her breast.

She closed her eyes in rising frustration. This couldn't get any stranger.

"It's...it's," she floundered, trying to think of a plausible story.

"No more lies," he warned.

"It's not from another, man. I'm not involved with anyone."

Des shook his head slowly.

"I wasn't thinking you were with another man. I know who put that mark on you, impossible as it seems. *I* did it. Last night. Right over there." He hitched his thumb to where she'd just been sitting on the armrest of the couch. "I did it while I had the orgasm of a lifetime deep inside you and you begged me to give you every last drop of my cum."

He shook his head in amazement at the same time that he reached down and swept her into his arms with one fluid motion. He grinned, slow and wicked, when he saw her open-mouthed shock.

"I would have never guessed in a million years that you had such a dirty mouth, Claire. I'm a lucky man."

Despite her surprise she flushed hotly at his words. "Des? What—what are you doing?"

He seemed genuinely surprised by her question. "Fucking you in a dream was fantastic but if you think I'm going to be satisfied with dream sex you've got another think coming."

"It wasn't the same for you as it was for me then," Claire said quietly as he raced down the hallway with her in his arms as if he were evacuating her from an inferno, except they were going in the opposite direction to create one. He paused with his first foot on the step of the grand staircase.

"Why would you say that, baby?"

"It wasn't like a dream to me," she whispered, her cheek against his chest. "And because there's no way it could get any better than that."

He paused at the foot of the grand staircase. "Here's to proving you wrong then, Claire."

He mounted the staircase two steps at a time.

Chapter Five

His breathing was barely escalated when he placed her on her feet in her bedroom. Her room was dark. Too dark. If she was risking her own life to get involved with this man she wanted to be able to see every bit of his beautiful naked body.

"Do you...want the light on?" she asked shakily. He didn't answer but moved through the darkness, switching her bedside lamp on to the most muted setting. He turned around, pinning her once again with his gaze.

She moved restlessly on her feet.

"Is this what you want, Claire?"

"Yes," she whispered.

"Then lower your hands from your breasts. You're beautiful. I don't want you to ever hide yourself from me."

Claire blinked. She hadn't even realized she'd been shielding herself. He waited, his eyes trailing her fingers as she lowered them. He moaned and unfastened several buttons on his jeans. Claire could see why—things were getting pretty full and pronounced behind that denim. He sat down on the edge of her bed.

"Are you hurting, Claire?" he asked in that seductive, husky voice.

For a second Claire didn't understand what he meant. Then she thought of the fevered pitch of her arousal last night and all day, the near-pain of an itch that couldn't be scratched. Yeah, she was hurting all right. The climax she'd had down in the library had been tremendous but it barely felt like it had even scratched the surface of her need. And he was the only thing that was going to cure that unbearable ache.

She nodded her head.

"I am too," he admitted with a small smile. "But that's not going to stop me from savoring every second with you. Take off your shorts. I want to see you completely naked."

Claire swallowed thickly at his request and the heavy-lidded look of almost tangible lust in his light eyes. She was struck by a fit of self-consciousness and yet—what a feeling of power, to know that *she* aroused him so much.

She slid her hands over her ribs and belly, utterly aware that he followed every move. Her nipples pinched in excitement. She undid the button fly on her shorts, stifling a gasp as the motion stimulated her clit.

Des didn't miss a thing.

"Go ahead. Touch yourself. Give yourself a little relief."

Claire's eyes widened at his request. The idea of pleasuring oneself in front of a lover seemed like the epitome of decadence. Wasn't that what the lover was there for?

But her pussy wasn't interested in all of that philosophizing. The ridge of her forefinger was already dipping down vertically between her moist labia. Des' attention on her was absolute.

Suddenly she longed to give him more.

She shoved her shorts and panties down to the tops of her thighs, shimmying her hips until the garments slowly dropped to her ankles. Satisfaction swelled in her breast when she saw his eyes widen at her wiggling hips and naked body. All the while she played her pussy for him, finally comprehending how his avid eyes on her completely eliminated the *auto* from *autoeroticism*.

"Come here."

When she approached him his long thighs opened and Claire stepped between them as if the movement had been orchestrated between them long ago and practiced countless times since. She stood still while he ran his hands lightly over the delicate skin beneath her armpits, over her ribs, skimming her narrow waist and finally settling on her naked hips.

His eyes fastened on the trim reddish-gold nest of pubic hair between her thighs. "God, you're gorgeous...like sex and sunshine. Play with that pretty pussy some more, Claire. Do it just like you do when you make yourself come."

"Des, *no*," she whispered. Her hands came up to bury in his hair and then traveled the width of his shoulders hungrily. She gripped at the white t-shirt at his chest and began to pull. He didn't protest when she lifted it over his head. His skin was such a beautiful color and texture, olive-toned and smooth, stretching tautly across defined, well-developed shoulder, chest and arm muscles.

Her fingers played over him in wonder, spellbound by the tautness of his skin and the hard muscle beneath it and the crisp texture of the hair on his chest. Her eyes followed the furrow of his rib cage and trailed over his ridged abdomen. Her mouth literally watered.

"I want to touch you. Everywhere."

He gave a slow smile that made her clench her thighs.

"And they say that miracles are dead," he teased.

He reached up and placed his hand behind her neck, pulling her to him for a scorching hot open-mouthed kiss. Claire moaned. No preamble to that kiss, no warm-up required. Who needed coy seduction when you could just jump straight to the good stuff—raw, intense desire? He held her steady while he possessed her, his agile tongue plundering her depths one moment, teasing and rubbing the next.

Claire could only imagine that the logical follow-up to the opening gambit of that erotic kiss was for him to toss her down on the bed and do the same thing with his cock inside her pussy that his tongue did to her mouth. She couldn't wait. So she was surprised when he gently sealed the kiss, leaned back from her blindly seeking lips and murmured, "Now touch yourself, baby. Show me how you like it."

"No," she groaned in frustration when she reached out to graze her fingertip across a stiff brown nipple and he caught her hand, stopping her.

"Yes. Come on, Claire, I want to see your technique." He grinned up at her as he stroked her hips, his touch causing her skin to roughen.

"Technique," she scoffed. "I don't have a *technique*."

He lowered his eyes to the thatch of hair between her thighs. "Usually I like a woman to shave her pussy. It increases the sensitivity to my touch…to my mouth." He looked up at her when she moaned softly. "But you're enough to make me change my mind, Claire. You've got the prettiest bush I've ever seen. I can't wait to spread you wide so I see if your pussy is as red as your hair."

Claire whimpered. She'd never known dirty talk would turn her on so much. Her pussy burned for him.

"Go on, baby," he coaxed with a naughty grin. "I'll show you my technique if you show me yours. Would you like that?"

When Claire nodded quickly his lips twitched even wider.

"I'm sort of shy about my toys. You show me yours first. Maybe that will make me feel more comfortable."

Claire swatted a rounded shoulder with amused exasperation. This was a different man than last night! Just as intense, just as domineering but so lighthearted. She never would have guessed that it would make her just as horny as his moody darkness had.

"Go on. Coax your little clit out to play and there's no way in hell I'm going to be able to resist not joining in on the fun."

That stiffened her resolve. "Okay."

She spread her legs and placed one knee up on his hard thigh. She tilted her hips slightly upward to give him better viewing and swept her hand slowly up her thigh. When she reached her pussy she slid her forefinger between her tender, damp labia.

A moan escaped her throat. She'd been intending to arouse him but her touch on her slick clit felt marvelous.

She'd never seen a more rapt audience than Des when she began to gyrate her hips in tiny circular motions, increasing the pressure of her rubbing, gliding finger on her clit. She imagined he knew just how wet she was. He could see her cream clinging to her pubic hair and glistening on her diddling finger.

"Slide a finger inside you," he directed.

He groaned as she parted her legs even more and penetrated her tight, slippery slit with one finger.

"You're doing a very nice job of convincing me to come out and play," he muttered thickly.

"You like?" Her voice surprised her, sounding like warm, flowing honey to her own ears.

He watched, hypnotized, as she spread her labia wide with one hand and slid her finger from her pussy, spreading the thick cream up her cleft, coaxing her clit out of its hood. Her thighs and ass tensed against the delicious burn.

"Oh *yeah*..."

He'd apparently gone mute at the sight of her exposed, erect clit just inches in front of his face. Her movements became more rapid. "It's getting kind of lonely out here. Are you going to join me on this playground or not?"

She smiled when she saw him tear at the fly of his pants. *Yes*. Claire wanted that cock. He'd created a fire of need in her last night that she was beginning to fear was damned near unquenchable. Her eyes were just as glued to his crotch as his were to hers. He reached inside his underwear and lifted himself free, holding himself at the base of the shaft. She waited with bated breath while he revealed inch after inch...after *inches* of cock.

Oh *God*. Her hand became more forceful in its actions between her legs. He was every bit as beautiful as he had been last night in the dream. *More* so. She hated being crude but that was one hell of a choice cock. Her fingers paused for a moment as she stared, awestruck.

His cock was big but so was his hand. He stroked himself slowly, surely, running his thumb along a thick purple vein and straight onto the bulbous head and catching some pre-cum with it. He smeared the clear fluid over the smooth surface, making the tip glisten before he moved his arm, stroking himself once again from full testicles to shiny head.

Never in a million years would she have guessed watching him touch himself would be such a tremendous turn-on.

He concentrated his efforts around the head for a few strokes, making a flicking motion with his wrist and twisting slightly just beneath the delineated crown.

"Isn't there something you're supposed to be doing, Claire?"

She started, realizing she'd gone completely still in fascination.

"Oh." She resumed stimulating herself, more enthusiastically this time, spurned on to further heights of desire by the sight of him stroking his beautiful cock. He smiled. "I-I see what you mean about *technique* now."

"You have a technique too," he said as he watched her intently. He leaned forward slightly and inhaled her scent, reminding her poignantly of the dream.

"Claire?"

"Yes?"

"Bring one of those pretty nipples into the game."

Claire moaned and pressed down greedily on her clit. "You're killing me, Des. Will you please just let me touch you?"

His nostrils flared and Claire got the impression he was considering doing a lot more than letting her touch him. "If I have to ask you again to play with your nipple, your ass is going to become very familiar with my palm."

"You're threatening to *spank* me if I don't do what you say?"

Des shook his head slowly, holding her gaze. "You're going to get used to me spanking you one way or another."

Claire felt her cheeks glow with heat, and she didn't even want to consider the flash flood in her pussy. She reached up and caressed her nipple, rolling it between her fingertips. At first she just did it because of the fixed, tense expression on his face as he watched her but then the stimulation really began to get to her and her efforts redoubled.

"God, those red nipples and red little pussy and all that white skin," Des muttered to himself. He stroked his erect penis harder.

"I don't want to be abused or beaten up, Des Alvarez. I won't stand for it."

His hand stilled. His eyebrows pinched together as he stared at her, aghast. "Why would you say that?"

"You threatened to spank me just now if I didn't do what you said. You did the same thing last night—in the dream," she hissed.

"You don't like the idea of me spanking you, huh?"

"No!"

He shrugged. His eyes returned to her pussy. "Fine. Enough said."

Claire felt a crazy urge to take it all back. "It turns you on? The idea of spanking me?"

"Claire, we don't have to get into this right now. We were in the midst of playing nicely together," he reminded her with a sexy grin.

Her tongue skimmed her lower lip uneasily but her curiosity won out. "It does turn you on though, doesn't it, Des?"

"You've got an ass that makes me itch to swat it...for starters. But if you don't want me to I won't."

"Animals get spanked, children get spanked...not grown women." She noticed his wry grin and realized she'd sounded like she was lecturing.

"Uh-huh. So why are you getting more excited thinking about it, Claire?"

Her eyes widened when she realized he was right. She'd been making small but forceful bucking motions with her hips against her rubbing fingers and squeezing a nipple lustily while she imagined what it would be like to have Des make her bottom sting beneath his palm.

He chuckled when he saw her reaction. He leaned forward and held her gaze, his silvery eyes gleaming. "Okay, here's another little aspect to our game. I'm going to tell you why I'd like to turn you over my knee and you're going to keep touching yourself. If you can make yourself come from listening to me talk I won't spank you now. If you can't though...I'm going to turn your ass pink."

Claire resumed rubbing herself when she heard that challenge uttered in a low, intimate tone.

"So you'll listen?" he asked.

She nodded her head quickly. A storm of arousal built in her. Her outer lips and clit were drenched with her juices.

And Des had hardly touched her yet!

He leaned back, bracing his long, muscular body with one hand on the bed while the other hand continued to stroke his long, straining cock.

"I've wanted to spank your ass ever since I first laid eyes on you. I might have you lie naked across my lap with your plump little ass in the air while my palm smacks those white cheeks repeatedly—not too hard, mind you, because your skin is very delicate, but hard enough to sting and make those plump cheeks blush. You're very firm. Can you imagine how sweet the sound would be when my hand popped your ass?" he muttered as his eyes traveled down over her breasts, pausing to appreciate her increasingly frantic stimulation of her nipple before moving on to her ribs and belly.

Claire was eerily focused as she listened to his deep voice.

"I might restrain your wrists before I spanked you…just to remind you that you were completely at my mercy. Depending on why I was punishing you, I might use a paddle or a crop with a sweet little slapper on the end. If I used those I might have you bend over with your ass in the air or even lie on your belly on the bed. Either way, you'd get turned on, Claire. Your pussy would get soaked while I spanked you."

Claire moaned and rubbed her burning clit madly.

"You would raise your ass up to meet each smack from my palm, you'd be so hungry for it. If you were tied up and lying in my lap you'd try to rub your little clit against my thigh but I wouldn't let you do that, baby. I'd make you keep still while you took your spanking until I was good and ready to let you have an orgasm. I'd make you wait until your ass blushed nice and pink before I touched your pussy…before I fucked you."

"*Ahhh*," Claire cried out. She shot off like a rocket, frantically stimulating her clit and pinching at her stiff nipple, all the while perfectly envisioning the picture painted by Des' erotic words. Pleasure shuddered through her again and again. Desperate, trapped little cries vibrated in her throat.

She heard Des' low growl and his voice through the blood thundering in her ears.

"Come here, baby. Turn around. You're gonna get fucked now."

Chapter Six

He spun her, not even certain that she'd heard him speak while she was in the midst of erupting like Mt. Vesuvius. Des was certain she didn't notice him reaching in his jean pocket for a condom. He fumbled while he rolled it on, mostly because he was distracted by his first sight of the enticing, plump ass he'd just been describing in so much detail. It was sexier than he'd even imagined.

Some semblance of reality must have been getting through to Claire because when he told her to bend over his lap, she complied. Even as he held her hip steady and brought the head of his cock to her pussy, however, she was still busy working every last spasm of pleasure out of her climax. Des paused, his nostrils flared wide, as he stared at her, bent over before him.

He gave her a light slap on the back of her thighs, garnering her attention.

"It's going to make your thighs burn in that position, but you're in charge here. I'm at your mercy."

That got her attention. She turned, her golden-red hair whipping around her shoulders as she met his gaze.

"I'm going to fuck you so hard I'm going to turn you inside out, Des Alvarez—just like you have me," she whispered with the fierceness of an Amazon warrior. She reached down and adjusted her delicate tissues around his cock.

"Calm down, Red," Des soothed, even as his eyes rolled back in his head from the visual stimulation and the sensation of having her dance her pussy around on the tip of his cock. He pushed back her satiny ass cheeks with both hands.

"You're very small. It will take some patience. Lift up just for a second."

"But you just fucked me last night and I took all of you!" she cried out in protest, gasping when he plunged first one finger and then two into her pussy. She rocked against him in growing excitement.

"We obviously need to talk. It was a *dream*, baby, not reality," he said through a clenched jaw, aroused to a fever pitch by the feeling of her hot, tight pussy enclosing his fingers. God, this was going to be good. "It was an incredibly hot, mutual dream but a dream nonetheless. *Dios*, you're tight."

"No, you don't understand, even though you saw your mark on me. You don't understand any of it, because I can't even understand it," she sobbed brokenly. "Ah God, Des, I need you inside me."

Des paused at her frantic plea. He *obviously* didn't understand, because he'd never seen a woman this desperate for him. The fact that it was *this* woman who was so needful battered at the limits of his usually rigid control. He brought her to him, carefully fitting the head of his cock into her slit and thrusting upward.

She clasped him like her pussy had been made to order for his cock. He reached blindly for her hips, seeing only the red haze of pure, maddening lust for several seconds. He bit his lip hard and shut his eyes. He felt her push down on him. His hands stilled her hips but not in enough time to stop her from sliding down a few more inches on his cock.

His hips thrust, seemingly of their own volition…and he was lost in her.

He gave a shout of primitive pleasure as he plunged his cock all the way into her snug sheath. She tensed her thighs and slid up his entire length until the head was still embedded in her. He placed his hands on her hips and drove her down on him again, her ass smacking loudly against his thighs.

"*Yeah*," he groaned, already lifting her and pounding her back down his length, his balls slapping against her wet tissues. God, she had the sweetest pussy in existence.

He couldn't get enough of the taut friction and it seemed that neither could she. Their coupling became furious, the pleasure beating at him almost brutally, taking him further, higher, faster into Claire's sweetness.

"Oh God, I'm going to come," she mumbled.

"Then *do* it, beautiful, give it all to me."

He shoved her back onto him at the same time that he thrust his pelvis up, slapping their flesh together, spearing her without mercy. He knew he was fucking her savagely but the knowledge couldn't save him. She was so damned beautiful, so sexy. He couldn't get enough of her.

Every muscle in his body bunched with restraint, his lips pulled across his teeth in a fixed snarl. But as relentlessly as he held himself at the crest of orgasm, he stretched his control impossibly further at the sensation of Claire's pussy climaxing around him, milking his cock rhythmically while he held himself steady at her heated core. Her cries fell past her lips at the same erotic rate that her muscular walls squeezed and tortured him.

He stood abruptly, catching Claire so that she didn't fall. Once she'd accepted her weight on her legs, Des firmly pressed down on her back.

"Bend over," he whispered harshly. Even the energy required to use his voice had been drained to give him just a second more of control.

Pulling his cock out of Claire's pussy felt like the equivalent of stripping buck-naked on a windy, subzero Chicago winter day and diving into Lake Michigan. He shucked off the condom, driving his slick cock between the deep crevice of her ass and along her spine. His fisted his cock at the head and let Claire's satiny soft, firm ass cheeks do the rest. He pumped his hips furiously, watching his ruddy cock slide in between Claire's white ass cheeks.

When the dam broke it did so thunderously. Orgasm blasted through him, the power of his climax commensurate with the immense energy he had utilized to hold it off. He clenched his eyelids shut as he came but it felt as if he jetted quarts of cum up Claire's back. Pleasure wracked his body, seemingly without end.

He eventually collapsed backward on the bed with Claire encircled in his arms. "Holy shit," was all he could manage to get out as he continued to gasp mightily for air.

Claire craned up at his curse and turned around to face him. Their sweat-dampened skin slid together erotically. She loved the feeling of his crisp chest hair abrading her tender skin. He must have become aware of her attempt to face him because he loosened his arms, his hands at her waist, until their bellies were flush. Then he scooted her up until her breasts crushed firmly against his chest and their faces were only inches apart. Claire saw that he was watching her steadily through eyelids weighted with satiation.

"Hey, Red."

"Hey," she whispered back.

"You're saying hello to my insides, Claire. You really did fuck me so hard that you turned me inside out."

Claire dipped her head and placed her cheek on his chest. He chuckled, obviously having seen her blush. She smiled as the lovely sound vibrated up to her ear.

"I know you have no reason to believe me, Des, but I don't usually fall into bed with strangers."

He reached up and prodded her chin gently until she looked up and met his eyes again. "I know you don't, but I'm glad you did this time. It was quite a gift."

Her mouth fell open. He'd seemed entirely genuine. "You're welcome," she mumbled as her cheek fell again to his chest.

"Why are you embarrassed?"

"I don't know. This is all so intense. I didn't even know that you actually existed until an hour ago. I don't even know you. And now look at us. We're all…inside out," she finished lamely.

Des just smoothed his hands reassuringly along the length of her sides, stroking the curve of her hips again and again.

"Your hands are so big," Claire sighed after a minute, as her muscles began to melt into his heat. He grunted in amusement.

"Or maybe it's just that you're so small." His hand swept up to her lower back. "Claire?"

"Yes?"

"Aren't you worried about safe sex?"

She'd practically been purring with contentment but her head sprang up at his words. "You used a condom."

"What about for other things?"

"I'm healthy. I had my annual a few months ago and everything was fine." Heat flooded her cheeks. "I haven't been with anybody for…almost two years now but even then—"

"Claire," Des abruptly halted her.

"What?"

"I wasn't worried about you giving me anything, Red," he murmured, his lips curving into a grin. "You hardly strike me as being the neighborhood tramp type, despite all that dirty talking you do when you get hot."

"*You're* the one who talks dirty, Des. I probably would never talk that way if…" What he was getting at finally breached her awareness. "You're not about to tell me that you're the neighborhood tramp, are you?"

"Scoot off me, just for a second, Claire. Don't get any ideas about going anywhere though. I'm not finished with you yet." His jeans were still bunched around his lower legs. He grabbed something out of the pocket and laid back on the bed, promptly sweeping Claire right back into his arms.

"What's this?" Claire asked in bewilderment when he gave her the folded piece of paper he'd retrieved from his jean pocket.

"Look and see."

She unfolded it and just stared for a few seconds, her bewilderment giving way to amazement then to vague suspicion. "Why did you bring the results of a blood workup that you had done...two days ago with you to my house today?"

"A guy can never be too prepared."

She saw that he was kidding. Her expression altered to a perplexed amusement. "I can only imagine that a man like you must have to make a lot of trips to the doctor if this is how you ensure women that sex with you is safe."

He scowled. "I practice safe sex like most sane men, Claire—by using a condom religiously."

"So why did you bring these papers with you?" she asked dubiously.

His fingers swept onto her back. He grimaced. "We need some tissues, Claire. Why didn't you say anything? You're soaked."

"Des?" Claire insisted even as his taut abdomen muscles flexed and he stretched, reaching for the box of tissues at the side of her bed. "Are you changing the subject, by chance?"

He didn't meet her gaze as he whipped out several tissues and began to mop up her back. It felt as if he'd spurted several quarts of semen on her back.

"Des?"

He sighed as he grabbed more tissues. "How much trouble am I going to be in if I say yes?"

"I don't know for sure. I'm still too stunned to say at the moment."

His eyes flickered up to hers. "I've known for a long time that what just happened was going to happen, Claire."

She gaped at him. "Don't tell me you're psychic too."

He smiled, showing off that deep dimple in his right cheek. Claire was quite sure he used that grin to disarm people. She was certain because it worked so effortlessly on her.

"No, I'm not a psychic. Too bad, I could really put that ability to use. I just meant that it wasn't a matter of whether or not we would get together. It was only a matter of when. Isabelle isn't here anymore to protest and even if she had been I wouldn't have waited much longer anyway. Let's just say the timing was right."

Claire stared at him in dawning amazement. "What made you think I would agree to go to bed with you?"

He merely shrugged. "I thought there was a good chance."

"Cocky," Claire muttered.

"You have some explaining to do yourself, Claire. About the dream," he added when he saw her bewildered expression.

"Oh, that." She shrugged and glanced away. "It was just a regular dream for you, wasn't it?"

"Are you telling me you have other kinds?"

"Last night's was different in a big way," she mumbled.

She sensed his attention on her as he waited for her to explain. She wanted to be honest with Des about her psychic ability. He'd respected her aunt and he loved his grandmother.

Still she hesitated. Old habits died hard. Claire had been shielding her psychic abilities from everyone, most importantly herself, for so long she couldn't bring herself to talk about them with ease.

Something else bothered her. When she'd had that dream about Des, he'd walked into her life the very next day. She shivered. How long would it be before the events that must have led up to the dead woman in the dumbwaiter would take place? Had their lovemaking just been the first of a series of actions that would inevitably lead to that end result, like tipping over the first domino lined up in a predesignated pattern?

No, she couldn't believe that. There had to be some choice, some freedom of action. That was what had made her try to take control of her dreaming to begin with, because she thought she might be able to make a difference.

"Claire, I want you to tell me what's going on with you. Why are you afraid?"

Claire looked at him with surprise. "I thought you said you weren't a psychic."

"I don't have to be a mind reader. It's like I said down in the library, nature didn't build you to keep secrets." He rubbed his big hands along her sides. "You just got goosebumps on your skin while you were thinking whatever you were thinking. Does any of this have to do with your psychic abilities?"

"How do you know about *that*?" Claire asked, wondering how many shocks she could withstand in one evening.

"Your aunt told me," he said quietly as he tossed aside the tissue and enclosed her again in his arms. He slid her several inches along his big, warm body. She felt his cock lurch and stiffen against her belly. "She said that you were even more powerful than she was but that you refused to acknowledge your gift."

Claire's laugh sounded brittle to her own ears. Knowing that Des had known about her freakish nature the whole time made her feel a hundred times more naked than she already was. "She really must have been trying to keep you away from me if she told you that."

He buried his hand into her hair, bringing the strands to his nose and inhaling appreciatively. "You smell like strawberries. Everywhere," he muttered distractedly. Once again she felt his cock jerk against her, arousing her despite her discomfort over the topic of conversation. He met her gaze. "You're the one who has an extreme prejudice against people with psychic abilities, baby. Don't project it onto me."

Claire scowled. She didn't relish being accused of intolerance against any group of people. She saw Des studying her and knew instinctively that he'd known that about her, and had used the knowledge against her.

"Why don't you tell me about it?" he suggested quietly.

"There's not that much to tell. Aunt Isabelle was always trying to get me to hone my skills instead of deny them. After she died I just…" Claire paused. She didn't want to tell him about those disturbing, claustrophobic dreams about the tiny room. He wasn't a part of those. What if her telling him dragged him into them somehow?

She noticed his eyes were narrowing on her as she hesitated. He seemed to have some kind of built-in lie detector. Just her luck to fall for a guy who could sense when she was lying. Not that she planned on making it a regular practice or anything.

Better to tell him at least *some* of the truth. That wasn't lying. Not really.

"I started to feel differently about my abilities after Isabelle died. Like maybe they weren't such a curse after all, more like they were a bond between Isabelle and me."

"You two were really close, weren't you?"

Claire nodded. She told him about looking in the library for a book to help her understand her psychic abilities more. She explained about finding the one Aunt Isabelle had left for her and about doing the exercise from the book before she fell asleep last night.

Once she started to describe how lucid, how hyperreal the dream was, Des interrupted her.

"Wait, Claire. You said that the exercise called for a point of focus. What did you ask to see in your vision?"

She licked her lower lip anxiously and glanced up at him. "I didn't know for sure what to ask for. I just wanted to learn how to use my abilities more. So I just thought—*Let me see whatever it is I most need*. And that's-that's when I saw you."

His eyes gleamed as he watched her. His cock lurched against her once again and Claire realized he was once again completely erect. Claire smiled and slid her body off him, reaching for him. She made a small sound of protest when he caught her wrist.

"Uh-uh. Not yet. First, tell me the rest," he insisted. But Claire didn't miss the new tension in his muscles. She sighed when she saw the resolution in the set of his jaw.

"You know the rest. We made love, there, in the library. You acted like you already knew me, which I guess you did, since like I told you, I'm a future dreamer. The sex was…phenomenal. What do you remember about it from your dream?" she asked him curiously.

He stroked her shoulder. When he spoke his voice sounded low, rough…intimate.

"I just remember little bits and pieces. I remember eating your pussy, sticking my tongue as high up in you as I possibly could, wishing that I was made longer so that I could taste your deepest honey. I remember thinking that I could drown in you, with your cum up my nose, in my mouth and down my throat…and die a very happy man."

"Des," she whispered, overwhelmed by his honesty. She leaned forward and caressed his lips softly with her own. "You told me to lick my cum off your face."

His eyebrows rose with prurient interest. "That's a detail I wish I remember. And did you?"

Claire licked delicately at the seam of his lips. "Yes," she whispered. He opened and their tongues touched lightly, tip to tip. Claire felt her juices start to flow again at the sensation of his teasing, warm tongue.

"And did you like the way you tasted, baby?"

Claire paused for several seconds, enjoying their dueling tongues and the sensation of his big cock throbbing hotly against her belly.

"Uh-huh. But I liked it more because I could taste you underneath. I loved the taste of us mixed together."

He stifled a groan. "Claire, stop a minute."

"Stop what?" she asked as she pressed small, eager kisses along his jawline. "You were the one who was telling me what you recalled about the dream."

"That's all I remember," he said shortly.

"Liar," Claire whispered. She looked up at him seductively beneath her eyelashes. "You said you remembered bending me over the couch and coming inside me while I…"

Despite her flirtatiousness she couldn't quite bring herself to repeat what he'd insisted she'd said in the ultimate heat of the moment. She gasped when a fierce expression hardened Des' face. He moved and she was suddenly looking up into those silvery eyes that reminded her impossibly of hot ice.

"Go ahead. Finish," he challenged with a slight lift of one dark eyebrow.

"While I begged you to give me every last drop of your cum," she whispered.

A taut silence ensued.

"What else did you say while I was fucking you, Claire?"

"I-I don't…really remember…Oh—*Des*," Claire cried out when he suddenly knelt between her legs and pushed back her thighs until she was spread wide.

He stared down at her exposed pussy for several seconds before he took his erect cock in his hand and began to trail the head from her creamy slit up along her clit.

"You have the prettiest pussy. Hold your thighs back with your hands. Make yourself completely available to me."

Claire's hands shot out to press her thighs back, wide open, when she registered his tone. He continued to stare at where he ran his cock over the swollen folds of her labia.

"Now that you've got what you wanted, tell me what else you said."

Claire moaned. She thrust her hips against the heavenly pressure of the hard velvety head of his cock rubbing against her simmering clit. He reached up and palmed one of her breasts surely in his big hand, running his thumb over the sensitive nipple. It immediately beaded tight beneath his fingertip.

She cried out in mounting excitement. Her hips pressed greedily against the hardness of his cock, feeling every texture—the turgid vein that ran on the underside, the thick ridge below the mushroom-shaped head, the very tip of him, as he slid up and over her clit again and again.

When her hips squirmed he stilled her with one hand. Still, he pressed the steely hard, smooth head directly on her clit, massaging the hungry kernel of flesh. Claire grunted softly when he increased the pressure of his cock on her delicate, hungry tissues, rubbing her more forcefully. She was so wet that his cock made a wet sound as he moved it in her juices.

"Oh, I'm going to come," she groaned.

"No, you're not. Not until you tell me what you said while I fucked you." One of his hands opened over her waist and caressed the sides of her torso before he took an aching breast in his hand again, running his big thumb over a peaking nipple.

"Christ you're beautiful," he whispered. He blinked as though waking from a trance and met her gaze. "Now tell me, baby. It's just you and me here. There's no right or wrong to it. It just *is*." He slowed his stimulation of her clit but pinched her nipple harder.

Claire writhed in pleasure, pushing herself up on him frantically. Her eyes clenched shut at the unbearable friction. "I-I told you to fuck me harder, even though you were already drilling into me so hard that I almost couldn't keep myself upright. I told you to..."

"You told me to what?" Des prodded. He thrust along her wet cleft more insistently. Claire cried out as orgasm loomed.

"I told you to...use me...to use me for your pleasure."

His face pulled tight with restraint. He fell over her and planted his arms beside her head, muttering one tense word.

"Come."

He ground his cock against her clit until she trembled and cried out in climax. He flexed his hips, stimulating her throughout her orgasm. Claire was distantly aware of him talking to her, of him telling her how beautiful she was, how responsive, precisely what he was going to do to her in a few seconds...and how much he was going to love it.

So Claire wasn't too shocked by the time she dazedly opened her eyes to see him rolling another condom down his magnificent cock.

Chapter Seven

He rolled back her hips and impaled himself in her with two long, hard strokes. "Such a hot little pussy," he muttered thickly as he watched himself penetrate her.

The sight of his small, male grin of supreme satisfaction made her clench around him even more hungrily.

His smile faded. He held her gaze and stroked her slowly, thoroughly. Claire felt just as penetrated, just as possessed by his light eyes as she was his thrusting cock.

He stretched her, overfilled her. The sensation was akin to pain but wasn't pain. Instead it was an almost unbearable, cruel pleasure. He rubbed someplace deep, reached a place she'd never known existed. She hung on a rack of agonized need.

He must have seen her torment because he increased his pace. The headboard of her bed began to bang rhythmically against the wall as their coupling segued from intense to frantic.

He pushed her legs back until toes hit the mattress on either side of her head. Claire was flexible but it wasn't her leg muscles that he stretched near the point of pain as he took her so fully. Her vagina squeezed him, pulling him deeper. She screamed in ecstasy at the tremendous impact of him pounding into her while her body was so open and vulnerable to him.

"Des! Oh *God*. It's too much..."

His answer was to press up into her, higher and deeper, to tell her with his body that she could...that she must. She cried out sharply, convulsing around him again in orgasm.

"Tell me what else you said," he demanded, his harsh tone breaching even the sensation overload of her climax. His continued relentless fucking amplified her orgasm, making it difficult for her to draw air let alone speak.

"Say it *now*, before I come."

Claire pried her eyelids open so she could see the man who so thoroughly filled her body and mind there was no room left for shame…no room left for *anything* but him.

"I told you to take what is yours," she said shakily. She reached up and smoothed her hand along his hard chest then pinched a dark brown, completely erect nipple. "And I meant it."

His lips curled into a feral snarl.

It was her turn to watch him in fascination as he growled deep in his chest and jerked his cock out of her. He peeled off the condom and tossed it aside. He pumped his engorged cock ruthlessly, his face and eyes clenched tight while he tottered for a second on the edge of climax. Then a deep roar erupted out of his throat as jets of thick white cum spurted on her belly, even arcing up to anoint the lower curve and nipple of her right breast.

Claire stared, awestruck. He looked so beautiful in that moment, so pure and raw, so elementally male. She dipped her finger into his hot fluid.

When she opened her eyes he was on hands and knees over her, still gasping for breath. But his magnificent eyes seemed to glow with unspoken emotion as he watched her slide her finger from her mouth.

"You undo me, little witch." A hand that personified strength trembled slightly when he reached up and palmed her jaw. "Are you all right, baby? I-I lost control. I never do that. Never. I don't know what…" Claire made a sound of protest when he abruptly stood up next to the bed.

"I'll get something to clean you up." He scooped up his jeans as he headed into her bathroom.

Claire lay there, stunned by his abrupt departure, his warm semen cooling on her skin. When he returned he was wearing his jeans, even though they were only partially buttoned. Claire began to sit up, suddenly feeling self-conscious when he was dressed and she was lying there naked and spread-eagle with his seed glistening all over her belly and breasts.

Something that looked like regret flickered across his handsome face. "Lie still. Let me clean you up."

He carried one of her washcloths and a towel. He sat on the edge of the bed and pressed the warm washcloth to her belly, wiping his semen off her carefully.

"What's wrong, Des?"

His eyes just followed his actions and he didn't speak for a minute as he cleaned her belly and breasts gently. "Just a second," he said gruffly.

Claire stopped him before he stood again. She felt it again and it alarmed her…just like she had in the dream—his withdrawal.

He was there with her, but he *wasn't*.

"I'll be right back," he muttered.

She dropped his hand reluctantly.

When he returned he'd switched washcloths. He sat down next to her, his eyes seeming to glow like banked flames.

"Spread your thighs, Claire."

Claire thought of refusing him but something in his expression made her open herself to him.

Again.

She closed her eyes, overwhelmed by the intimacy of him gently washing her pussy with the warm, wet cloth and then drying her, his actions focused and tender. Claire felt both cherished and uncertain. He'd pulled away from her but she couldn't say how exactly…or why.

She watched him as he bent his dark head and examined her pussy when he was finished. She couldn't believe it when he pursed his lips and shot a focused stream of cool air on her enflamed, damp cunt. He'd meant it to be soothing…calming. She could tell by his manner.

A low moan escaped her throat, the intimate caress heating instead of cooling her. Why did every damned thing he did make her want him all over again?

Des heard her and glanced up into her face. "Are you sore? I was so rough with you…and you're so small."

"*You* were there. I was hardly complaining. Des, what's really wrong?"

He tossed the towel aside and came onto the bed, bringing her into his arms.

"Are you really that concerned about it?" Claire whispered. "I'm not *breakable*. I liked it as much as you did, trust me."

He sighed. His voice was a low, husky rumble against her ear when he brought her back next to him. "You must have liked it a hell of a lot then."

She smiled, sensing some of the tension easing out of his muscles.

"Finish telling me about the dream," he said. "I want all the details…not the ones about the sex, at least not right now. I want to keep my focus."

Claire couldn't say exactly why his withdrawal bothered her so much but it had to do with the dream last night, how desperate she'd been to reach out to him in his stark desolation. She sighed, telling herself she was just imagining things. Didn't lots of men withdraw emotionally after sex, feeling vulnerable and exposed after the intimacy of the act? If that were true in general then she was surprised Des wasn't racing out the front door after the degree of intimacy they'd just shared.

She leaned back, studying his impassive, handsome face. *Maybe* that was why he was behaving this way...but she doubted it, for some reason.

"I saw you sitting in front of the fireplace in the library," she began softly. "You were so sad, so alone. Something told me I was supposed to warn you, get you to help me—"

She felt him tense. "Warn me about what?"

"Something bad," Claire whispered. "You weren't aware of me in the dream. So I sort of...made a conduit between us, using my attraction to you. Then you saw me. You felt me. I let it get out hand though."

"Are you trying to tell me that we had that mutual dream of having sex because you were trying to *warn* me about something?"

She nodded. "It worked...a little better than I expected it would. I connected to you but in the dream it was too late to stop...what happened."

His brow creased with confusion. "I don't know what you're talking about."

"You don't remember in the dream? After we made love, there was that woman...hanging dead in the dumbwaiter?"

"*What?*" He sat up on the bed, his eyes blazing. He gripped her shoulders. "What the hell are you talking about, Claire?"

She gave a helpless shrug beneath his hands. "I think that the tragedy that I was trying to prevent in the dream was my own. You and I went up to Aunt Isabelle's room and I was...hanging there, lifeless...in the dumbwaiter."

Claire almost backed away from Des' intensity when he suddenly reached up and held her face. His tortured, incredulous expression stunned her.

"Christ, is that what you've been thinking? That it was *you* hanging there in that dumbwaiter? You thought you were *foreseeing your own death?*"

Claire nodded, overwhelmed by his palpable anxiety.

"It doesn't mean that it's going to happen, Des. I'm going to do everything to make sure it doesn't. I've thought a lot about it. Maybe there are some things that are predestined but very few, I have a feeling. I don't believe in fixed destiny. Most things in future dreams are probabilities, not absolutes."

"But why? Why in the world would you think that was *you*?"

"B-because I saw…"

"What? What did you see?"

"I saw the hair. I saw my bracelet."

Des' eyes looked a little wild as he shook his head.

"No, *no*, you've misunderstood, baby. What you saw…that wasn't *you*. It wasn't the future, it was the past. You saw something that happened here in this house eighteen years ago."

Chapter Eight

Claire stared at him, stunned.

"Your aunt, your parents, nobody ever told you about what happened here?"

She shook her head.

He closed his eyes, trying to still his chaotic thoughts. Jesus, this was the last thing he'd expected. He felt rattled to the core at the idea of her seeing something so frightening.

Something so personal.

And then she'd thought it'd been *her*.

"I guess you couldn't have been any more than eleven or twelve years old at the time," he muttered, trying to piece things together in his whirling mind. "I can see why they would have kept it from you, to protect you. Still, it was in the news—"

"It wouldn't have been that hard to keep me ignorant of what was on the news," Claire interrupted. "When I was eleven I never watched the news unless I walked in the room and my father had it turned on. It wasn't as if I read the newspaper then either. What happened, Des?"

He opened his eyes slowly, bringing Claire into focus. "A girl killed herself here, in this house. It was when Kevin and I were both seventeen years old. Kevin had a party one night after a basketball game. Your aunt was on one of her trips to China. A girl committed suicide that night…just like you saw it."

"You know my cousin Kevin?"

He nodded, carefully examining her reaction. What did Claire think of Isabelle's only son?

"We were in the same year at the University Lab School," he said, referring to the high school where many University of Chicago professors' children were enrolled. "We played sports together."

"How did they know it was a suicide?" Claire asked reluctantly.

"She left a note."

"You knew her well, didn't you?"

Des nodded, schooling his features into impassivity. "Yeah. I'd known her since we were in the sixth grade. We'd dated for about a year and a half. I'd just broken up with her right before it happened."

"Oh Des, *no*," Claire whispered, her tone laced with dread. She reached out and touched his shoulder. "Is that…is that why you have nightmares?"

He glanced away, feeling uncomfortably exposed under Claire's compassionate gaze. "Her name was Alanna Hartfield. She obviously was a lot less emotionally stable then I'd imagined, but I didn't really imagine much about other people's issues. I was seventeen years old—stupid and selfish."

Claire put both her hands on his shoulders and molded the muscle soothingly.

"What seventeen-year-old kid isn't self-centered? Des, when people end their lives it's a terrible tragedy and loss. But Alanna made that choice. She must have had so many problems to take her own life in such a violent way. Please, believe me when I say this—her issues had to have been much deeper and more serious than just having her boyfriend break up with her in order for her to do what she did. Think of how many times boys and girls break up with each other every day and they survive, move on, heal from heartbreak and live their lives."

He felt Claire's searching stare on his averted face.

"Did Alanna mention you in the note, Des?"

Claire waited for what felt like a tense eternity for Des to answer her question.

"Not specifically, no," he eventually said. "She just said she didn't want to go on living any more."

Claire hugged him tightly, pressing her lips to his neck. *Of course.* Everything made more sense to her now. Because she had this close, unexplainable connection with him, Claire had seen him suffer during his own dreams.

But Claire couldn't protect him from the pain. Des had already been experiencing the pain of that night for almost half of his life. His arms came around her after a moment and they just held each other for a while in silence. Her heart was beating rapidly. After a moment she realized her anxiety stemmed from feeling his withdrawal, his distance, just like she'd felt in the dream…when he'd seemed so locked away from her.

Eventually she felt some of the tension leave his muscles. How traumatic it must have been for him. It would be bad enough to lose a friend or close acquaintance at the impressionable age of seventeen but to lose a girlfriend, and to find her in such horrific circumstances, would have been downright life-altering.

Claire knew that there were plenty of cases when females killed themselves violently but such violent suicides—hanging, intentional car crashes, gunshots—were more commonly committed by men. Alanna Hartfield had certainly left life shaking her fist in anger at the people she'd left behind, perhaps most especially in Des Alvarez's face.

"What about my bracelet, Des?" she asked, leaning back to look at his face.

Des slid his hands up and down her back. Claire was touched that he tried to soothe her even though he was the one who had clearly been more affected by the revelation of her dream.

"I gave Alanna that bracelet when I was sixteen years old. She had it on when she died." When he saw the question in her eyes Des shrugged. "I don't know, Claire. The bracelet must have fallen off sometime when I pulled her out of the dumbwaiter or during the investigation and your aunt found it."

"No wonder you were so freaked out when you saw it on me."

Des' hands spanned her waist. "What I experienced when I saw that bracelet is *nothing* compared to what you must have been thinking when you saw me at your door today."

A part of Claire realized that he was shifting the topic away from himself, uncomfortable discussing his private pain. The dream memory of trying to reach him when he was so locked away in his grief filled her awareness again, bringing all of the helplessness and desperation that she experienced with it. Tears stung her eyes.

"You believed that you were possibly going to die and that your death was somehow connected to me and yet you still made love with me?" he asked in amazement.

Claire had the impression that he was torn between being touched by the fact that she'd shared herself with him under those circumstances and giving her a lecture on taking such a risk with her life, even if the assumption she'd made turned out to be invalid.

"Why? Why would you do something like that?" he demanded.

She shook her head, causing a tear to spill down her cheek. "I don't know. I kept telling myself it was crazy. But my fear wasn't enough to overcome how much I wanted you."

He just stared at her for a long moment. Finally he gently released himself from her arms and stood up.

"Where are you going?" she asked, surprised when he headed for the door.

"I need a drink, and you look like you could use one too. You're extremely pale. I assume that the bar is still down in the game room?"

By the time he had returned with two highball glasses partially filled with amber liquid, Claire had changed into some comfortable sweats and a tank top, brushed her teeth and washed her face. She felt drained. Maybe Des was right. What had happened tonight, what she'd learned tonight, had gotten to her.

Her eyes flickered warily to Des. He'd given her a glass and sat in a chair, sipping his drink. A shadow partially covered his face. She experienced a sense of distance from him that wasn't entirely related to the physical space that parted them.

"Are you leaving?" she asked, sounding calmer than she felt. Claire suddenly was poignantly aware of everything that had passed between them. Maybe he was feeling a little exposed, like she had intruded on what had always been a private experience for him. Was he thinking she was weird, abnormal? He was probably imagining she was a lot more than he'd bargained for.

But Claire couldn't validate or disconfirm her fears based on anything Des gave away in his expression.

"Do you want me to go?" he asked quietly.

Claire met his gaze and shook her head.

A shadow of a smile ghosted his lips. "Claire, before you came to live here, did you ever dream or have any visions about this house or your family members?"

"Why do you ask me that?" she asked slowly. "Aunt Isabelle asked me the same thing a couple days before she died."

Des just watched her impassively. "You're a psychic. Considering there was a tragedy here years ago, it seems like a logical question to ask. You used to come here fairly frequently as a child, didn't you?"

"Yes."

"So the question is—why did you see the vision now?"

"I don't know. But I never dreamed of this house until I inherited it. I always felt comfortable here before…"

"Before what?" he asked sharply when she trailed off.

"Before Aunt Isabel died. To be honest, I've felt watched since I've moved in here. Sometimes the presence feels comforting, protective…sort of like, well, it reminds me of Aunt Isabelle. At other times it's creepy, like whoever is watching me is angry. Like they don't want me in this house."

"Are you saying you think the house is haunted?"

"*Haunted*? Oh come on, Des," she scoffed. It was bad enough that she'd started to take her psychic abilities seriously, surely she wasn't going to start believing in ghosts, was she?

Des touched his fingers to his eyes. Claire realized that he looked even more exhausted then she felt.

"I'm going to go clean up, if that's okay," he murmured as he stood.

Claire cuddled down into the pillows, sleepiness slowly beginning to slide across her awareness. When he emerged from the bathroom he was only wearing a pair of white boxer briefs that made a sensual contrast to his dusky, smooth skin.

What an incredibly beautiful man, she thought dazedly. She held her breath as she watched him carefully drape his clothes on the chair and approach the bed, her mind reliving every detail of the amazing sex they'd just had.

Her sleepiness vanished instantly.

He paused next to the bed, looking down at her. "You should finish the rest of your drink."

Claire frowned but took the final swallow of the bourbon, wincing only a little at the burn in her throat and chest.

Des took her glass, set it on the bedside table and switched off the lamp. He got into bed and reached for her.

Claire settled against his chest, his arms closing around her. She shut her eyes, savoring the sensation of his solid warmth and nearness.

She felt uncertain about where they stood. He seemed so preoccupied, distant. Claire moved her hand, ready to stroke his chest, his stomach, wanting to arouse him to a place where no barriers could exist between them. But before she could Des gripped her hand as if he could see her in the dark. He caressed the center of her open palm slowly, making shivers of pleasure run up her spine.

"Go to sleep, Claire. You should rest."

Claire paused, uncertainty filling her. More than likely he was feeling as if his privacy had been tread upon with her psychic knowledge.

She'd judged herself harshly for the majority of her life for possessing psychic abilities. It wasn't hard for her to imagine that somebody else would judge her in return. But Des was here with her, in her arms. At least he hadn't fled in disgust.

With that thought, she fell into a deep sleep.

Something poked Claire sharply in the back.

She turned abruptly in the darkness. The scent of Des and their lovemaking filled her nose, bringing her immediately into wakefulness. Her hand shot out on the bed...but no.

She was alone.

Her heart began to beat rapidly when she saw the opened bathroom door. No light shone from within. Where the heck was Des?

She turned on the light and searched the bed for what had jabbed her. Her gaze fell on the book, *Dreams, Prophecy and the Future*. It had been placed just inside the bedcovers in the spot where Des had been when she'd fallen asleep. Claire would have taken an oath that she'd moved the book to the bureau at the far side of her room. Did Des put it there?

It was still several hours until dawn. He wouldn't just leave without waking her. Would he? Memories of their lovemaking swamped her. Mild panic followed on the coattails of all those graphic, arousing images.

He paused just inside the door when he saw her sitting there with the light on. His gaze flickered across her naked body before he closed the door.

"Sorry, I hope I didn't wake you."

"What's wrong?" Claire whispered. He felt a burst of irritation surge through him when she covered her beautiful body from his gaze with the sheet. What should he expect, after all? The circumstances would surely make her feel vulnerable and uncertain. She'd caught him returning from searching her house. He was completely dressed—including wearing his socks and shoes. Meanwhile she was gloriously nude, looking soft and sexy in a bed rumpled from their lovemaking—

"I thought I heard something downstairs," he said gruffly, forcing his stare away from the sight of her nipples pressing against the thin sheet.

"Is everything okay?"

Des nodded as he headed for the bathroom. "Must have been some kids out on the street or something. I searched the house, everything seems fine," he said before he shut the bathroom door.

He grimaced at his reflection in the bathroom mirror. Lying to her was really starting to bug him. He'd been searching the house all right, but not because he'd heard a noise. How could he explain himself when he wasn't sure what exactly he was searching for in the Preskill mansion? He'd awakened earlier feeling edgy, like he'd forgotten something important, even though he rationally knew he hadn't.

He must be losing his fucking mind, he thought as he quickly shed his shoes and socks and stripped out of his clothes. He'd gone out to his car and retrieved his gun. Maybe he couldn't rest in this house unless he had his weapon in close proximity. He made sure the safety was on before he carefully concealed the gun in his clothing.

His cock was erect when he peeled off his boxer briefs. That was what just one, all-too-brief glance at Claire's white skin, bare breasts and the sexy spill of her strawberry blonde hair falling around her naked shoulders had done to him.

He placed his clothing on an upholstered chair and approached the bed. Claire's sapphire-blue eyes flickered down over his naked body, feeling like the equivalent of a light electric current buzzing under his skin. His cock jerked in arousal.

"Why are you holding that book?"

She stared down at *Dreams, Prophecy and the Future* as though surprised at the sight of it. "Did you put this book in the bed before you left?"

He grinned before he switched out the lamp. "No, I wasn't really up for any late-night reading."

He grabbed the book from her and placed it on her bedside table. His arms were around her almost instantly, turning her on her side and molding his front to her back, spooning her. Claire moaned shakily when he pressed his cock against her ass.

He was *up* for something all right, just not reading.

His hand caressed her waist and stomach. He experienced a fresh wave of awe and delight at the incredible softness of her skin. He skimmed his fingers along the lower curve of a breast. She whimpered. He leaned forward, pressing his lips into the back of her neck before he spoke.

"Is it okay?"

"Yes," she said, turning her face toward him.

He hardly waited for her acquiescence before covering her lips with his own. Their mouths mated feverishly, desperately, both of them unable to quite satisfy their need for the taste and sensation of the other. Des pressed his cock into the crevice of her ass and flexed his hips. Claire trembled beneath his hand. She felt hot, feverish.

He reached around her and eased his forefinger between her labia, dipping into warm cream.

"You're so wet. You're ready for me already," he groaned in amazed satisfaction.

She sought out his mouth in the pale moonlight that bathed the room. He kissed her upturned lips with cherishment. Then he pillaged and plundered, ravaging the sweet cove of her mouth without restraint. He stroked her cunt, pulling her taut, coaxing gasps and cries from her throat.

They went on that like that, kissing voraciously while his cock throbbed hotly between her ass cheeks and he built the friction in her flesh. He caressed a breast, rolling the nipple between his calloused fingertips until she screamed.

He couldn't figure out how the feeling of her shaking in orgasm against him made him want to cherish and protect her and fuck her mercilessly, both at once. Des nursed her through her climax, his fingers coaxing every last shiver of pleasure from her body, enthralled by the intensity and honesty of her response.

He suddenly groaned, his forehead dropping against her shoulder.

"What's wrong?" Claire asked breathlessly.

"Please tell me you've got a condom somewhere."

"Oh...I don't. I'm sorry." Her whimper mixed with his moan of frustration.

"You can still fuck me," she whispered, as though what she said was a great secret—an intimacy shared between them and them alone. "Just don't come inside me. I just finished my period. The chances of me getting pregnant are negligible."

He raised his head slowly. "Are you sure?"

Claire nodded quickly. His cock jerked against her ass.

Des knew he shouldn't but he was just that fucking desperate to be enfolded in Claire's sweetness that he ignored his mental misgivings. What she did to him was akin to a madness.

He *had* to have her, hard and deep. They were both healthy. He wouldn't come inside her, but it would feel so damned *good* for his cock to be naked in her tight pussy.

Her heat penetrated him as he slowly drove into her. He thrust forcefully, deeper and deeper into her sweetness. Claire felt like life itself to him at that moment, hot, encompassing, primal. He held her steady and slammed into her again and again until he thought not just his cock would explode but his head, his heart...his whole damn world.

He didn't want to come before her but he found he couldn't control himself. His seed boiled in his balls. He whipped his cock out of her, almost too late. "Hold your ass up for me, baby," he grated out.

He growled like an animal at the erotic moonlit image of her tilting up her pale, round bottom in offering to him. His shout shattered the silence, harsh and anguished. He cupped one plump cheek tautly in his hand and bathed the luminescent globe with his seed.

Afterward he realized he was still erect. It stunned him.

Part of his original plan in coming there that evening had been not just to make love to Claire but to overwhelm her...to *force* her to accept him. He could only protect her if she allowed him to be with her, especially when she was alone in that house at night. His body seemed more than willing to follow his plans for overwhelming her. Still, he should watch himself. His need was almost savage at times.

He was almost painfully aware of his seed glistening on her round bottom. beckoning to him in the darkness. Her ribs expanding and contracting rapidly as she tried to catch her breath. He stroked the beguiling curve of her hip and waist and cradled a suspended breast, caressing a nipple. With his other hand he reached between her thighs.

He listened intently to her catchy sighs and whimpers, using them as evidence to amplify her pleasure, enraptured by the experience of learning Claire's body. Hearing her cry out as she came was his rich reward.

Awhile later she opened her eyes to see his face just inches from her own.

"Are you smiling?"

"Yes," he said huskily.

"Why?"

"Because I'm a hell of a lucky man, that's why," he murmured. He felt her smile pressed into his neck after he'd dried her off and rolled her into his arms.

"Are you okay, Red? Was I too rough?"

"You were definitely rough. Good thing I loved it."

"You're so sexy," he murmured, puzzled by the strength of his physical attraction to her. He spread his hand over the back of her skull and ran his fingers through her hair. "I'm a little worried about losing control with you. I don't want to."

"I like it—*love* it when you get wild," she whispered. He realized with an upsurge of tenderness that she was embarrassed by her admission.

She was so sweet, sexy…fresh.

He closed his eyes, feeling calmed by the unique scent of strawberries and sex rising off Claire's hair and skin. He kissed her once on her forehead.

"You won't love it so much tomorrow when you're dead on your feet at work because I kept you up all night ravishing your body. Go to sleep, Claire. Sweet dreams."

Claire murmured contentedly, already heeding Des' advice as she inhaled his rich male scent and her muscles grew warm and heavy.

But her dreams were far from sweet.

Chapter Nine

She first became aware that she was dreaming when she was blind despite her eyes being wide open.

It was such a disturbing effect that her hands went out to grasp at something—anything—to gain her bearings. She reached out, encountering walls before her arms were fully outstretched. She was in the familiar trapped space...the tiny, claustrophobic room.

No, not this dream again.

But even as the feeling of familiarity struck her she couldn't recall any other details...just the familiar sense of airlessness and dread.

Her senses sharpened in the darkness. She reached out and touched walls on each side of her. Was it a closet? She realized that she could see a faint but definite issuance of light. It streamed through a narrow rectangular pattern about three feet above her head.

She wanted *out* of there. There was something disturbing, a feeling of heavy tension in the unmoving air. A shadow flitted in front of the rectangle of light. Her heart seemed to cease beating a moment before it continued with a throbbing beat in her ears. She recognized the outline of hair. She bit her lip to stifle a gasp.

Someone shared this tiny space with her.

She went very still, a hunted animal suddenly aware of the proximity of a hunter.

The hair was cut short, leading Claire to believe it was a man. He must have been standing on something to reach the rectangular opening. He moved stealthily, causing a slight rustling of clothing.

Whoever she shared this hellishly small space with seemed to be making an effort to breathe quietly, occasionally holding their breath. For a moment Claire thought it meant that her presence was known. Slowly, she realized that the breathing was irregular because he was trying to listen, not to her, but to something that was taking place outside of the narrow room. Despite his efforts to control his breath it continued uneven and choppy, as though the person was excited.

Or aroused.

Claire mentally focused her own hearing, and as if in response to her unspoken request muted noises began to enter her awareness. At first she just heard a scraping sound, as if a piece of furniture or a bed had given slightly when someone sat on it or got off it. Then there was a slight rustling of bedclothes or fabric. She made out a plaintive female voice but Claire couldn't tell exactly what she was saying. It took her a minute to discern two voices—a man's and a woman's.

A conversation ensued. She couldn't decipher the actual words, just the tones and cadence. The woman sounded desperate, as if she was pleading for something. The man's tone was tense, unhappy. Once she heard him say, "It was a mistake," but Claire couldn't hear the rest of the words, as if the speaker had temporarily turned toward the closet and then away again, the tone apologetic but firm.

A door closed and silence followed. There were moans and then the distinct sounds of crying.

Claire had been so focused on hearing the exchange that she'd temporarily forgotten that someone else had been listening to the muted conversation. The man near her moved slightly now. Her fellow voyeur. A feeling of guilt washed through her at the thought, even though she knew her participation was far from being something she wanted or chose.

The man, on the other hand, had hidden himself with full intent on eavesdropping on the couple in the outside room. Claire sensed eagerness on his part...anticipation. He'd done this before. It was a type of foreplay to him, Claire realized with distaste. She wasn't sure how she knew but she didn't think to question the knowledge.

That was when she realized that the woman was alone in the outer room and that she didn't know that someone was spying on her, someone seeming to enjoy her vulnerability while relishing a unique position of power. Her crying was fading now. Only an occasional whimper punctuated the quiet but Claire sensed that the woman's focus was on something else. Claire heard a rattling noise like pills being shaken from a plastic bottle. The man moved, as though aware that the wait was almost over. The rectangle of muted light slowly began to shrink and then disappeared.

Claire's heart thundered. She was utterly blind in the pitch blackness but she heard a rustling above her and to her right. She cringed back, repulsed at the idea of the man touching her. Heavy air pressed down on her lungs, sucking all her breath. She was wet with sweat on her neck.

Something was about to happen and she couldn't even inhale the sickly air, let alone move. She gasped and cried out shakily when something brushed against her face, as if a rope had been uncoiled from above her.

A fear like she'd never before experienced temporarily immobilized her. Although no light entered the dreadful place, Claire distinctly heard a click and then a sliding noise. The air moving across her face brought her no relief, instead increased her panic. Despite her blindness and fear she flailed forward in the blackness, determined to warn the woman, help her if she could.

But the clutches of the nightmare squeezed their grip on her, mocking her efforts. Although her feet moved, she could never reach the end of the narrow space. Her hands sought wildly for something solid but there was nothing. She shouted out in surprise and anger, feeling tricked and betrayed.

Why was she being forced to see these dreams, only to be left useless and ineffective time and again? She would *not* allow it. She would *not* –

"Claire! Wake up, baby."

Her eyes flew open. She raised her hands and fought wildly against the shadow leaning over her in the darkened room.

"Hey...calm down. It's me. Des."

"I will *not* be used by you!" she cried out bitterly when he caught her flailing arms and secured her wrists with one hand.

The lamp switched on. She blinked in disorientation at the sight of Des leaning over her, his dark hair falling on his forehead, his face tight with concern.

"You were dreaming." He caressed her cheek, drying scattered tears. Claire was mortified to realize she couldn't stop her shaking. Des slowly released her wrists and lightly touched her neck and shoulder in a soothing gesture.

"You're soaked." His eyes scoured her face. Claire wondered what he saw when his big hand froze on her neck. "Claire...are you all right?"

She nodded but she *wasn't* all right. Her stomach cramped painfully, as if her body needed to physically rid itself of the violence and twisted energy she'd been exposed to in the dream.

"Bathroom," she whispered shakily.

Des moved off the bed quickly. Damn, she must look like hell if his rigid, worried expression was any indication. She tottered when she stood but his hands were immediately there to steady her. He helped her to the bathroom and switched on the light.

"Claire?"

She made an incoherent sound of misery, dropped to the floor in front of the toilet and became violently ill. After a tortuous span of time, which was likely only thirty seconds, she came to the mortifying realization that Des held back her long hair while she vomited.

Great way to impress the man of your dreams—puke out your guts while he watches, she thought woozily. God, this sucked.

She spit and inhaled raggedly. She ached. Her insides felt like they'd been scraped raw.

"Please go, Des. This is so embarrassing," she whispered miserably.

"No, baby, I'm not going anywhere." He touched her neck gently. "Do you think you'll be sick more?"

She waited before she answered, testing the sensations of her body. "No, I'm okay now." She started to get up and Des instantly rose to help her. "I just…need to shower and brush my teeth."

God, this was so embarrassing. Tears filled her eyes when she finally dared to glance up and saw the expression on his face. His features were as hard as ever but his light eyes looked a little wild with what she recognized as worry. It was that look in his eyes that emotionally undid her even more than the nightmare or the fact that he'd just observed her upchuck what felt like everything she'd eaten for the past week.

"I'll just start the shower for you and leave you alone then. If you're sure you'll be okay?"

Claire nodded.

Something caught her eye when Des opened the frosted pane of her shower door. She blinked, trying to bring her eyes into focus.

"What the fuck?" Des asked in amazement as he turned to Claire.

A frisson of fear ran through her at the anomaly of what they both saw. She looked up at Des helplessly. "Des, don't look at me like that. I don't understand it any more than you do. I don't understand anything about what's been happening lately."

His mouth sagged. He must have sensed her desperation. "Come here, Claire."

Claire went into his comforting embrace, pressing a tear-soaked cheek to his chest. But she couldn't stop herself from peering past him to see the white ceramic bottom of the shower. Hundreds, thousands of oak leaves covered her shower floor, looking as green and freshly fallen as if they'd just blown off a tree moments ago.

"I don't even have a window in this bathroom," Claire laughed hysterically against his chest.

"Claire, have you had nightmares like that before?"

Reassuring daylight flooded the foyer where they were standing as Des prepared to leave. Claire had gotten ready for work the in the guest bathroom, avoiding the bizarre sight of the leaves and her thoughts about the nightmare. She'd felt embarrassed but thankful when he'd casually told her a short while ago that he'd cleaned up all of the leaves. For some reason the thought of doing it herself had filled her with dread. At the time he'd said it Des had been casually leaning against her kitchen counter sipping a cup of black coffee, looking incredibly sexy with a light morning stubble shadowing his jaw.

She glanced downward, avoiding his gaze. "A few. They started after Isabelle died."

Des' eyebrows pulled into a frown as he studied her. He put his hand to her jaw, tilting her face up so that he could see her wide eyes.

"I want to know about them, Claire. I want to know about what's scaring you."

"They're not like the other dream, the dumbwaiter dream, Des. You're not a part of them." *And I'd prefer to keep it that way,* Claire added silently. His expression hardened.

"You're going to tell me about them. I know you have to go to work right now. You can tell me tonight."

She opened her lips to protest, but he cut her off by kissing her, deep and thorough. Her toes curled into the oriental carpet.

"I'll be by at six-thirty tonight to pick you up. You can tell me about the dreams after dinner."

Claire was left staring stupidly as he walked out her front door, her well-kissed mouth hanging open. What an insufferable man. He'd just assumed she would tell him about the claustrophobic dreams because he *said* it was so.

She sighed as she went back upstairs. Stubborn or not, he'd been gone for all of fifteen seconds and she missed him already.

Claire suddenly detoured to Aunt Isabelle's room. She wasn't aware of making a decision to go in there. All she knew was that she was suddenly standing a few feet inside of the door. A chill went through her. That increasingly familiar feeling had returned. She felt watched by an angry, wrathful presence. The hair on her arms prickled. An animal-like fear caused her to start toward the door but she paused suddenly, frowning when her eyes fell on the hammer. It was still where she'd left it on a dresser yesterday morning after pulling the nails out of the dumbwaiter door. She specifically remembered leaving the extracted nails next to the hammer. She'd been late in preparing for work and she'd told herself she would retrieve the hammer and dispose of the nails another time.

Her gaze flashed to the dumbwaiter door. She didn't inhale a breath for a full fifteen seconds as she went closer and ran her fingers over the wood. Every nail had been replaced. Claire tugged with disbelief but the door was shut so tightly it was like it was vacuum sealed, despite the fact that the nails had been put back in their original ragged holes. Claire backed away, her expression rigid and incredulous in the face of the unexplained phenomenon.

There was no way those nails could have gotten back into the dumbwaiter door.

"Of course there's a way," she muttered to herself thickly. "The same way that those leaves got in my shower—someone had to put them there."

Claire glanced around nervously, not liking that possibility any more than she did the option of a supernatural explanation. Her feet couldn't move fast enough as she raced out of Isabelle's room.

She flew down the grand staircase too quickly for safety, pausing suddenly at the bottom.

Of course. Des must have put the nails back in the dumbwaiter. It wouldn't have been a shocking thing for him to do, especially considering what he'd told her about Alanna Hartfield last night.

But what about those leaves in her shower? He had been up last night in the middle of the night. Who knew how long he'd been gone before Claire awoke, alone. She scoffed at the idea even as she made sure her front door was locked and exited the house.

While she could at least remotely imagine that he might nail up the dumbwaiter again, why in the world would he put all those leaves in her shower? Why would *anybody* for that matter? Claire peered at the trees that lined her street. It was midsummer, for God's sake. The leaves wouldn't fall for several months still. Someone would have had to have climbed up into the branches of a tree and pluck off all of those leaves one by one, collect them and put them in her shower. And what the heck for? Just to freak her out?

If that was their motive, they'd certainly succeeded.

Her gaze fell on a blond man watching her in a car parked across the street. She stared, her footsteps slowing on the sidewalk. He started the engine and drove away.

Claire shook her head in frustration as she got behind the wheel of her car. God, she was getting twitchy and paranoid.

The next thing she knew she was going to start believing in aliens and that the FBI was spying on her, she thought with a disgusted roll of her eyes. Des already had her considering the idea of a ghost in her house.

She managed to stay focused at work that day but barely. When she got home she pulled one outfit after another out of her closet, not completely satisfied with the thought of wearing any of them for an evening with Des.

"I'm acting like a giddy teenager on her first date," she mumbled to herself.

But even as she said it, she knew it wasn't true. Claire had never been so acutely anticipatory in her life about spending an evening with any man as she was with Des Alvarez. And the level of sexual tension that was growing in her was far from being appropriate for a sixteen-year-old girl.

She finally settled on a soft, feminine, knee-length light pink skirt and a matching sleeveless blouse that managed to both complement her coloring and cover the hickey on her shoulder. Claire smiled ruefully, thinking how embarrassing it would be if Carlos Alvarez saw her son's teeth marks on her skin.

How is it possible that you became such an insatiable slut in such a short period of time? Claire amusedly asked her reflection in the mirror. The woman who stared back at her didn't look like a wanton. In fact, she looked downright tame.

She grinned widely. Maybe her carnal thoughts were what made her leave her wavy hair loose and falling around her shoulders. She'd just fastened a pair of small diamonds in her ears and grabbed some heels when she heard her doorbell ring.

"Hi," she said, breathless from running down the stairs to answer the door. The sight of Des standing there on her front porch didn't do much to calm her breathing. He was wearing a light blue button-down shirt this evening but the sleeves were rolled back casually. Her eyes lingered hungrily at the sight of his strong, veined forearms lightly sprinkled with dark hair.

He wore a casual pair of khakis instead of jeans but Claire noticed that they still rode enticingly low on his flat stomach and narrow hips.

"Des," Claire laughed when, without returning her greeting, he lowered his head to her neck and inhaled. He pressed his body to her, backing her up into the foyer. His mouth had already taken possession of hers by the time he slammed the front door behind him. His tongue speared into her mouth again and again, as if he were firmly re-establishing his claim on her, before he finally slowed enough to toy and tangle his tongue with hers.

Claire moaned into his mouth when she felt his palms cradle the side of her breasts and his thumbs slide erotically over her nipples.

"Des?" she questioned shakily as she hesitantly broke their kiss. "Aren't we going to be late for your dad's birthday dinner?"

"Probably. You make me so hot though," he muttered against her neck. "I've been walking around with a hard-on all day. I almost jacked off a dozen different times but I held off. Well, except for that one time in the bathroom at lunchtime, but nobody's perfect, right?" he teased against her lips. He must have noticed how red her cheeks went at his casual admission. He grinned as he touched his lips to the telltale signs of her embarrassment.

She cleared her throat hesitantly. She may be embarrassed but as usual, his stark honesty aroused her like nothing she'd ever experienced.

"Do you want me to make you come before we go?" she asked, pleased by the evenness of her voice.

Des rarely ever looked surprised at this point in his life but those words coming out of elegant Claire Allen's lips unhinged his jaw. He just watched, speechless, as she unbuckled his belt. Her eager hands worked quickly, stretching his briefs carefully over his erection and then sliding them and his pants down over his ass and thighs. He groaned desperately when she caressed his ass cheeks before she fisted his cock.

"*Dios mio,*" Des muttered in a choked voice. They both watched as she began to stroke and play with him. Just the sight of her small, white hand on his ruddy erection almost had him emptying himself into her palm.

Claire smoothed her hand up and down his length then paused to linger at the head, fascinated by the sensation of him. His skin was so soft, and it stretched impossibly tight over his steely length. She ran a fingertip over a distended purple vein. Her tongue flicked over her lips hungrily. She longed to trace it with her tongue. She pressed her thumb rhythmically beneath his swollen head, as she'd watched him do when he pleasured himself. Des gasped.

"Do you like that?" she asked as she looked up at him wide-eyed.

"Yes, little witch," he managed through clenched teeth as he continued to watch her steadily. He felt the sweat popping out on his brow. God help him, he was going to come any second. Just like that. The arousal that had coiled in him all day, the pleasure of seeing her play with him and the sensation of her stroking hand were more than sufficient stimuli. He began to pulse his hips, thrusting into her gripping fist. His jaw clenched tight.

"Ah, Claire, harder. Please."

Claire glanced up at his face with surprise, aroused beyond measure by the honest desperation in his voice. She firmly grasped his cock at the base and stroked him long and firm at the same time she dropped to her knees before him. "I want you to come in my mouth."

"Holy..." Des couldn't finish. He wavered on the edge of orgasm at feeling her whispering breath on the head of his cock. She continued to fist him with rapid, surefire strokes as she leaned toward him, her red, lush lips growing tantalizingly nearer. He groaned.

"Open your lips just a little at first, Claire, just for a moment." Her hand flicked up on him in a hard stroke. He clenched his teeth and buried his fingers in her hair, holding her slightly parted mouth steady at the tip of his cock. The first burst of semen jetted across her lips.

He grunted and thrust forward into her moist heat. A variety of curses and prayers flowed out of his mouth as he had a mind-boggling orgasm to the acutely erotic sensation of her tongue running over him and her mouth sucking so sweetly on the head of his cock. Her hand efficiently emptied him. When she'd sucked him dry she began to explore him in earnest, running her tongue down to his balls. She cried out in disappointment when Des put his hands beneath her armpits, lifting her.

"That's enough, Red. You're making me hard all over again."

She licked her lips. God, she loved the way he made love. She loved the way he tasted. Her smile was slow and satisfied. "I suppose that would defeat the purpose of this whole exercise, wouldn't it?"

Des narrowed his eyes on her moist mouth. "I think you're teasing me, baby."

Claire's eyes were wide with innocence when she met his but her grin was sin itself. "I was just trying to make you more comfortable."

"Uh-huh." His eyes glittered at her dangerously as he pulled up his briefs and pants. "As if the image that's burned on the back of my eyelids, of shooting onto your lips before my cock plunged in your mouth, is going to be *soothing* me as we make small talk all evening."

He refastened his belt while he watched Claire's cat-that-ate-the-canary grin widen. She smoothed her hair and checked her image in the foyer mirror. He leaned down and grazed his lips over her ear, feeling her shiver.

"Enjoy your moment, Claire. Tonight it'll be payback time."

Her eyes went wide at his sensual threat. He chuckled. "But right now I have to think about more mundane matters, like my dad's birthday dinner."

"Oh wait. I was going to bring a bottle of wine. Red or white?" Claire asked anxiously as she hurried toward the kitchen.

* * * * *

Carlos Rivera Alvarez greeted Claire as though she were a long-lost family member returned to the fold at last. Des was right. She was utterly charmed by the tall man, his accented English, his melodious deep voice and the way he kissed her hand as though it were the most natural of everyday gestures. Claire definitely saw the similarities between Carlos and his son—the height, the handsome, classical-looking features, a deep inner vitality that refused to be repressed or stilted by convention.

"Happy birthday, Mr. Alvarez," Claire said, giving him her gift of a bottle of wine.

He still held one of her hands warmly as he accepted the bottle. "Ah, that's lovely, thank you, Claire. But please, call me Carl. I'm an American now, and it's the American way to abbreviate everything. Des told you it's my birthday? Well, I suppose they don't stop at sixty, much as I would like them to, hey, Desi?"

Carl kissed his son on both cheeks. Much to her surprise Des kissed him back and hugged him with an equal lack of reserve. Claire was touched by the open demonstration of love and warmth between two such masculine men. She recalled the easy manner in which Des would touch her at times, or the intimate, erotic things he could say with no embarrassment.

She was beginning to think Des had some of that old-world magic too.

Carl Alvarez led them back to the kitchen, where Claire was introduced to Des' younger sister. Angie Alvarez was an attractive, animated woman of about Claire's age. When Carl went to open the bottle of wine Claire asked Angie if she could help prepare dinner.

Angie shook her head, smiling. "I *am* the help. Didn't Desi tell you he was doing most of the cooking?"

Claire raised her eyebrows in disbelief as she watched Des who, true to his sister's word, was opening the large stainless steel oven.

"I think he did say something about it being a dual venture but I have to admit I didn't really believe it until now."

Des heard her from across the room and gave her a fake wounded look.

"Desi is a wonderful cook," Carl insisted with a brisk shake of his head, as though he were stating the obvious. Claire couldn't help but smile at his parental pride. He handed Claire and Angie a glass of wine and raised his hand in a toast.

"To new friendships."

"To new friendships," Claire agreed. When Angie raised her wineglass to her lips Claire saw the bracelet on her wrist, so similar to Claire's own. Angie saw the direction of her gaze. She held her arm out and Claire aligned her wrist with Angie's so that the bracelets could be examined side by side.

"Des told me that you had one of Mother's bracelets. I can't believe it," Angie said.

Carl looked on with interest.

"I hope you don't mind me having it. I tried to give it back to Des but he insisted…"

"Of course he did," Carl Alvarez assured robustly. "I'm happy to see something my Ellen made giving someone pleasure." Angie nodded warmly in agreement and Claire found her discomfort fading.

"Claire, how would you like a tour of my beautiful home? There are some photos of Desi in the den that I'm sure you will find very interesting."

Claire allowed herself to be formally escorted away by the charming Carl. She noticed he glanced at Des with a sparkle in his eyes. She heard Angie's delighted laughter and saw Des give her a big brother scowl. She was delighted to see his usually impassive face flushed slightly in embarrassment at his father's teasing.

"Ten bucks he'll blow your cover," Angie murmured with amusement when Claire had left the room.

"I'm not undercover, Ang," Des said irritably. "It's just…sort of complicated."

"Not according to *Abuela* Anita." She grinned as she popped a slice of cucumber in her mouth.

"If you say a word about that to her, brat, I swear to God I'll—"

"Enough with the threats, Desi. Your payoff is sufficient for now. My cats are going to come to love your surly face."

Twenty minutes later Des went to retrieve his father and Claire from the den. They were having an in-depth discussion about one of Carl's short stories, "American Dreaming".

"Guess you guys never got around to the tour," Des interrupted wryly from the doorway.

"Is it dinnertime already?" a shocked Carl asked. Des merely nodded as his father passed him. He didn't allow Claire to get past without a kiss.

"What did I tell you, Red? Neck deep in it, aren't you?"

"He's wonderful," Claire whispered back. "And he's incredibly proud of you."

Claire had to admit she was a little surprised that Carl's bragging about his son's cooking was actually entirely warranted though. Her eyes widened when she bit into the rare-grilled flank steak, marveling at the tenderness of the meat and the burst of flavor from the spicy juices. Des' eyes were on her as she took the first bite, catching her look of unexpected pleasure.

"I've been the victim of sexism." The sad shake of his head said it was all tragically predictable.

Claire laughed. "I'm sorry, you're right. How did you get the meat so tender?" she asked, already taking another bite.

"A woman who enjoys her food. I love to see it," Carl beamed.

"Des came over last night to prepare it," Angie explained. "The meat has been marinating overnight."

Claire glanced at Des while she chewed, remembering how he'd said last night that he was in the neighborhood, visiting his father.

She enjoyed the meal excessively, relishing the whipped potato casserole that was as subtly flavored as the beef was spicy, Angie's huge salad and, finally, a delicious raspberry and chocolate torte, complete with candles. Mostly, Claire appreciated the warm environment of their family, the way they teased each other, the good conversation. She'd been alone too much in that old house lately. No wonder she was having nightmares.

Later, as they lingered over coffee and dessert, Angie asked, "So, Claire, how long have you known Desi?"

"Oh, I just met him yesterday," Claire murmured. She took a sip of coffee to hide her embarrassment.

Angie feigned amazement. "Just yesterday. And he's already brought you home to meet Dad? Jeez, that's the kind of thing a man does when he's really serious."

Des cleared his throat loudly and shot his sister a threatening look. Claire shrank in her chair. Angie raised her eyes in staged misunderstanding at Des and smiled sweetly. "Well, at the very least it's very un-Desi-like behavior, wouldn't you say, Dad?"

"Hush, Angela," Carl said calmly. "Tease your brother another time. You're embarrassing Claire."

Angie apologized for it later while Claire was helping her put dishes in the dishwasher. "I'm sorry, Claire, I couldn't resist. Des always mortifies me in front of my boyfriends. Once, when I was in college, he told this guy that I had a real crush on that I had a venereal disease."

"I *never* said that, Angie," Des said as he came in from the dining room carrying some plates and overheard the last part of his sister's explanation. "I told him that you had a *serious* disease. It was his own dirty mind that made him think it was something sexual. That guy had sex on the brain, Ang. You think one guy can't see it in another one?"

Claire blinked when Des waggled his eyebrows at her before sauntering out of the kitchen again.

"What a jerk," Angie muttered as she washed the casserole dish. "The guy I mean, not Des. Des was right about him but don't tell him that I told you," Angie whispered conspiratorially. "The thing is—Des really likes you."

Claire felt at a loss for words at the sudden topic change. "Oh well..."

She was saved from having to respond to Des' irrepressible sister by the sound of the phone ringing. Angie went to answer it and Des took over at the kitchen sink.

"*Abuela* Anita! How nice to hear from you," Angie greeted with obvious delight. A moment of silence ensued and then, to Claire's surprise, Angie looked directly at her and smiled.

"Yes, she's here, Grandmother."

Claire glanced at Des in bewilderment but he only shrugged.

"Noooo, *Tia* Maria didn't say that, did she?" Angie asked in feigned disbelief, all the while grinning at Des and Claire. She seemed to be enjoying the conversation with her grandmother immensely.

"Aunt Maria is Anita's sister," Des said quietly. "They've fought over everything their entire life, including which one of them was going to be the one to marry my grandfather. It still goes on today, even though Maria has been dead for five years."

Claire was still choking back laughter when Des left to take a turn talking to his grandmother on the phone. He had suggested that they would leave following the after-dinner cleanup. As a result, Clair was chatting on the front porch with Angie and Carl a few minutes later while they waited for Des to finish the phone call.

"Did Desi ever tell you his full name, Claire?" Angie asked.

"No. What is it?"

"His name is Desiderio," Carl supplied with a matter-of-fact, professorial air. "It stems from the Latin, meaning desire and longing."

"Oh my God, that suits him so perfectly," Claire murmured before she had a chance to censor her words. She noticed Angie's suppressed laughter and Carl's tender smile. Claire turned around slowly, already guessing that Des must have come onto the porch and was standing quietly behind her, hearing every word of the exchange. His face gave away nothing but his grayish-silver eyes were several degrees past warm as they rested on her blushing face.

"Are you ready to go, Claire?" he asked quietly.

Claire nodded, momentarily struck dumb by the message in his gaze. Thankfully she managed to rally enough to say her thanks and bid her farewells with all the genuine feeling that the lovely evening had inspired.

Chapter Ten

Des caught her hand when she moved past him in the foyer of her house a few minutes later. "I was going to get us something to drink. Don't you want something?"

He shook his head as he wound a skein of reddish-gold hair around his hand. When his fist finally reached her scalp he tugged, tilting her back to give his mouth access. He pressed firm lips along her jaw line.

"Yes. I want you, in the bedroom, naked. Right now," he said huskily between light kisses.

"Oh. Okay." At what point in time would she cease blushing around him like a fifteen-year-old did around her first crush, anyway? She turned away so that he wouldn't see her heated cheeks and headed for the stairs.

He was right behind her as they started up. Claire had the sneaking suspicion that his eyes were right on her ass. Her suspicion was confirmed when she felt him cup a cheek in his palm then trail it down over her thigh. He stopped her abruptly with a hand on her hip.

"Are you wearing a garter and stockings, Claire?"

"Yes. Des?"

He was already lifting up her skirt, exposing her thighs and rear end. "Des!" she protested, struck by the indecency of him exposing her like that while they were on the stairs…even though that was ridiculous, because she was about to strip for him in a few seconds anyway.

Des ignored her protests until he'd looked his fill. Then he slapped upward on one ass cheek before he pushed her skirt down. Claire's eyes sprang wide. His voice was a sexy growl next to her ear.

"Correction. I want you, in the bedroom, right now, naked except for the stockings and garters. Go on, Red, or you're going to get another swat on your sweet ass even before we get to the bedroom."

Claire gasped and hurried up the stairs. Her heartbeat began pounding loudly in her ears. The place where he'd spanked her tingled. It hadn't hurt. But she could still feel the warm imprint of his hand on her flesh.

And he'd hinted that he was going to spank her again in the bedroom. Heat scalded her cheeks again but this time it wasn't from embarrassment. It was from pure arousal.

Still, she had her pride. She glanced over her shoulder at him as they reached the landing. He looked gorgeous as he stalked behind her, hard and male and determined.

His eyes narrowed when he recognized the wariness and excitement on her face.

Claire tried to shut the door on him, pushing with all of her might and weight as her heart beat almost painfully in her chest. She eventually sighed with exasperation when she glanced up through the crack in the door and saw the effortless way Des held it in place and the almost bored expression on his face.

Damn it. He could have pushed that door wide at any second, he was just amusing himself by watching her spend all that energy trying to close it. She growled in frustration and hurried to the far side of the bed. She watched him flip on the light and close the door behind him calmly. Her eyes narrowed accusingly when she saw his lips twitch with incipient laughter.

"It's not funny, Des. I don't want to be spanked."

He casually opened her top dresser drawer, closed it, then opened the second. He pulled out a silk scarf. Claire edged toward the far side of the bed as he slowly approached. "What are you doing?"

"How do you know that you don't want to be spanked? You seemed pretty...taken with the idea when I described it to you yesterday."

"Hmph," Claire snorted. "I should have known you would stoop to bringing up that little incident."

He trailed his hand along the wood railing at the end of the bed as he slowly stalked her. "By little incident, I assume you mean the way you worked yourself until you exploded while I described spanking you."

"Stay right there, Des Alvarez," Claire pointed her finger. Her pulse felt like it was going to pop right out of her neck. "I was turned on yesterday, that's true, but it wasn't because of that."

Des rolled his eyes as he took a few more steps toward her. "Please. Don't insult me."

Despite the situation, she felt like cracking up at his response. She held up her hand in a placating manner. "Okay. You can spank me, but I get to say exactly how and the number of times."

"No."

Claire's mouth fell open in disbelief. "What do you mean, *no*?"

Des circled the end of the bed and kept coming. "You might have bargained earlier, before you ran away from me, but you've lost that right, baby. Now I'm going to tie you up and have my way with you."

"You will not," Claire said hotly, but her eyes went wide when she looked down at the scarf in his hand. Obviously he would. The sound that bubbled out of her throat was a mixture of nervous laughter and panic. She flung herself onto the bed in an attempt to get to the other side.

Des whipped out a hand and caught an ankle. He pulled her toward him, waiting until she reached up to claw at the bedding to gently grab one wrist and put it to the small of her back, then the other.

"I can't believe you're tying me up," Claire shouted. In fact, she was more outraged at being so easily subdued than she was about being tied up.

"I can't believe you ran away from me," Des said almost conversationally as he flipped her over on the bed like a flapjack on a griddle. As she spit a lock of hair out of her mouth and glared at him, he went on in the same tone, "In addition to being a psychic, you're a smart woman. You must know that I would never really hurt you. If I ever cause you a little sting of pain, it'll only be within the context of a lot of pleasure. I'm not even remotely interested in causing you pain just for pain's sake. So I can only assume that it's your pride that's really at issue here."

He reached down and circled the tip of his forefinger around one large nipple and smiled when she instantly pebbled up beneath him. His grayish-silver eyes rose to hers in challenge. "I don't particularly like you putting pride before desire, Claire."

Claire bit her lip to keep from moaning in pleasure at what he was doing to her nipple. "Let's just get this over with, Alvarez."

"By all means," he agreed. Claire tried to ignore his wicked grin but her pussy wasn't cooperative. Her thighs clamped together hard to alleviate the pressure as Des examined her for a few seconds.

"I wanted to spank you the first time while you were completely naked, except for the stockings and heels, of course. But I guess I'll just have to compromise now that I've tied you up already." He grabbed her shoulders and raised her to a sitting position.

"I was going to do a little striptease for you when we got up here before you started all of this ridiculous spanking business," Claire told him in a bored tone of voice. "I guess you've missed out."

Des smirked as he raised her blouse over her breasts and tucked the bottom through the neck hole to keep it in place. "You'll strip for me plenty of times in the future."

Claire stared in disbelief. "No wonder you drive your sister so crazy. I wouldn't strip for you now if... Oh, oh!"

He'd peeled down the nylon cups of her bra while leaving it fastened, fully exposing her breasts and pushing them up into further pronouncement, then calmly leaned over and helped himself to a nipple. Damn the man, he knew how to use his mouth. Claire's eyes rolled back into her head as his wet, rough tongue lashed at her repeatedly. She arched her back, granting him more access. When he closed his mouth and drew on her strongly enough to hollow out his cheeks, Claire wiggled her hips frantically to appease the arrow of desire that shot from her nipple to her aching pussy.

"Beautiful," Des praised gruffly as he studied his handiwork awhile later. Claire glanced down and made a choking sound when she saw the glistening, distended nipple. He combed his fingers through her long hair as he looked down at her. "Have I told you yet how much that turned me on when you came yesterday, just from the stimulation of me sucking on your nipple?"

Claire bit her lip. "No."

"Well it did, Red. Have you ever come like that before?"

She thought of lying. She was supposed to be resisting him, after all. But then she looked into his beautiful eyes and saw desire, pure and undiluted, shining there. "No," she whispered.

He just nodded as if satisfied by her response. "Come here. Lie across my lap, baby. I'll help you."

He held her steady as she clumsily put her knees up on the bed and came down over his hard thighs. He guided her so that her bottom was centered on his lap. She moaned with embarrassment and arousal when she realized that wasn't the only thing in this scenario that was aligned. Her pussy rested on the enormous bulge in his pants. Claire resisted an urge to press down on him. She turned her cheek into the cool bedding to calm herself at the recollection of him describing how she would rub against his cock and try to come as he spanked her. Damn. He'd put those ideas in her head just to torture her.

"Make it so that your nipples just barely brush the bed. I like to be able to see them. What is it?" he asked when she moaned.

"You...you made me do that in the dream too. My nipples...against the leather of the armrest," she said brokenly as she scooted back her shoulders, positioning her nipples so they just tickled the material of her cool duvet. They immediately tightened pleasurably, making her want to move them over the bedding rhythmically.

"Damn. Another juicy detail I can't remember. I'll bet that felt good, having your nipples scrape against that hard leather while I fucked you," Des said warmly.

He saw her clamp her eyes shut as he began to raise her skirt over her thighs and then her ass. He transferred his eyes to the vision in his lap, fully enthralled by the sight of the pearly luster of her white thighs and bottom, the lacy little pink garter that matched her panties. His hand looked starkly dark in contrast to her paleness as he caressed her thighs and palmed the bottom curve of a cheek.

"I'm going to leave your panties on at first to give you some protection. Your skin is delicate. Just the last spankings will be bare-assed."

Claire whimpered. Her pussy liquefied at his words. An unbearable anticipation built in her. She didn't have long to wait before he landed the first stinging slap on one cheek, only to quickly be followed by a lusty spanking on the other. Claire's eyes went wide at the sensation coupled with the heady eroticism of feeling his cock lurch up as he smacked her bottom each time.

"Des," she moaned.

"All right, Claire?"

She just nodded then gasped when he popped her again on each cheek. Claire panted like an overheated dog. Oh God, it was humiliating, but it was making her incredibly hot. She was soaking her panties. Claire ground her pussy into him in small, circular motions as he continued to swat her.

Des noticed that she was pleasuring herself on him but he was too mesmerized by the experience of spanking her perfect ass to say anything for the moment. Besides, her writhing against his cock felt fantastic, not that he needed the extra stimulation. He used his left hand to pull her panties into a narrow line of material that he worked deeply into her crack, leaving her ass cheeks exposed to him.

"You're so beautiful, baby," he praised as he gently caressed her bottom. He pulled up on her panties firmly with his other hand then rocked the material so that it stimulated her clit, pussy and anus all at once.

"Oh, that feels so good."

Des stared hotly as she rotated her bottom, grinding herself into his erection and against the pressure of the tightly drawn panties. He lifted his hand and spanked her bare buttocks soundly. She gasped.

"No more getting off on me, Claire." He jerked on the underwear and her pelvis sprang up. "Stay like that, with your bottom in the air, while you take the rest of it. Put your nipples back where they're supposed to be, baby."

He waited patiently while she readjusted her angle so that the crests of her breasts scraped the bedding again. Her nipples were fully erect. His eyes remained glued on them as he swatted her ass twice, enjoying the sight of them bouncing against the bed.

Claire bit her lip to prevent herself from begging him to let her come. He kept her underwear pulled tight against her pussy and asshole but he wasn't rubbing it against her tissues anymore. Her ass felt like it was on fire, the sensation was incredibly erotic. She could just imagine how pink she must be getting.

Des spanked her again then pressed his big hand to the plump cheek, rubbing soothingly. He heard her aroused groan. "Are you turned on?"

Claire clamped her eyes shut. "Yes," she finally admitted.

"You want to come, don't you?"

"Des, don't. Why are you trying to humiliate me?" she cried unevenly.

His jaw hardened. "I'm not trying to humiliate you, Claire. I'm trying to get you to let go of all this pride bullshit and just accept yourself the way you are. Why should you feel embarrassed that getting spanked is making you want to come?"

"I never said that it was."

Des abruptly yanked her underwear down over her legs. He brought her panties to his nose and inhaled. She put her chin on her shoulder, watching him. He held her gaze as he rubbed the panties over her ass cheek. She choked back a groan of arousal.

"Do you feel that, Claire? All that sweet, hot cream? You want to come, baby, why don't you just admit it? If you ask for it, I'll give you what you need."

"Go to hell," she sputtered. "Isn't this almost over?"

His jaw leapt with tension. He slapped her thigh lightly. "Spread your thighs."

Claire gritted her teeth as she did what he said. Even the cool air seemed to stimulate her swollen, overheated pussy. Des slapped her inner thigh lightly again and she exposed herself even further to him.

"I'm going to spank you five more times and then we'll be done. Claire?"

"Yes?"

"I'm going to spank your pussy on number five."

Claire went entirely still at that proclamation. Her heart started to pound unbearably loud in her ears. She prayed that Des didn't notice the surge of wetness that flooded her pussy. He was evil incarnate. She gasped when he grabbed a handful of ass with one hand and held the flesh steady for a brisk slap by the other. She was panting by the time he spanked upward on the bottom curve of the other then held down on her stinging flesh, circling it beneath his pressing hand, soothing her stinging flesh.

Her moan wasn't muffled by the bedding when he spread her cheeks wide. Claire stilled, knowing instinctively that he was staring at her asshole.

"Des," she cried out desperately when he rubbed his fingertip over the tight, puckered bud.

"Have you ever let a man fuck you in the ass, Claire?" he asked thickly.

"No," she mumbled into the bedding.

"Good. I'll be the first. Are you going to bitch and moan about that too?"

"No," Claire admitted slowly.

"I'm shocked. Why not?" he teased as he continued to stimulate her sensitive asshole.

She rocked against him. "Because…because in the dream you finger-fucked me hard. I've never let a man touch me there. It set everything on fire. Ever since then I kept thinking about what it would be like. Oh," she cried out sharply when he pinned back her ass cheeks firmly with his left hand and spanked her directly over her asshole with a curved palm.

"You'll find out soon enough. Maybe tomorrow night. Now—one more over your little asshole and one left for your pussy."

He spanked her again, noticing how her thighs quivered with arousal and her ribs expanded as she panted. He lifted her knees suddenly and ducked under her.

"Why did you stand up?" she asked him in confusion when he placed her back on the bed.

He didn't answer her. He was too awestruck at how beautiful she looked with her blushing pink ass up in the air and her hair tousled wildly around her shoulders. Her cheeks were the rosy color that he'd quickly learned meant that she was on the brink of orgasm. He drew up her ass cheeks with his left hand, fully exposing her swollen pussy.

"Are you ready, baby?"

"I'm ready," Claire said, thinking that it was the understatement of the century.

"Ask for it."

She pressed her face into the bedding, overwhelmed by desire. He wouldn't. He wouldn't make her…

"Ask for it, Claire."

"Spank it. Spank my pussy, please," Claire begged, forgetting her shame.

He brought his hand down and gently but firmly swatted her swollen cunt.

She jerked. It was like he'd set off a firework. She screamed as orgasm exploded, the energy traveling all the way from her feet and from her head, converging on her sex before it zipped up her spine again. Her head snapped back.

Des watched her convulse and quiver under the power of an enormously powerful climax. He held his hand against her, massaging her while she continued to scream and come. Never in a million years would he be able to tell her how beautiful she was at that moment, as she fully surrendered to desire.

He cursed under his breath and grabbed desperately for his wallet and a condom. He shoved his pants and briefs down his legs while Claire's keening slowly began to fade. His hand shook when he straddled her with one knee on the mattress, leaving the other foot on the floor.

His eyes darkened with intense arousal as he brought his cock head to her dripping sex. He slid into her tight channel slowly, savoring the moment.

"Christ, Claire, you've never been this wet for me before. You're so fucking sweet." His facial muscles bunched as though he were in pain at the sensation of her enfolding him.

Claire moaned. "Oh God, you feel so good. Fuck me hard, Desi. Please."

He growled deep in his throat and went a little crazy for the next few minutes as Claire filled every corner of his existence. He grabbed her hips and plunged her back on his thrusting cock repeatedly while she begged him to give it to her harder. He thought he was having desire-induced hallucinations when she asked him to spank her again. He gave her a brisk slap on an already pink ass cheek, feeling her convulse around him as she came again, milking him while he moaned in desperate pleasure. His eyes rolled back in his head at the exquisite sensation. He slammed into her then pressed his groin against her thighs and ass, placing himself at Claire's furthest reaches while he exploded in climax.

He leaned over her, gulping for air. After several dazed moments he gritted his teeth as he withdrew. Claire lay there limply when he untied the scarf that bound her hands.

"You okay, baby?" he murmured as he rubbed her arms.

Claire couldn't answer at first. After a moment she rose up on all fours. "I think people's brains can get seriously fried from orgasms that intense."

Des came down on the bed and pulled her into his arms. He pressed his mouth to her warm neck. "Trust me, I know."

"Desi?" she asked groggily after a moment.

He smiled, liking the sound of his intimate family name on her lips. "Yes, baby?"

"Do you do this to all of your lovers?"

Des paused in the action of running his fingers through her hair. "Do what, exactly?"

"Make them all into spineless, quivering, brainless blobs of lust?"

He snorted. "You're not back to playing that tune, are you? Was it really that awful to get spanked?"

"No."

"You wish that it had been though, don't you?" he asked with grim amusement.

Claire nodded into his chest.

He stroked her hair again, relishing her sigh of contentment. He thought of telling her not to go to sleep because she hadn't told him about the dreams yet. But she seemed so relaxed and he hated to stress her out even more than he had tonight.

"Claire?"

"Yes?" she asked sleepily.

"I knew that you would end up liking getting spanked as much as you did. Do you know how I knew?"

"Because you can read me like an open book?"

"Well, there is that too," he agreed with amusement. "But mostly I knew it would get you horny because you're so perfect."

"I'm not perfect," Claire mumbled into his chest, embarrassed.

"To me you are. Go to sleep, baby."

Claire didn't think she'd be able to sleep ever again after hearing Des say so casually that she was perfect for him. Well, not casually really, more like naturally. She closed her eyes and drifted as warmth and contentment filled her.

He must have some kind of dark, terrible secret that would ruin him for her. Because Claire was too logical to believe in perfect. And that's precisely what Des Alvarez felt like to her too.

That night she dreamed again, but thankfully not of the disturbing image of the dumbwaiter or the warped activities of the man in the closet.

In many ways though, the experience was worse than those nightmares.

She dreamed as though she were only a pair of eyes, not a corporeal, living presence. In her dream she saw Des the way she'd first seen him in the library. He sat in the armchair by the fireplace, his elbows resting on his knees, his forehead in his hands. She saw the darkness around him again with some sensory organ that wasn't her eyes.

Claire experienced his pain and desolation with unbearable intensity. He seemed so vulnerable, so lost to her in his misery. The thought struck her that this darkness that surrounded him, this palpable misery, was blinding him when he most needed to see. But she couldn't be sure what her thought actually meant. She felt desperate to comfort him. Tonight, however, he was as unreachable to her as he had been before she was able to touch him through the channel of passion. Only his image and his suffering were available to her, poignant and sharp. And this time Claire had no body to enforce her will. She was just a ghost, as ineffective as vapor. The realization made her want to scream with frustration and helplessness.

"Claire. *Claire*." Des shook her shoulder and turned on the bedside lamp. He'd awakened a moment ago to the noise of her whimpering softly. The sound had cut at him deeply. He held her jaw and smoothed his thumb along her damp cheek. "Wake up, baby."

"You need to see through the black veil. I can't reach you."

His breath whooshed out of his lungs when Claire abruptly launched herself at him, holding him tight. When his surprise had passed he returned her desperate hug. After a moment he pushed her back so that he could see her face.

"Are you actually awake?" he asked incredulously.

Claire nodded her head. She looked terrified.

"Enough of this. Tell me what's upsetting you so much in your dreams."

Claire reached up and touched his face. "Why are you so alone in my dreams, Des? Why are you so sad?"

His thumb paused in its caress. "What are you talking about?"

Another tear skipped over his thumb. "I dream about you. You're sitting there in the library, just like when I first saw you. And you're so shut away I can't reach you. Is it because of what happened to Alanna Hartfield? Des, that wasn't your fault," Claire insisted, stumbling over her words when he didn't respond.

"You were dreaming about me?" he asked stiffly.

Claire nodded. "It really bothers me in those dreams that you're so sad and alone. You seem lost to me. Untouchable. Why, Des?"

For a brief moment the familiar feeling of panic flashed through her. No, he was holding her in his arms, caressing her. Des wasn't locked away from her. Or was he? His grayish-silver eyes steadily held her gaze but shades seemed to temporarily block his inner soul.

He finally inhaled slowly. "I don't have the dreams every night anymore. After Alanna died I dreamed every night, usually much more intensely. These dreams that I've been having lately are sort of shadows of what they once were. They don't even bother me that much. Trust me, Claire, I can live with them."

Claire glanced away, hating that he was lying to her. She knew that the dreams—or some emotion woven into the dream—did bother him excessively. She knew because she experienced them with him. The thing she couldn't completely get a handle on was *why*.

"Des...do you still feel guilty about Alanna?" When he stared at her stonily, she continued breathlessly, "Because you shouldn't. You shouldn't, Desi. You were no more responsible for her death than I am."

Des shook his head before he turned out the light. "You're wrong. I'm not worried about that. I have enough to be worried about in the present without dredging up that old skeleton."

Chapter Eleven

∽

When Claire returned home from her lunch with her friend on Saturday she noticed Lisa's bag in the foyer.

"Lisa? Are you up there?" she called up the stairs.

After a moment, Lisa's voice floated from the upper regions of the house. "I'm here, Claire, getting Kevin's room ready. I'll come down in a jiff."

Claire put on the teakettle, thinking of how Lisa liked to have a cup of tea sometimes before she left. Her once-a-week maid was actually a University of Chicago archaeology student who cleaned houses in the area to help pay her way through college.

Claire flipped through her mail, most of her attention on deciding what she should wear for dinner with Des.

She'd hesitated at first when he'd asked her to go out with him tonight. It had been this morning, they had just made love, and their limbs had still been entwined.

"I don't know. My cousin Kevin is arriving this afternoon. He still needs to sort through a bunch of junk from when he lived here and Isabelle left him quite a few things that he still needs to collect."

"Kevin is coming here today?"

"Yes," Claire had murmured into his chest, hoping that he didn't hear the resignation in her tone. But he obviously had. He'd touched her chin so that she would meet his eyes.

"You don't like it when he's here?"

Claire had shrugged. "You knew him. You must at least have an idea what he's like. If I remember correctly what Kevin was like as a teenager, I think I can say that there haven't been any major improvements. But...he's family. That's just the way it is sometimes, right?"

Des hadn't replied for a moment and Claire had thought she felt tension rising in his body. "Not necessarily, Claire. If he bothers you, you shouldn't feel obligated to have him in your own home. Especially when you're here alone. Maybe..."

"What?" Claire had asked, confused by his sudden preoccupation.

"Nothing."

"I guess it would be okay if we went out to dinner. I don't know why I'm feeling like I should play hostess. He grew up in this house. I've only lived here for a month or so. He won't be here all that long though. Hopefully. Besides, I'll be with you most of the night if we go out to dinner and—"

Des had just massaged her scalp, deep in thought. "I'll be with you, Claire. Don't worry about it."

Claire smiled like an idiot at the memory. She tossed a catalog in the trash and gathered her mail in a neat pile. She didn't even look up when she sensed the presence of someone standing at the kitchen entry.

"I put some tea on for you, Lisa, but I'm afraid I can't join you at the moment. I have a million things to do and guess what? I have a date tonight," Claire said, cheered for the hundredth time that day at the thought of her date with Des. She glanced up in distractedly when Lisa didn't move or answer her.

The mail in her hands clattered to the floor. She locked gazes with Isabelle Preskill. Claire reached out to steady herself on the counter as a wave of dizziness struck her. The skin all over her body pulled tight, prickling painfully.

"Aunt Isabelle?" Her aunt looked real enough as she stood there, if very pale and drawn. Claire recognized the expression of sternness that she'd seen on her aunt's face from the dream. Her dark eyes glittered with intense emotion.

"What do you want?" Claire whispered. Deep within her, sadness stirred that she should feel fear at the sight of Isabelle. But she *did* feel afraid, with every animal instinct in her body. She closed her eyes to break the powerful impact of her aunt's stare, attempting to regain the equilibrium she'd lost.

"What kind of tea do I want, do you mean?"

When Claire reopened her eyes Lisa was standing several feet away from her, looking at her with puzzlement. "Are you okay, Claire?" Her kind brown eyes were wide with concern.

Claire blinked several times and glanced around the room uncertainly. With the exception of the mail spilled on the floor, everything appeared to be just as it should be in the room. She shivered with a bone-deep cold.

"Here, let me help you with that." Lisa stooped and gathered the mail, placing it on the counter. "Gosh, you're pale, Claire. Maybe you'd better lie down?"

Claire felt like she had to pry her lips apart to speak. "I...no, I'm okay. I must be tired. Maybe I will lie down after all."

She picked up her bag from the counter, her movements stiff and robotic. The shivers continued to rack her bones. "You didn't see anything when you came in the room, did you, Lisa?"

"Just you standing there like you'd seen a ghost or something," Lisa replied uncomfortably.

She couldn't help but laugh grimly at Lisa's unexpectedly accurate description.

"Claire? It's me."

"*Shit,*" Claire mumbled. It still felt like her bone marrow had been replaced by icicles. How could Kevin's timing be any worse? "I'm in here, Kevin," she called resignedly.

Kevin Preskill sauntered into the kitchen, tossed the newspaper that Claire had left on the front porch that morning onto the counter and approached her with a smile. *Just like the lord of the manor,* Claire thought, trying to unclench her teeth when he leaned down and lingered just a second too long when he kissed her cheek.

"Hello, cousin," he murmured.

"Kevin. Welcome back," Claire greeted briskly, moving subtly away from his embrace. She introduced Lisa to Kevin, trying not to scowl when Kevin gave her maid an appreciative once-over and Lisa gave him a dark-eyed, seductive look and coy smile.

Kevin was dressed to the nines, as usual. He wore a pair of black pants that fit his trim, athletic build perfectly, which wasn't a surprise, because Claire knew that Kevin had all his suits and pants tailored. His shirt was a European-cut, sage silk knit that practically screamed money and showed off the fruits of Kevin's endeavors at the gym without seeming too obvious. That was Kevin to a T. He never wanted to give the impression that he cared enough to try for anything. His brown hair hung just a tad too long but Kevin could pull that off too, making even a shaggy hairstyle look like the epitome of preppy chic.

"How was your trip to Tanzania?" she asked dutifully. She sidled away after a few minutes of his description of hunting elephants and zebra and poured him a glass of tea. Claire figured her presence wasn't actually required. Kevin just needed an interested audience and Lisa seemed to be fulfilling the requirement admirably. As she placed the glass on the island next to Kevin he suddenly grabbed her hand and kissed it. Claire fought the urge to rip her hand away.

"And how is the beautiful reason that I came to Chicago doing?"

Claire scowled. "I'd hardly call all of that junk that you have stored in your room and in the attic beautiful, although some of the paintings and artwork that Isabelle left you certainly apply."

He caressed her palm. Claire's already severe chill worsened. She never recalled him doing anything quite so flagrant before.

"You know very well I was referring to you, cousin, the heiress of this fabulous house."

Claire went still with anxiety. "*Fabulous*? I thought you were okay with Isabelle leaving me this house."

Lisa was sensitive enough to make her excuses at that point.

Kevin faced Claire again after Lisa had gone. "Of course I'm okay with Mom leaving it to you. You and I both know that Chicago isn't my favorite place in the world. Besides, having the house in common will keep us close, don't you think?" He glanced at her hand before he dropped it. "You're as cold as a corpse, cousin."

Claire's chill overtook her heart at his words. She didn't have the energy to lay things on the line with him presently. Setting some firm limits would have to wait. Thankfully he moved away from her. She watched him root around in his sport jacket for cigarettes. She knew he would be back at his old smoking haunt in the backyard within minutes. Smokers were so predictable.

"Listen, Kevin, about tonight, I—"

"Don't worry. I made plans. We're having dinner at Charlie Trotter's."

"Kevin, you shouldn't have. I have a date tonight. That's what I was trying to tell you."

His expression cooled momentarily but by the time he stood with the package of cigarettes in his hand he was grinning. "Cousin has a date? My, things certainly have warmed up in the Windy City."

While normally Claire would have steamed out the ears at the comment, she only had the energy to droop. "Funny, Kevin. One can never hear too many frigid cracks in her lifetime. And you're right. I am currently completely and utterly frigid. I'm going to take a hot shower. Your room is ready for you. Do you still have a key so you can get in and out?"

Kevin brushed her cheek before he headed for the back door. "Don't worry, Claire. I was a teenager here, remember? Even if I'd forgotten my key, you'd probably be shocked if I showed you my knowledge of how to access this house."

Claire spent a long time in the shower, letting the hot jets of heat beat some of the intense chill out of her. By the time she emerged she'd regained much of her calm, telling herself repeatedly that even if she had seen a ghost—which she was *not* willing to entirely concede—it was only Isabelle. Isabelle would never harm her. There was obviously some serious, unusual psychic phenomenon going on but that didn't imply that Claire was in some sort of immediate danger, did it?

After her shower she was completely drained, as if the experience of seeing Isabelle had leached the life force out of her. She crawled into bed and fell asleep almost instantly. The next thing she knew she was blinking, once, twice, three times. She was still blind.

Before panic overcame her she recalled the sensation and recognized she was dreaming. Her eyes flickered upward and saw the rectangle of barely perceptible light. She knew immediately where she was.

She was in the closed, claustrophobic space with a pervert.

She tried to breathe slowly, to calm her escalating heart and her rising sense of panic. Helplessness pulled tight at her like a strangling rope around her neck. She forced breath into her reluctant, fear-frozen lungs and the sensation disappeared. As in the previous dreams, she became aware of the man's presence, his soft movements, his eager listening. Claire slowly became aware of the muted noises emanating from the outer room. She closed her eyes, willing back the bile that was rising in her throat.

He was listening—*she* was listening—to someone making love.

Claire's stomach cramped. She gasped raggedly then froze in panic. Was the man able to hear her? But no, it was just a dream. Besides, she doubted anything could have distracted his fixed attention from the sounds in the outer room, a woman's cries of pleasure, the unmistakable thump of the bed rocking against the wall. Claire wanted to be anywhere in the world but there at that moment. She felt both painfully intrusive and shamefully violated at once. She closed her eyes and willed herself out of the dream. But she couldn't escape. Even with her eyes closed tightly she could still hear the tumult of the couple's passion, the increased pace of the bed as it struck the wall again and again.

Worse, she didn't need to have her vision to fully sense the voyeur's piqued excitement, didn't need her eyes to recognize the sound of a zipper being lowered furtively. She prayed for release from the dream, even allowing the acid bile to rise in her throat as a welcome sensation that might pull her out of the nightmare.

It worked. When she awoke in her bed she was doubled over with nausea, the now-familiar clammy sweat covering her body. She stumbled to her bathroom and had a repeat performance of the other night, this time thankfully without Des as a witness.

* * * * *

The only remnant that was visible of her nightmarish afternoon by the time evening rolled around was the extreme pallor of her face. She was hoping Des wouldn't notice it but, of course, his hawk-like eyes missed nothing.

She opened the front door that evening at a little after seven. She barely had time to notice how handsome Des looked in dress pants, a crisp white button-down shirt and a summer-weight sport jacket when he placed his hand on her cheek. As usual, his silver-gray eyes studied her with a knee-melting intensity.

"You're pale, baby. How come?"

Claire tried to disarm his seriousness. "I'm wearing a new dress. And you should feel damn special because I actually used a curling iron tonight, which is unheard-of behavior for me. You're supposed to say how nice I look, not notice that I didn't apply my blush perfectly."

His gaze swept down her slowly. Claire felt her body heat notch up to a slow burn. All remnants of the chill she'd had when she'd seen Aunt Isabelle's ghost disappeared when Des smiled. The combination of warmth in his silvery eyes and that dimple in his right cheek were like a one-two punch that left Claire reeling time and again.

Earlier that spring, during one of her parents' visits while Aunt Isabelle was ill, her mother had insisted on taking Claire shopping. At the time Claire had vehemently protested Cecilia Allen's intention to buy her an expensive dress from Prada, arguing that she would never have the opportunity to wear it. Claire was glad now that she finally allowed it so that she had something nice to wear to go out with Des.

It was a midnight-blue wrap, deceptively simple in its design. The material was soft, clinging to the curves of her body in a way that Claire hoped looked as sexy as it felt. It was low-cut, sexy but tasteful, allowing just a shadowy glimpse of cleavage. A single ruffle at the hem slanted upward at her knees to become the wrap at her waist. Although the length of the dress was essentially modest, the cut in the front created an inverted V from her lower thighs to her knees, allowing a glimpse of her legs. Claire liked the effect when she paired the dress with a pair of strappy high-heeled sandals.

She'd inspected herself in the mirror earlier and been satisfied. The dress was conservative and sophisticated enough to fit her style but sexy and fun too. She'd rooted around in her jewelry box and located a pair of sapphire earrings that her parents had given her when she had completed her undergraduate degree.

"They match your eyes perfectly," her father had said when she had opened the box.

"Is this okay for the restaurant you picked?" she whispered, suddenly self-conscious under Des' steady gaze.

"Of course it's okay." He leaned down and kissed her cheek softly. The caress and the breath in her ear when he spoke caused a delicious shiver to run down her spine. "You're beautiful."

Claire craned up, inhaling his masculine, clean scent. Their lips clung and then their tongues. "How long has it been since I saw you?" she breathed out as she kissed his strong neck hungrily.

"Too long, apparently. Claire?"

"Hmmm?" She asked, nibbling at the delicious skin above his collar.

"Why are you whispering?" Her gaze skittered to the back of the house. "Is it Kevin?"

"Wha… Oh yes. I think he's in the kitchen. Do you…want to say hello to him?" Claire segued from a whisper to a low speaking voice when she noticed his stare on her.

"Yes, but not just yet." He growled softly before he leaned down and parted her lips again with his tongue. His kiss was a delicious sensual assault. Claire moaned at his heat and intensity. Her back arched as he leaned over her.

They were so involved in each other that they didn't notice that they were being watched.

"I see you're still a lady-killer, Alvarez."

Claire started when Kevin spoke in a cold voice. "Oh, I didn't know you were there, Kevin," Claire said, flustered. She started to move out of Des' arms but he refused to allow her flight of embarrassment. He flexed his biceps to keep her body fully in contact with his. Claire glanced uneasily at the two men. They were eyeing each other with varying degrees of unconcealed animosity.

"I see that you two remember each other," she said grimly. When neither one of them spoke, Claire whispered desperately, "Des?"

Her appeal broke through his intense focus and his light eyes flickered to her face. When he saw her look of dismay he muttered stiffly, "Kevin. It's been a long time."

Kevin smiled but his eyes remained cold. "Yeah, but some things never change, do they?" His gaze ran over them as though he'd caught them in the flagrant act of making love instead of kissing. He looked at Claire with cool speculation. "I practically didn't recognize you, cousin."

Claire glared at him. He was making another crack about the fact that he'd always assumed she was sexually cold. All based on the unassailable evidence that she didn't respond to him, of course.

"When Claire said that you were coming by, Alvarez, I have to admit that I didn't understand the nature of your relationship," Kevin said quietly. Suddenly the coldness and animosity that had been in his expression were gone and he was coming forward to shake Des' hand. "What's it been, Des, eighteen years?"

"Something like that," Des said, shaking Kevin's hand when Claire softly nudged him into cooperation.

Claire cleared her throat uncomfortably when nobody said anything else and the men resumed their staring contest.

"What are you kids planning for the evening?" Kevin asked with abrupt cheerfulness.

Claire eyed her cousin warily. The behavior was so typical of Kevin—angry one moment, charming the next. She'd seen it so many times over the years that it failed to surprise her now.

"We're going to a French Vietnamese place in the city," Des answered.

Kevin arched his eyebrows in a show of polite interest. "Oh. Well, I told Claire that I have reservations for us at Charlie Trotter's. But she seems to prefer something a little more ethnic."

She felt Des coil even tighter next to her. Kevin just smiled charmingly, making it difficult to accuse him of the subtle racial slur. "I'm telling you, cousin, you should watch out for this guy. He's a real heartbreaker."

"Why don't you explain exactly what you mean by that, Kevin?" Des said.

A chill went down Claire's spine at his tone. She glanced up at him in rising alarm, clearly feeling the tension in his hard muscles, seeing the whiteness around his mouth, the piercing anger in his eyes. He appeared dangerous at that moment. Claire didn't doubt that he was perfectly capable of causing Kevin some serious harm. Was Kevin crazy? Her cousin might be tall and fit but of the two there was no doubt that Des was clearly the larger and more powerful man.

But Kevin seemed entirely ignorant of the incipient threat, or at least he gave that impression. He moved toward the coat tree where his jacket hung and pulled out his pack of cigarettes. He turned away, tossing over his shoulder, "Don't even tell me you don't remember Alanna," he said mockingly. "You really are a heartbreaker, Alvarez. Well, you two enjoy your evening. Don't wait up for me, Claire."

"Des?" Claire said quietly after Kevin was gone. He stared down the hallway. He had the oddest expression on his face. Claire still saw the vestiges of anger but there was also a faraway look in his eyes. She repeated his name again and he finally glanced down at her, blinking as though he'd been momentarily blinded.

"Don't let him get to you, Des. He's obnoxious, I know. Who better? You should have told me how much you disliked him though. It might have been nice to be a little better prepared for," she waved her hand around, momentarily speechless, "whatever that just was. God, Des, I thought you were going to kill him."

Des regained his composure as she spoke but his expression was still grim. "Sorry. I know I was stupid when I was a teenager but I still can't believe I could ever stand to be around him."

The fact of the matter was Preskill and he had never been anything but loose acquaintances, and they had become less than that when Kevin made a racial insult after football practice once when they were kids. The coach had pulled them apart and Des had been especially wary of Kevin afterward. He'd steered clear of Kevin since they were teenagers, repulsed by some of the things he'd heard him tell the guys in the locker room about girls he'd had sex with.

After a moment he became aware of Claire's look of concern. "It'll be okay, Red. Let me get a glass of water in the kitchen and we'll get going."

He really needed to get out of that house.

Chapter Twelve

Des had chosen a new colonial French Vietnamese restaurant on West Randolph Street. The near west side of Chicago was a hot location for upscale lofts, bars, art galleries and restaurants. Previously it had been exclusively Chicago's food manufacturing and meat-packing district, and this still was its primary purpose. But now instead of being desolate and abandoned in the evening the streets were filled with cars and taxis, and well-heeled men and women strolled by sidewalk cafés on warm summer nights.

The restaurant that Des had picked was farther west on Randolph than many of its trendy neighbors. They lingered over their meal, savoring each other's presence even more than the delicious food and mood-mellowing wine. Claire learned that Des didn't live that far from the restaurant and that he'd found out about it while passing it on his morning jog.

After Des told her he lived close by, he bit back a strong desire to ask Claire to stay at his place for the next few nights. He needed to know that she was safe. But he'd be with her tonight at the Preskill mansion, right? He didn't want to blow the one opportunity he was going to get to check out some of Kevin Preskill's personal items while Kevin was out of the house.

He'd been near panicked today as he'd watched Claire's house and watched Kevin arrive, especially when he saw the maid leave. Luckily, Kevin left the premises soon afterward, or Des would have had to pay Claire an unexpected visit that would have been hard to explain since he was supposed to be picking her up for dinner in a few hours. She'd never know how relieved he'd been to see her standing at the front door awhile ago.

"Your father is so easy to talk to," Claire mused later over coffee. Her cheeks were flushed, possibly from the wine but more likely due to the presence of the man across the table. It had been a wonderful dinner. She was fully entranced by Des, finding him to be smarter, funnier and more insightful that she'd already imagined. "He's not at all intimidating, like you would think a famous writer would be. He's just like his books, approachable, warm and colorful. Was your mother like that too?"

"She was more of an intellectual than my father. When I say she was an intellectual, I mean she was the type of person who was great in a debate. She had a good fund of knowledge but it was the way that she could synthesize her ideas and emotions that characterized her. I always thought it was interesting that she was an artist, because she was very verbal."

Claire nodded. She'd admired several of Ellen Alvarez's paintings while she was in Carl's home. "It is an interesting contrast. There was a narrative quality to her work but she still captured so much emotion. It's as if she painted right at the border between the unconscious and rational thought. It takes a special person to be able to transmute those two very different energies."

"You're like that too," Des said quietly, after a moment.

Claire opened her mouth to argue. She hadn't felt like much of an expert lately in being able to handle her own unconscious mind. But then she reconsidered. Much of what a psychotherapist did was to help an individual to translate information from the unconscious, nonverbal, feeling mind into a language that incorporated those emotions with the rational, verbal, thinking mind. She recalled a professor once saying that psychotherapy was about assisting people in finding words for what had previously been left unacknowledged, unnamed and unhonored. Those shadowy and nebulous parts were so packed with power but without translation had no channel for expression. Without assistance they would eventually find expression through the type of behaviors that brought people to psychotherapy—chronic relationship problems, self-destructive behavior, addiction. Even though she had always been adamant about denying her psychic abilities, she had to admit that possessing them probably helped her to move about so skillfully within the world of her patients' unconscious minds.

Instead of commenting on Des' intimate remark she said, "I'll bet Isabelle left me some of your mother's paintings. We should look tonight. She gave Kevin the ones he admired and left the rest to me with the house. They're stacked in the library. I haven't had a chance to look—"

She paused abruptly, realizing that if Des' mother's paintings were still in the library, it was the equivalent of saying that Kevin didn't care for them.

Des saw the mortified look on her face. He brushed aside a lock of hair that had fallen onto her cheek. His fingertips caressed her skin warmly, lingering briefly on her earlobe after he'd tucked the hair behind her ear.

"It's okay, Claire. I'd rather see you own my mother's paintings than Kevin Preskill any day." She swallowed when she looked into his eyes. His touch set her body aflame so effortlessly. He gave her a small, slow smile that told Claire that his thoughts had traveled the same path as her own.

"Are you ready to go?" he asked in a low, husky voice.

Claire nodded, unable to break their gaze. "Just let me run to the ladies' room first."

She was still smiling goofily when she came out of the bathroom. As she reached the entrance to the hallway where the restrooms were located, a strange man stopped her with a touch on her shoulder. Claire peered up at him curiously.

"Excuse me. Are you Claire Allen?"

"Uh...yes," Claire answered, perplexed. The man looked vaguely familiar. Was he one of her former patients or something? No, that wasn't it. She'd just seen him recently.

But where?

"I saw you here with one of my colleagues from the FBI. Des Alvarez? I was wondering how you two met."

She wrinkled her brow in confusion. "Des? The FBI? No, you're mistaken. Des renovates homes. He doesn't work for the FBI."

"Is that what he told you?" The blond man's expression was patronizing.

"Yes, that's what he told me," she said irritably. Her lips fell open as recognition dawned. He was the man she'd seen watching her from the street the other morning. "Excuse me, but why are you talking to me?"

"That's a damned good question, Malkovic. Come on, Claire."

She choked in disbelief at the sound of Des' low, furious voice and the feeling of him grabbing her elbow and hauling her out of the restaurant.

"Des, what are you doing?" she asked in disbelief. He'd practically shoved her through the revolving door in front of him. Claire spun around so quickly when they reached the sidewalk that she tripped on her high-heeled shoes. Des steadied her at the same time that he passed the parking token to the attendant along with several bills.

"Hurry up," he said in a low, tense voice that made the valet's eyes spring wide as he muttered a "yes sir". Des pushed Claire behind him as he turned to face the tall blond man who surged through the revolving doors behind them. "Is this how low you've sunk, Malkovic? You're so jealous of me that you're stalking me on my dates now?"

Malkovic's eyes flared with hatred. "Why should I be jealous of a man who would stoop so low as to seduce an innocent woman just to position himself to capture a man whom he delusionally believes to be a serial killer? You've accused me of being willing to do anything to climb the ladder at the Bureau, Alvarez, but even I would have never agreed to fuck my way into an inside position." Malkovic threw a demeaning, lecherous glance back at Claire. "Though I'm sure you've been enjoying every second of getting inside Ms. Allen."

Des' teeth ground together when he heard Claire's soft gasp behind him. He didn't give a second thought to clocking Malkovic's smug face. The precise, powerful jab to his jaw was only partially a product of unmitigated fury. He couldn't think of a better way to temporarily shut up the son of a bitch before he said something even more misleading and insulting to Claire.

"Des, what the—"

But Claire didn't have a chance to get any more of her question out before Des opened up the passenger door of his newly arrived car and pushed her into the seat. Claire was left staring back wide-eyed through the car window at the man sprawled on the sidewalk who was struggling to stand.

"I can explain," he said gruffly.

"You don't have to explain anything. It'll be sufficient to know that man was a raving lunatic and all of the stuff about you working for the FBI and using me to get some kind of inside line on a case you're working on was just his paranoid delusion or something." She studied him closely. A shiver ran over her bare arms when he didn't meet her gaze and she saw the way his jaw clenched with tension.

"Des?"

"Andre Malkovic is a power-hungry pain in my ass but I don't know if I'd necessarily call him a lunatic."

"Why would he say that you worked for the FBI then?" Claire asked slowly.

"Stop the car," she said abruptly when he didn't speak for several seconds.

"What?"

"Stop this damn car."

His eyes sliced over to her in the darkness. "What? You're going to believe everything that asshole says about me just like that?"

"Why shouldn't I? You aren't denying any of it. Do you or do you not work for the FBI?"

"I do. But—"

"Let me out. I'll take a cab home."

"The hell you will!"

"The hell I will," Claire shot back just as passionately. When they pulled up to the stoplight at Randolph and Halsted she heard a clicking sound a millisecond before she reached for her car door. "Why won't my door open?"

Des' voice was cold. "I have a master lock over here."

"Are you putting me under arrest or something?" Without batting an eyelash, she lunged across him and tried to hit the lock. Des caught her wrists. Claire couldn't help but feel a measure of satisfaction when she saw the look of sheer frustration on his handsome face. She'd teach him to think he could fuck around with her life like she was a mere chess piece that he manipulated toward his own ends.

"No. But I am going to handcuff you if you keep acting like such an impulsive child. Are you going to sit still so I can drive safely and explain?"

She stared at him mutinously. "I can't believe you've been lying to me all this time." Her eyes glittered with anger but her face flinched in pain as she said the words.

Damn Malkovic straight to hell, Des seethed. The light changed. "Are you going to sit still or not, Claire? I expect an answer."

Fury bloomed in her at that. Tears stung her eyes. It had been enough of a battle for her to overcome her better judgment and be with this man in the intimate ways that she had been, ways she had never even considering giving herself to another man. But she'd trusted her instincts to be with him even when she thought her involvement with him might mysteriously involve her own death.

"I don't give a fuck what you expect. I trusted you and you're nothing but a god-damned liar." She struggled to get her wrists free of his vise-like grip. He'd flipped open the glove box, slapped her left wrist in a pair of handcuffs and had her cuffed to the handle of her locked car door in a matter of seconds. He did it so quickly and so efficiently that Claire was manacled before they were halfway down the next block.

"*Des*." She rattled the handle, the sound and pressure on her wrist only increasing her fury and helplessness. "Let me go right this second or I'll never speak to you again in my life."

"Right now that sounds pretty damn promising," he muttered under his breath.

"And I'll have you arrested, you lying bastard FBI..." A flicker of curiosity passed over her otherwise impassioned features. Her eyelids narrowed. "What is it that you do at the FBI exactly?"

He looked straight ahead as he drove. His heart was pounding loudly in his ears. He was almost blind with rage at what Malkovic had done. He needed to be careful not to misdirect it at Claire. "I was a special agent in the Violent Crimes Unit. Just recently, I was offered a promotion. If Malkovic has his way after what just happened back there, I'll never get it though."

"Serves you right," Claire spat out, trying to ignore the way her heart squeezed when she saw briefly beneath his cold veneer and realized how much his casually spoken words were actually paining him. "So *what*? Do you think I'm some kind of a crazed killer or something? You must be a really crappy agent. No wonder they—"

"Just be *quiet*, Claire," he barked abruptly. "I've had more than I can take right now. Do you understand?"

Claire's jaw snapped shut when she saw his icy, indomitable stare and felt it penetrate straight through her. She turned her head and stared out the window, seeing nothing. Neither of them spoke again until they reached Claire's house as they both tried to get their emotions under control.

After Des had parked, he shut off the engine and glanced over at her partially averted face. He sighed. "Don't you even want to hear my side of the story?"

"Is it true what that man said? Did you seduce me just to get an inside track on some kind of assignment that you're working on?"

"The answer to that is a lot more complicated than it seems."

Claire turned to look at him, surprised at how hard it was under the circumstances. "Yes or no, Des. I deserve an answer."

He leaned toward her. "Listen, I realize how much this must hurt. I knew that I was going to be very attracted to you, but even knowing what I knew I never expected it would be like this."

Claire tugged on the cool metal of the handcuffs to try to steel herself against his admission. Of course he would try to flatter her. Whatever he was trying to accomplish on his assignment hadn't yet been achieved. He still needed her cooperation. "You told me the other day that you purposely came to the house to seduce me. You even brought your official paperwork to convince me," Claire recalled with a grimace. "Did you, or did you not, do that so that you could position yourself with some personal agenda in mind?"

Des closed his eyes briefly. "Yes."

"Let me out of this damned car. If the FBI has something they need to speak with me about they can make an appointment at my office and present themselves with badges bared, in what I hope is the normal, ethical manner required. I'll be the first to tell them that tomorrow morning when I call and file a complaint against you."

"You want to get out of the car? Fine. I've had enough of your smart mouth."

When he opened her door her cuffed wrist pulled her into even more of an awkward angle. Her eyes widened in rising dismay while Des searched around in her purse for her house key.

"What the... *Hey,* what are you doing?" Claire blurted out when he released her left wrist from the door handle only to place the other cuff on her right one. Air whooshed out of her lungs when Des abruptly lifted her out of the passenger seat and tossed her over his shoulder. Claire was so shocked by his actions she didn't have the ability to protest until he was up the front steps.

"Put me down, you animal!" She struggled and struck his back with her fists. He swatted her fanny once. Hard. It surprised Claire enough she stiffened and gasped in rising rage. It was all he needed to get the front door unlocked. Claire threatened all manner of dire consequences and fought him continually as he carried her up the stairs in that ignominious position. Her curses and kicks might as well have been aimed at a mountain of ice for all the good it did her.

"You cold son of a bitch," she ranted when he dumped her on her bed and she landed gracelessly. She screamed in fury. He pulled her arms back and released her left wrist long enough to lace the cuffs through one of her bedposts.

He stood back and examined her calmly while she struggled. "You're going to scratch up your bed."

She stilled. He stared down at her, his face impassive.

"Why in the world are you doing this?"

"Because I'm trying to protect you."

She choked out a humorless bark of laughter. "*This* is what you call protecting me? You manhandle me and handcuff me to a bed?"

Her dress had become mussed and tangled during her struggle, exposing her thigh-high stockings and the edge of her dark blue panties. She stiffened when Des' silver eyes traveled the same path that hers had. Her cheeks flamed. "I insist that you release me from these handcuffs. If you won't, then for God's sake at least put my dress down."

"No," Des said simply as he removed his jacket and draped it on the chair.

"Where are you going?" Claire asked desperately when he headed for the door.

"I'm giving you a chance to cool off. I guess it's true what they say about redheads and their tempers, huh?"

He slammed the door on Claire's howl of outrage.

Afterward he searched the house carefully, guessing that Kevin was still gone but needing to make sure. He went through Kevin's personal items but there was nothing to cause undue interest.

By the time he'd returned to Claire's bedroom, he hoped that he'd calmed down sufficiently to face her again and vice versa. He knew she had a right to be pissed off. But the fact that she'd so easily believed that asshole Malkovic's allegations about him stung more than he cared to admit. Was he entirely alone in believing that the chemistry that bubbled between the two of them was not only unique but also precious? She wouldn't even let him explain, for God's sake. He met her furious stare steadily when he reentered the bedroom. At least she didn't start insulting him immediately.

Stubborn woman.

Stubborn bastard, Claire thought at the same moment as she took in the arrogant tilt of Des' chin as he came and sat down on the edge of the bed. She wasn't going to give him the satisfaction of shouting at him anymore. He'd handcuffed her to her own bed! Claire still couldn't believe it.

"Are you ready to listen to me now?"

"What if I'm not?" she asked coldly. "I didn't realize that the FBI used tactics like this on innocent women."

"This," he glanced down meaningfully at the bed, "doesn't have anything to do with the FBI or my investigation. This has everything to do with *us*, Claire. My primary motive is to keep you safe. I couldn't do that with you going all cockeyed with self-righteous indignation and refusing to let me protect you."

She regarded him coldly even though inside she was boiling over with anger and hurt. How could he have turned her inside out like this? Where was her old self, the calm, rational, analytical woman who would never in a million years let a caveman like Des Alvarez turn her into a simpering slut who only wanted to know how far when he told her to bend over? And he'd been lying the whole time. She hated him, *hated* him for doing this.

"What are you going to do to me? Why are you keeping me tied to this bed? Are you planning on raping me or something?"

Claire flinched, her eyes opening wide, when she saw his reaction. *Shit*. She bit her lip to force herself not to apologize. All right, maybe she shouldn't have said that. She didn't really believe Des was capable of something so heinous. But he'd left her not only furious but helpless. She wanted to beat at him with her fists, hurt him, but all he left her was words to use as missiles. And from the incredulous look that segued to a fury even greater than what she'd seen when he hit that Malkovic guy, her blow had just hit below the belt indeed.

He straddled her on the bed and lowered until their faces were barely an inch apart. Claire couldn't breathe at first at being so close to the anger that seemed to roll off his body like hot waves. When her lungs finally did work she inhaled the rich, masculine scent that was unique to him alone, the scent that made her body come to life entirely of its own will. Claire shut her eyes. Christ, why did she respond to him so powerfully, as if the subtle chemicals of his body had been made in some heavenly laboratory to perfectly mix with and arouse her own essence?

"I'm going to make you pay for that, Claire."

Her eyes sprang open at that steely, softly muttered threat. She didn't have to ask him what he meant. His meaning was as clear as the heat that was already building between their bodies.

"No."

"Yes," he assured her as he stood again next to the bed. "I've offered to explain myself almost half a dozen times now but instead you just want to insult me and everything that's happened between us." He headed for the door again. "I'll make you listen to me, Claire, and I'm not going to have to resort to rape to do it."

"Des, wait. I'm...*damn*." Claire's head fell back on the pillows in frustration when he walked out of her room again and shut the door. What was he doing?

Her eyes were huge with anxiety and anticipation when he opened the door a minute later, carrying a plastic bag. He didn't speak to or acknowledge her, just set the bag on the bedside table. Her eyes grew even larger when she saw him calmly reach into his jacket pocket and remove a gun that looked entirely too concealed to have been hidden in there. He scowled when he saw her expression.

"What? Are you going to accuse me of planning on forcing you at gunpoint now?" he asked testily before he opened up her bedside table drawer and dropped the gun inside it. "Now that you know what I do for a living I'm not going to hide it anymore, Claire. The safety is on, and in the future I'll lock it up. I need it close by while we're in this house though."

"Des, I don't really believe that you'd rape me or hold me at gunpoint," she began, as diplomatically as possible given the fact that she was boiling mad. "But I also didn't expect that you would lie so outrageously and seduce me for your own purposes." She rolled her eyes in exasperation when she saw the flame of fury leap again into his light eyes. She hadn't meant her attempt at communication to end up that way. She watched warily as Des kneeled over her thighs again.

"Well I wouldn't have expected that you were so ashamed of your feelings for me that you would betray them completely at the first sign of potential conflict."

Claire's mouth fell open. Is that how he saw this whole situation? He answered as though he read her mind at the same time that he reached down to untie the belt that wrapped her dress around her waist.

"Yeah, babe, that's exactly what I see happening here. You're the psychiatrist, think about it for a minute. You know *shit* about Andre Malkovic. And yet you're willing to believe a few nasty accusations that he made against me without blinking an eye. You know what I think, Claire?" he asked smoothly as he peeled back both sides of her dress, leaving her exposed to his hungry gaze with the exception of her bra, panties, heels and thigh highs. "I think you've been waiting to find out something bad about me so that you could dump me, along with all these new feelings and thoughts you've been having about yourself."

He leaned forward and ran a thumb over her collarbone, gauging her reaction to his touch. She gasped. His fingertips slid over her neck and shoulder. He felt her shiver. "They're downright bothersome, some of those feelings. Aren't they, baby?"

Claire couldn't respond. She was too hyperaware of the proximity of his big, hard body, of the deftness of his touch as he soothed his fingertips over her shoulder. She made a trapped sound in her throat when she realized that he was hypnotically caressing his mark on her, the one that he'd made to such eye-opening effect during the dream.

Her eyes clamped shut but it was a fragile form of protection. Had she just called Des Alvarez a caveman in her thoughts? What a joke. His subtlety was genius. Not only did his touch cause liquid to surge from her pussy, he reminded her without words of the strange, powerful bond that was between them.

He felt her jump slightly when he trailed his fingers along the sensitive skin beneath her armpit. Her nipples instantly peaked beneath the clinging satin fabric of her bra, telling Des that she was more aroused than anxious. He flicked his wrist beneath her, unfastening the garment. She made a strangled sound.

"Des, don't do this. I told you that I know you would never force me. You don't have to prove—"

"What, Claire?" he asked, focusing most of his attention on his actions as he moved the fabric of her bra, exposing her lovely, tender breasts. He felt his cock surge almost painfully. Every time he saw her he felt overwhelmed anew by her perfection, her shape, her coloring. After a moment his eyes lifted to meet hers. "Prove what?"

"That you can make me respond to you."

Their gazes remained locked while he shook his head. "I don't have to prove it to me. Apparently it's necessary for me to prove it to you. You know, there are some things that it's a sacrilege to deny."

Claire couldn't form a coherent response. His fierce gaze, the lightest, feathery touch across his mark on her shoulder, made her speechless. Without ever noticing that he'd actually moved, he was suddenly shadowing hers within an inch. But he didn't touch her anywhere—except for on his brand on her shoulder, and there so lightly that Claire almost thought she was imagining it. The mark of passion took on a strange significance. Her entire self seemed focused there, just beneath his lightly brushing, calloused fingertips.

"Don't, Desi. Please."

One dark brow rose enigmatically. "I'm hardly touching you, Claire. Do you want me to stop touching your shoulder?"

Claire licked her dry lips. "No."

His mouth came to within a quarter inch of hers, grazing her lips. The thought struck her that he was likely inhaling her desire and her dread all at once. Her eyes clenched shut as she skimmed on the knife's edge of uncertainty.

Des saw. "Don't. Open your eyes."

His were only inches away. She noticed the black ring of his iris, which stood in such stark contrast to the silvery center. She felt herself being pulled down into their depths, further and further. Her resistance to him faded faster by the second but her anger fought to survive. "I'm not your toy, Des. I'm not your sex slave either. Take off these handcuffs."

"I don't think so."

Claire swallowed heavily as his eyes moved slowly down her body, seemingly burning a trail on her exposed skin wherever his gaze touched. Her nipples pulled tightly, painfully even, under his hot stare. She was acutely aware of him moving his hand. *Please touch me,* she thought. Claire turned her head away from him, mortified by her weakness. She whimpered softly when his calloused fingers circled the delicate skin on the lower swell of her breast. Her nipple tugged even stiffer, creating a sensation she felt deep down in her womb. He leaned down close to her chest, his breath caressing her sensitive skin.

"And as for the other, perhaps you're not my slave, precisely…but there is something that holds authority over you. Best you give in to it once and for all," Des muttered distractedly, most of his attention on how exquisitely soft her skin felt, like warm, flowing silk beneath his fingertips. He continued to finesse her breast, deliberately avoiding the erect nipple, all the while studying his effect on the pouting flesh. He heard Claire moan in growing arousal and glanced up at her beautiful, strained face.

"Do you want something, Claire?" He watched as she harried her full lower lip with small, white teeth. Des' nostrils flared.

Even the image of her rebellion was potent.

Claire finally bit her lip hard, saying "no" in the wake of the pain. It was the only way she could manage it, because she felt as if she wanted, needed, his rough yet soothing tongue, the warm caress of his suckling mouth, more than she needed breath at that moment. Des looked darkly amused at her response. She watched as he sat up and reached for the bag that he'd set on the bedside table. Her eyes widened when he removed a small bowl of strawberries.

"Remember these?" The look of dazed desire followed by wariness in her eyes told him that she'd recalled the reference from their shared dream all right...and her discomfort when he'd offered them to her the first day they'd met.

Your nipples would be hard, sweet, ripe berries just begging to be eaten.

"I washed them when I was downstairs but they're still pretty much frozen."

"Frozen?" Claire asked slowly.

"Mmm hmm."

He took one of the berries and positioned himself over her again. "I put them in the freezer before we left tonight." A single droplet of water poised thickly at the end of the berry. Both of them watched as he held it an inch from her nipple. When the drop finally fell Claire whimpered at the icy sensation. She didn't have time to recover from that small shock before Des pressed the entire strawberry to her nipple.

She gasped, but her protest was followed by a groan of arousal at the sensation of him stimulating her with the icy-cold fruit. He rolled it against her tight nipple, pressed it and circled it around the tip. The slightly roughened, cold surface abraded every bump and crevice on the painfully taut peak. She shivered at the pleasure of the hard, cool caress.

"Cold?" he asked gently when he saw her tremble. Without preamble, he abruptly removed the frozen strawberry and took her nipple into his hot mouth.

Claire cried out brokenly. Prickles of heat ran like electricity from her breasts to her sex and from there down to resonate in a tension-filled tingling sensation on the soles of her feet.

"Oh *yes*," she panted. She wondered dazedly if he was going to push her over the edge of orgasm just from nipple stimulation like he had the other day. The pleasure that his raspy, warm tongue wrought on her was enormous. Then he sucked her lustily, pressing her nipple up against the roof of his mouth. Claire's back bowed off the bed. She didn't have to wonder about whether or not she was going to come again. It took her a moment to realize that the torn, keening noise that echoed in her ear was her own. Pleasure wracked her in relentless waves. When it ebbed Claire cracked open her eyes hesitantly.

Des stared at her steadily, all the while lapping at her nipple with his long tongue. Claire almost choked when she glanced down to see him waggling his tongue rapidly, flicking the erect, bobbing flesh, giving it a gentle thrashing yet never moving his silvery gaze from her eyes. The knowledge that he'd just been a spectator to her orgasm filled her with both renewed arousal and anxiety.

Was this the real Claire Allen—this weak, spineless creature that this man transformed her into with so much ease?

"What are you thinking?" he asked thickly, after he'd released her nipple from his enclosing mouth with a popping noise.

"I'm weak," Claire whispered. Suddenly she didn't care if he knew the depths of her despair. He wouldn't understand it anyway. How could he, when Claire herself couldn't understand the wild, insatiable desires he awakened in her? Her nostrils flared with anger when she saw both his smile and that dimple that ought to be outlawed in order to give an independent woman like Claire the freedom she deserved. Her anger came from so many places but first and foremost it was the knowledge that his smile always made her his slave that made her furious and panicked.

And so confused.

Des saw her bewildered expression. His smile faded. "Baby, you're so *weak* that you could knock me over with a feather right now. Do you know what that does to me? To watch you come like that? To know that you're so sensual, so responsive to my touch, so damned perfect that you explode from me touching your nipple?"

He leaned up abruptly and brought his face close to hers.

Claire's eyes widened at seeing the hard, harsh angles of his face in such close proximity. His heat and hardness vibrated into her flesh. She struggled to inhale when she realized how aroused he was. "What, Desi?"

"It makes me feel like a king. You make me feel like the most powerful man on Earth when you shake for me."

Tears sprang to her eyes. Why did he have to say things like that? She had a powerful memory of how she'd felt when he came in her mouth yesterday, muttering every curse known to man and a few comical made-up ones too. Yes, she knew what he meant. That had made her feel like a queen…a goddess. She suddenly felt overwhelmed with a need to touch his hard muscles and smooth skin.

"Des, let me out of these handcuffs. I want to touch you." She saw his face relax slightly at her words, giving her a clue just how much tension he was carrying in his body, despite his impassive features.

"Are you uncomfortable?" he asked as he stood next to the bed and began to remove his clothing.

Claire hesitated as he peeled off his shirt, her eyes detailing all that smooth, hard male flesh. God, he was beautiful. "I'm uncomfortable because I want to touch you and I can't."

That was the understatement of the year, she thought as he peeled his boxer briefs over his erection. He stood before her a second later, inspecting her calmly. Claire salivated at the sight of his long penis. Her pussy contracted. She longed to have him fill her emptiness. She wanted him even more than she had on that first night, in the dream...when she had chosen to rub against him and come instead of breathe. God, the shame of it all...and the glory. How could both feelings exist at once? One of them was going to have to give way. She couldn't exist with such a paradox at her core.

He knelt over her again.

"If the handcuffs aren't actually hurting you, I don't think I'll take them off." He placed his finger at her lips, stilling her protest. At the same time he lowered his pelvis so that the long, velvety length of his erection brushed along her belly and the furrow of her ribs.

Des felt her go still beneath him. He waited until her midnight eyes met his. "I haven't been able to convince you yet that there's no shame in surrendering yourself to me, Claire. I know you're a strong woman. Do you think I don't know how much courage it takes for you to give yourself to me, especially when I ask you to do things that challenge you here in the bedroom?" He shook his head in amazement. "You gave yourself to me when you thought that doing so might somehow lead to your own death. You're the most courageous person I know, baby."

A tear slid down her flushed cheeks. "I'm going to show you that there's no place for shame between us. I'm going to prove to you that your trust in me isn't misplaced, even though you don't fully understand all of the circumstances of what's been happening here. I have far too little control when it comes to you."

He scooted up on the bed and placed his knees on the outside of her shoulders. His cock felt impossibly heavy and achy in his palm. "Do you see that? That's how much I burn for you. That's what seeing you restrained on this bed with your beautiful body bared for the pleasure of my eyes and my hands and my mouth, what the sight of you screaming out in orgasm, does to me. Do you think I'm *depraved* because that turns me on? Do you?"

Claire felt herself melting with a feeling that went way beyond desire as she looked into his silver eyes and saw his stark need. She could lie to him right now, and she knew instinctively that it would wound him deeply.

That was what she'd wanted to do, more than anything, just a short while ago.

"No, Desi. Come here."

"Ah Christ, baby," he moaned in tense ecstasy as he brought his cock to her lips and pushed the first few inches into her. He saw her struggle with the angle and he propped a pillow beneath her neck. He groaned loudly as her tongue darted over him and she took him deeper into her wet, warm heat.

The pleasure bordered on being cruel. Des leaned forward, bracing his upper body on the rail of her headboard. The need to fuck her tight, clasping mouth was almost overwhelming but he resisted the savage urge. The energy that he expended in doing so made his thighs quiver. He clenched his eyelids tight, refusing to allow himself the flagrantly erotic vision before him — Claire handcuffed to the bed with his cock stretching her red lips wide.

But it was no good. The image remained behind his eyelids. Christ. He'd had more experienced women then Claire, women who were used to taking a large penis deep and hard. But nothing, nothing could ever...*would* ever compare to Claire's generosity at that moment. And although she hadn't learned yet how to take him deeply, the suction she created was heavenly, her quick, darting tongue a torment. Des felt his eyes roll back in his head, felt his balls draw up. Her strong, relentless sucking told him how much she wanted him, despite everything that happened earlier.

It was that knowledge that had him sweating and grunting and gasping on the edge.

"Claire, baby, I need to fuck your sweet little mouth. Please, just a...ahh!"

Claire answered him by straining up her head, determinedly swallowing down another inch of him. Her action made her gag and tears flowed down her face. She vaguely heard Des' moan of sympathy, felt one of his hands fall to her head. But Claire had already forgotten about the discomfort. *God,* she wanted him. She wanted him so badly it was a physical pain.

"Shhh, Claire. Just let me...like this. Ah baby, that's fucking great," he muttered mindlessly as he kept her head steady and fucked just the first half of his cock into her suctioning heat. Five strokes was all it took and he was shouting, his cock jerking in orgasm, his cum shooting powerfully into her mouth. His cry of completion sounded a little shocked and desperate at the extremity of his pleasure.

He regretfully slid his cock out of her harboring heat and leaned down, kissing her wet lips softly. He met her liquid eyes.

"Thank you." Despite his recent release, his cock twitched at the sight of her damp, swollen lips curving into a smile. "Witch," he whispered gruffly. "You like having me at your mercy, don't you?"

She nodded. It was silly to try to hide the truth from him at this point. Not that she could if she wanted to. Des smiled. He kissed her lips once more before he leaned over the bed and snagged his pants. He withdrew something from the pocket that she couldn't see and then reached for the bowl of berries, placing them by her head on the bed.

"Getting the best blowjob of my life has me hungry for dessert," he told her with a wicked upthrust of his eyebrows. He flicked open his pocket knife and cored one of the still-icy strawberries. He was encouraged by the small smile on her lips, but he wished he could see the sparkle in her dark eyes that he loved so much. He wanted her to relish the singular electricity between them as much as he did. He knew that he was using caveman tactics to get her to accept him here in this house—accept him, period—but what the hell else could he do? Part of him was just a stupid, primitive savage, after all.

Claire watched him with fascination as he removed the cores from the strawberries. What he did next puzzled her. He studied her nipple, as though he were taking her measure, before he made a couple slits in the center of the core of the strawberry. She gasped when he slid the icy cold core of the fruit over her left nipple.

"Des."

The frozen strawberry teased her nipple with its chill and weight. Laughter bubbled across her lips when she saw the way he was inspecting his handiwork with lecherous satisfaction. "Where do you come up with these kinky ideas anyway?"

He was busy fitting the second large berry over her other lush crest. "Your nipples inspired me." He grinned as he took both of her breasts in his palms and squeezed, loving the picture of her creamy, strawberry-tipped breasts protruding up at him.

"They're freezing my nipples," Claire murmured dazedly. Despite what she said, heat flooded her pussy.

His face looked tense as he picked up another berry and pressed it to her swollen lips. "I want to eat one. Heat this one up for me with your mouth."

Claire moaned as he gently slid the large strawberry between her lips. "That's right. Good girl," he said thickly after a moment. His gaze on her was like a palpable touch. He brought the thawed fruit to his mouth and bit. The juice ran over his lips before he removed it. "Keep your lips still," he whispered. He trailed the strawberry over her wet lips, letting the juices stain her mouth even darker red than nature had. Only then did he pop the fruit into his mouth and chew.

"Sweet. Want one, baby?"

Claire trailed the tip of her tongue over her lips slowly, tasting the mixture of Des' semen and sweet juice. "Yes."

He dipped his dark head and fitted his entire mouth over her strawberry nipple. The fruit came unfastened in the confines of his mouth. She choked with arousal as he skillfully manipulated the cold fruit over her straining breast. The contrast between the icy cold, meaty texture of the fruit and the heat of his pleasuring tongue was electrifying. She arched her back, offering more of her breast to him.

He pressed the fruit to her nipple, holding it steady, and bit. She felt the cold juice dribble over her, the gentle scrape of his teeth over her tender flesh. Her pussy clenched with need. She wouldn't be able to take much more of this torture.

"Desi!" she cried out desperately.

He withdrew from her breasts. "Yes, baby. Here's your sweet."

She moaned into his mouth when he kissed her deeply, transferring the fruit between her lips. He withdrew, dipping his dark head to her other strawberry-tipped breast.

Claire whimpered and writhed against the handcuffs. Her thighs pressed together tightly to still her growing ache but still he tortured her other breast, the pleasure stretching and swelling.

Please, please, please! I can't survive this. Let me come, Desi.

It was her own wanton cries that echoed in her ears, her own need, her own desire. Tonight they still sounded strange to her, but nowhere near as alien to her as they had when Des first made love to her.

He pushed the second berry in her mouth before he made his way down her belly. He ripped away her flimsy underwear without a thought. No barriers would be allowed to exist between them tonight. He kissed the insides of her tender thighs, aroused beyond measure by how damp they were from her arousal. His tongue flicked over her hungrily, glorying in her unique flavor.

"You know what I want, Claire. Don't deny me."

Claire groaned with intense arousal as she spread her thighs as wide as she could, knowing how he liked her to be fully exposed to him. She was rewarded almost immediately by the sensation of his rough tongue stroking the length of her clit. He rubbed her ruthlessly with a rigid tongue. She screamed. His hand came up to hold her hips and ass steady as she thrashed against him in the tumult of orgasm. The reward was rich but he wouldn't allow her to rest until she'd taken every last ounce of pleasure that his marauding tongue and suctioning mouth had to offer.

"Okay, baby?" Des asked roughly a minute later. He spoke in the interim between tonguing her still-sensitive labia.

"Oh God, yes. It felt so good," Claire said unevenly between gasping breaths. "It *feels* so good," she corrected as he continued his onslaught on her senses. She moaned helplessly when he put a finger to her soaking slit and penetrated her. The sliding in-and-out motion and his continued ministrations with his talented tongue had her straining toward release yet again.

"Des."

"What? You need more? Tell me what you want." He sounded harsh, desire-bitten. It was a demand, not a request.

"I need more of you in me. Ah, oh *yes!*" Claire keened as he squeezed another finger into her and thrust hard.

"Your juices are running down my knuckles, baby. You're tight but you're so hot. Take another." She made an incoherent sound of desire as he carefully fit another finger into her. He began to probe and rub her clit again with his tongue. Claire thrashed wildly, her body strung tight like a bow, straining against the handcuffs.

Des noticed the way she pulled frantically at the bedpost, how the hard metal of the cuffs bit at her wrists as she writhed in pleasure. He muttered a curse and slanted his mouth over her tumescent clit. His teeth bit ever so gently at the nerve-packed kernel of flesh, sending her over the edge, ending her torment abruptly.

She cried out as orgasm slammed into her.

He nursed her tumultuous orgasm with his hand while he leaned over for the keys to the cuffs. The thought struck him that she might run away from him again if he let her loose, but he would have to take the chance.

Desire bound her at this point even more than the restraints.

Claire blinked dazedly when she felt Des release her wrists. He rubbed her wrists soothingly. She loved the feeling of his calloused fingers equally as much whether they were gentle and calming or thrusting and relentless.

"Desi?" she whispered as she looked into his steady gaze.

"Yes, baby."

"How do you do that to me?"

He paused as he gazed into her sweat-dampened features, hearing the broken entreaty in her voice. He came down next to her and took her into his arms, kissing her swollen lips softly. His own desire throbbed powerfully but he knew how important it was to be patient with her, especially now, when she was so confused.

"You make it sound so one-sided," he murmured next to her lips.

He kissed her again, this time letting some of his passion unfurl. Their tongues tangled hotly. His cock surged painfully against her silky thigh.

"I'm sorry for lying to you, Claire. This is all my fault. I should have said to hell with Isabelle's wishes. I should have met you sooner, before all of this other crap came into play. But I didn't. Now you'll just have to believe me when I say that I would have sought you out sooner or later, no matter what happened on this case."

He studied her expression carefully, drowning in the depths of her midnight blue eyes. "Trust your instincts. Give yourself to me or don't. But if you do give yourself, do it without resentment. You decide."

She reached up and entwined her fingers in his silky hair. To be able to touch him was heaven. Her sensitized fingertips sought out the skin on his neck. She loved the way his breath drew in sharply at her touch. She skimmed her fingernails across his muscular chest and teased a dark brown nipple. Des groaned. He immediately stiffened beneath her eager ministrations.

She dragged her tongue over his sensitive flesh. He groaned again. No, there was no inequity here, not in the way she'd been imagining. He gasped and drew her up to face him. His eyes were like glowing, silvery crescents of desire when she met his gaze.

"It feels right, being with you." She kissed him hotly, her tongue teasing and swirling in his mouth. "I give myself. Whatever way you want me."

Their kiss turned voracious and carnal, both of them giving and taking in equal measure. He never made a conscious decision to do it. He couldn't stand the thought of parting from her lips. But suddenly he was fumbling desperately for a condom.

He thrust and they moaned into each other's mouth. His strokes were slow and deep.

Claire closed her eyes and luxuriated in the sensation. "I love being filled by you."

His lips brushed hers softly even as his body surged into her with increased force. She was so aroused, and he thrust so powerfully, that the sound of her pussy sucking and slurping eagerly on his cock filled the silent room.

Des groaned in excitement and dropped his head next to her shoulder. "Do you remember how I said I might make love to you tonight?"

She tensed with excited anxiety. Her hips surged up against him, taking him into her deeper. "Yes."

"Are you ready to give yourself, even in that way?"

She exhaled with a puff of air. "Take me any way you like."

Des forced himself to slow, to try to regain a measure of control. Her pussy was like a tight velvet clasp. Her juices ran abundantly, wetting his balls with every deep thrust. He wanted to fuck her little pussy until they both found bliss. But he also had an overwhelming need to take her on this night in a way that she'd never before been taken by a man. He had a primitive need to be her first in some manner. He made a low hissing sound when he pulled out of her.

"No, don't."

"Only for a moment," Des managed between panting breaths. Christ, he needed to get control of himself if he was going to make this a good experience for Claire. After a few seconds he reached down and thrust two fingers into her hot, soaking pussy. "I never knew that a woman could get this wet for a man."

Claire moaned and instinctively thrust up against him. He gave her what she needed for a few moments as he slid his body to the side of her and drew up her knees. She made a sigh of protest when he withdrew. But then he was pressing a creamy finger to her asshole and telling her to press up on him. She did so without thinking, taking him into her body. There was no pain this time, as there had been in the dream. She began to move her hips against him as he slid in and out of her. She threw back her head and moaned at the erotic sensation as the nerves along her sacrum began to tingle with life.

"Open your eyes, baby," he ordered as he pressed a second finger to her tight, muscular entry.

Claire complied, gasping loudly as his second finger penetrated her. "Oh," she exclaimed.

"What does it feel like?"

"Different...good. It feels like..."

"What?"

"It feels like you're making me yours."

Des craned down and kissed her. "I am." He began to plunge into her harder, occasionally twisting his fingers, stretching her. All the while he watched her face carefully, assessing her experience and using the feedback to attenuate his actions.

"Your ass is on fire, and you're so tight. It's going to feel so damned good."

"It is?" Claire asked with breathless arousal. She loved seeing the tense desire on his face, the naked need. It made her feel powerful.

"Oh yeah."

"You're so big," she whispered. "Won't it hurt?"

Des paused in his action of gently spreading her with his two fingers. "It might," he admitted. "I hope not, Claire. But if it does, you only need to tell me and I'll stop. Okay?"

She nodded. They gazed into each other's eyes while he stroked her so intimately, cocooned in their own private world of sensuality. Suddenly they both froze at the sound of the front door slamming shut.

"*Kevin,*" Claire whispered.

Tension pulled Des' already strained muscles impossibly tighter.

Even though she should have been confused when he stood abruptly and turned off the light in the room, she wasn't. Nor was she shocked when she heard him flip the lock on the bedroom door.

She was relieved.

She heard him next to the bed, the sound of him rustling in a plastic bag, and then a scraping noise as he opened the bedside table.

"Des?" she asked nervously.

"It's okay. I was just making my gun easily available."

His warm, hard body was next to her almost immediately, reassuring her. He caressed her shoulders and waist. "It's because of *Kevin*?" Claire asked in dawning wonder. "*He's* the reason you're here?"

"He's the reason I'm in this house, Claire, to protect you from him. But he's not the reason I'm in this bed with you. Shhh, relax," he soothed when he felt her muscles bunch with tension. "I'll explain later. It's safe for now. He's not going to do anything with me here. He's too much of a coward. Kiss me, Claire. I'm too far gone. I need to have you, and soon."

Claire moaned at the impact of his heat when he took her mouth. He felt like a furnace. He pressed his fingers back to her ass. This time they were covered with a cool lubricant. When she got over her shock, Claire moaned at the erotic feeling of him sliding into her so easily. Then he pressed a third finger into her and began to fuck her steadily.

"Oh," Claire cried out in arousal. Her pussy swelled with new life. She could feel her heartbeat pulse in her clit.

He paused. Christ, he wished he could see her face. He needed the feedback in this delicate procedure. "Pain?" he asked roughly.

"No. I want more. I want you in me."

He groaned. His cock felt like it weighed a ton, it was so engorged with blood. He was going to explode with no other stimulation than the sound of Claire's aroused, catchy breaths in the darkness. "Ah, baby, you're going to have me." He positioned himself between her thighs.

"Spread your legs and hold back your thighs for me," he whispered tautly. His hand skimmed her body position in the darkness. "Farther back," he muttered as he repositioned her. "I should take you from behind but I want to be able to kiss you the first time I come in your body."

Claire bit her lip to stifle her sounds of arousal but she couldn't prevent her fingers from sliding around her thighs as she held them back, massaging her clit under cover of darkness when she heard his erotic words. But she should have known she couldn't hide anything from Des.

"Are you touching yourself?" he asked as he lubricated his cock in preparation for penetrating her. He didn't know how he knew she was. It was as if he'd been given the gift of not only reading the most minute details of her expression, but also the energy waves that surged around her body.

"Yes," she admitted into the darkness. Something about the pitch blackness, their bodies touching, the smell of sex and arousal, their hushed voices and the anticipation of what was to come created an almost unbearable excitement in Claire.

She stroked herself more rapidly.

"I wish I had ten hands, baby. I want to be doing it for you. But go ahead and pleasure yourself. It will ease things for you."

He found her with his fingers in the darkness. Her low moan, penetrating the black veil that surrounded them as he lubricated her asshole, was an incredible turn-on for him. He'd reached his limit. He pressed the head to her small, puckered entry. If he didn't know better he'd think what he planned to do to her was a sure impossibility.

He paused next to the warm, tight entry. He clenched his teeth tightly at the erotic sensation.

"Claire, listen to me," he muttered thickly into the darkness. "You said that you would give yourself to me, but you must do it in reality now. If I pushed there would be pain. You have to give yourself, offer yourself to me. Relax and push up on me, baby. Show me with your body that you meant what you said."

"I did mean it," she whispered determinedly. She thrust her hips up, felt the initial resistance then the quick stab of pain. God, he felt huge. It would never work.

"You're too big. But I want you so much." She gritted her teeth and pushed again, hard. They gasped in unison when the thick head of his cock slid into her body with the assistance of the generously applied lubrication.

He felt her tension and heard her animal-like cry. The pleasure of her tight embrace was cruel in its intensity but his overwhelming emotion was regret. "I'm sorry. Is it bad?"

For a second she couldn't respond. The pain was so overwhelming she felt like her body had been cleaved. It surprised her how quickly the acute sensation segued to excitement. A tingling sensation electrified her entire sacrum and sex. The need for friction and movement overcame her. She thrust her hips up on him again. This time when they groaned together it was mutually, in pleasure.

"The pain passed," Claire assured him as he sank farther into her. "Now it feels wonderful."

Des flexed his hips then, unable to resist the temptation of her tight, hot channel. He had to thrust hard to gain further entry into her narrow pathway. He braced his hands on the bed and began to rock in her gently. "You feel so fucking good, baby. Better even than I imagined. Ah, God help me, I need to—"

"Yes. Deeper."

It was all she could say. She was inundated with sensation and pleasure. She rubbed her clit desperately at the same time that he stuffed himself into her farther. There was a brief slice of pain but her excitement as she pleasured herself was far greater.

She almost choked in surprise as orgasm thundered through her.

She momentarily lost all sense of herself as wave after wave of pleasure inundated her existence. When she came to awareness it was to the incredibly erotic feeling of him fucking her most private place deep and hard. The sensation of his cock in her ass boggled her mind. She felt him more acutely here than in her pussy, clearly feeling him throb and jerk and lengthen within her body. He didn't speak but Claire could perfectly imagine the desperate tension on his face, the hard edge of his jaw as pleasure swamped him, his muscles delineated and tight as he thrust, the glint of wildness in his silvery eyes.

"Feel good, baby?"

"Yes. So good."

He smacked into her ass. "Give me your mouth. I'm going to come inside you in a second."

Claire raised her mouth to him. His movements were controlled and restrained but he still pounded her ass thoroughly. His hot mouth completed his possession of her. She heard that unique, desperate sound of his impending small death, felt his cock lengthen inside of her body, felt it jerking.

When he came he threw his head back and roared. All thoughts of subtlety and secrecy evaporated in a blinding rush of pleasure. The shudders of sensation seemed to go on and on, singeing him from the inside out. His arms gave way and he barely caught himself from falling heavily onto Claire.

He vaguely became aware of her tiny, jagged cries as she rocked her pelvis. "Ah baby, I'm sorry," he murmured, touched by her mindless need as she sought to satisfy herself by rocking up against him. He reached down with his left hand and glided his finger across her slick petals until she was shaking again in orgasm and crying out in release.

"You're so sweet," he murmured next to her lips when she eventually calmed. He kissed the fragile shell of her ear.

Her arms came up around his neck and she hugged him tightly. She realized that her cheeks were wet as she pressed her face against his neck. It had been such an emotionally charged exchange between them. So strange. To consider they'd only met days ago.

Des Alvarez had the power to make her question some essential, elemental concepts about herself. And the proven fact that her inner self was shifting and altering to accommodate this gorgeous, sexy, stubborn man was the equivalent of having the earth move under her feet, and in the earthquake way. It scared the crap out of her.

She felt him smile. His gravelly voice was like a sensual rake against the nape of her neck.

"You're not saying anything, Claire. That doesn't make what you're thinking any less true though."

Chapter Thirteen

ಬ

God damn that Alvarez. Who fucked with the lights off anyway, especially when the woman had a body like Claire did? Stupid Mexican son of a bitch, or whatever the hell he was. What a show he must be missing, Kevin thought bitterly.

He recalled all too clearly that Alvarez was hung like a horse, not only from their locker room days but from watching a few sessions between him and the lovely Alanna as well.

What a kick in the gut it had been to find out that Claire, his frigid but nevertheless way-hot little cousin, was dating Alvarez. What a kick in the god damned nuts it had been to find out that not only was she dating him but apparently letting him fuck her brains out via the pathway of her ass. He knew the sound of a woman being fucked in the ass when heard it. The moan was different—deeper, more primitive.

Kevin's face pulled tight with lust and pure unadulterated hate as he listened avidly to Claire's low moans. She'd already come once while Alvarez fucked her.

Who would have thought it? His ice princess cousin loved being pounded in the ass with a big cock. Ice princess? From the sounds of things, Claire could become a horny little bitch in heat the second Des Alvarez told her to assume the position.

His mouth twisted into a grin. If only his mother had known about *this*, she might not have thought Claire was so damn perfect.

He stroked his cock. He'd hated Alvarez for almost twenty years. Listening to him make his brainy, aloof cousin come and pant like an animal really twisted the knife, but it was also making him hard enough to pound nails.

Just like listening to that jerk years ago had—

Claire whimpered and then cried out sharply, as though surprised. Kevin panted and pumped with more force.

He was furious at being denied the visuals on this but the audio was hotter than anything he'd experienced in years. Something about the secrecy, the blackness, their hushed voices and low moans, was hotter than watching the most graphic sex being enacted strictly for his benefit.

Envy didn't dull his sexual gratification when he heard Alvarez roar like an animal. Jesus, he must have dropped a load of boiling cum in his cousin's sweet ass. He closed his eyes and imagined Alvarez's big hands tightly gripping Claire's slender throat as he came.

Women were such sluts down deep. That was the one thing this house had taught him very young. He'd been a fool to think that Claire was any different.

As much as he'd hated to discover Alvarez in the process of fucking his cousin, Kevin had been thrilled to feel himself getting such a hearty erection. And when he spilled his semen into his rapidly pumping hand while listening to Alvarez shout out to the high heavens as he came, Kevin felt all of his doubts about his manhood evaporate.

He felt good when he returned to his room, almost carefree as he searched around in his closet until he located an elaborate tackle box. He smirked. It'd been a guilt gift from his father. He'd told Kevin the two of them were going to spend more time together fishing out at Medford or Spy Pond.

What a joke.

His father had always been too happy to buy him expensive things, but how many times had the old geezer ever bothered to follow through on his promises with regard to his time? Once, that Kevin could recall. And even then he'd suddenly recalled a critical phone call he needed to make for work.

Sure enough, there was a roll of good strong fishing line in the corner of the box. Kevin's grin was almost boyish as he held the twine up before him. It was transparent—almost invisible. Such an innocent, innocuous little thing, fishing line.

He wondered just how much hell he could wreak with it.

Claire listened intently to Des' hushed explanations in the darkness.

She'd passed doubt long ago and had recently segued from confusion to a vague, amorphous feeling of horror.

Des had been telling her about the recent murder by strangulation of a woman named Clarisse Myer. She had been found in a riverbed northeast of San Francisco.

"There are several differences between this murder and the other six by the so-called Morningside Murderer. So many differences, in fact, that the regional office of the FBI hasn't picked up the case. The investigation is still being headed by the San Francisco Police Department."

"What are the differences?" Claire asked in a whisper.

This night had taken such a bizarre turn. She'd only just begun to accept that Des was an FBI agent. Considering the possibility that Kevin was a serial murderer was just too weird and frightening.

She shivered. Des felt it and pulled her tighter into his arms.

"One of the biggest is that Clarisse Myers tested positive for Rohypnol."

"The date rape drug?" She felt Des nod in the darkness. "Had she been raped?"

"No. That was another glaring difference between this case and the Morningside Murders."

Claire sensed his hesitation. "What, Des? What else was different?"

Des didn't speak for several seconds. Claire heard him sigh.

"None of the Morningside murders were pretty, trust me. But the brutality of this most recent murder was beyond anything I've ever seen as far as strangulation." She waited patiently as he paused again. "The son of a bitch practically took Clarisse Myer's head off with that rope, Claire. Her trachea was nearly severed along with a good portion of the muscle tissue. Calling it a strangulation-murder is more a matter of convenience than accuracy."

"God, that's horrible," Claire murmured in revulsion. "Why do you think Clarisse Myer was killed by the Morningside Murderer?"

"Keep in mind I'm one of the few people who does," he said wryly. "I told you there were differences, but there were similarities too. The most significant is that the murderer took one of Clarisse Myer's earrings."

"The Morningside Murderer takes tokens from his victims?"

Des nodded, reminding himself that although Claire wasn't a forensic psychiatrist, she'd still have a firm understanding of antisocial personality disorders. "One piece of jewelry from each victim," he told her quietly. "Also, the victims thus far have all had physical similarities. They've all been women with fair hair, slender, attractive. Clarisse Myer fit that description. But with all of that, it's not enough for Special Agent Dawson, the guy who's in charge of the Morningside Murders at the San Francisco office of the FBI, to think that the Myer murder is related."

"What am I not getting here? Why are you convinced?"

Des stroked her shoulder distractedly. "What you're not getting is the connection to Kevin Preskill. See, Clarisse Myer was the girlfriend of one of Kevin's gallery employees in San Francisco. A woman who works across the street from Kevin's gallery saw Kevin and Clarisse talking next to this car on the day she disappeared."

"That's all?" she wondered, confused.

He sighed. "Yeah, unfortunately. The witness never saw Clarisse get in his car. Kevin was questioned about it by a detective with the SFPD when he returned to Boston. I spoke with Emile Peterson, the detective, and he told me that Kevin was as smooth as silk when the situation was brought to his attention. Peterson doesn't like your cousin, and I can tell that he thinks Kevin knows more than he's giving away. But unfortunately that's no reason to arrest him."

Des felt Claire shake her head against his chest.

"I still don't get it. What could possibly make you suspect Kevin of being the Morningside Murderer?"

Des grimaced in the darkness. "Because I know things about Kevin, things from when we were young. He used to treat not only his friends like they were objects for his pleasure but girls too. Once, when we were both seniors, he bragged to a bunch of guys in the locker room how he'd…"

"What, Des?" Claire whispered.

He shifted uncomfortably.

"Des, remember what I do for a living. I've heard my share of bizarre and scary stories," she said quietly.

"Maybe, but none of them related to a family member, I assume," Des said grimly. "Kevin said that he'd choked this girl, one of our classmates, while they were having sex. Not enough to kill her," Des said when he felt Claire tense next to him. "You know about autoerotic asphyxiation, right? Well your cousin seemed to have a thing for doing something similar, just not the 'auto' portion of it. He liked doing it to his partners in the midst of having sex. Snuff in the making.

"Claire?" he asked after a long silence.

"I'm here," Claire whispered. She shivered again. "Is that all? You're basing your suspicions on that story and the witness who saw Kevin with Clarisse Myer?"

"No. Not completely. Because I knew Kevin, I noticed a little detail about one of the Morningside Murders that others wouldn't have. One of the victims, Sandra Dross, was a real estate agent from the suburb right next to the neighborhood of Morningside. Three nights before she was murdered, she was visiting a friend on the East Coast. They attended a high-profile gallery opening in Boston."

"Kevin's gallery?" Claire asked in rising disbelief.

"No. But I've since found out that the owner of the gallery was a young man who Kevin had taken under his wing. Preskill footed most of the bill for this guy to open his gallery. And another thing—Kevin was definitely there for that party, the same one that Sandra Dross attended. There are other things too, Claire. Maybe not things that are telling when taken in isolation but when they're viewed as part of a bigger picture they're enough to make me more than just suspicious of your cousin. I might be wrong about this but I don't think so. In any case, I couldn't afford to be cautious. Not when it came to you. I tracked Kevin's travel records. I knew that he was coming to Chicago today."

He felt her stiffen in his arms. "And so you contrived to meet me, knowing that Kevin would be staying in this house?"

Christ, was this going to the beginning of another argument? He sighed. "And so I contrived to meet you, knowing that Kevin would be staying in this house," he answered flatly.

A tense silence followed. "You're going to have to trust me, Claire. Can you do that?"

The question hung between them like a swinging blade.

"I don't think I want to be here, Desi."

Des sat up in bed, bringing her with him. "Why do you say that?"

"Because," she replied shakily. "I do trust you. And if what you said is true, the last place I want to be falling asleep is in the same house as Kevin."

Des reached up and tangled his hand in her hair. "Then pack some things. I'm taking you to my place. I don't believe for a second that Kevin would do anything to harm you when

I'm here next to you. But you're right. It's stupid to take the chance of being wrong. Go on, Red. Get dressed."

Claire seemed preoccupied and subdued while they got ready. But Des would always recall the bright smile that she gave him when she looked over her shoulder before she reached for her bedroom door, an overnight bag slung over her shoulder.

He stopped Claire abruptly and signaled with his head for her to get behind him as he scoped out the empty hallway. He went to the rail of the grand staircase and glanced down. The large hall was still and vacant but Kevin had left the dim stairway light on, making it impossible for anyone to hide in the shadows.

"Wait," he ordered sharply when he saw Claire hurry past him to the stairs. He quickly moved to follow her rapid descent. "I said to *wait* a second."

"What?" Claire asked over her shoulder.

"*Claire.*"

He watched in stunned horror as she flew through the air headfirst, as if she'd suddenly decided to take a nosedive off the top of the stairs. He lunged forward but he was several feet behind her. He was moving with his feet and she was flying, unhindered.

She seemed to hit an invisible wall. She fell to the stairs at the place of impact. Impact into *what*, Des couldn't say. He didn't have time to figure it out. Her body struck the wooden stairs with a series of sickening thumps.

He used both banisters to leap down several stairs at a time. Blood trickled on the right side of her forehead where she'd struck the railing. He quickly checked her pulse. It was rapid but strong.

He became vaguely aware of the sound of someone questioning him. Kevin stood at the top of the stairs, looking half asleep and concerned.

Des didn't respond. The whole time he placed a 9-1-1 call, he stood guard over Claire. His gaze never wavered off Kevin Preskill. At one point Kevin started hesitantly down the stairs.

His foot drew back abruptly when he saw the expression that leapt into Des' eyes.

Claire had a headache that vibrated her eyeballs, and it was only partially associated with the good-sized bump and stitches she had on her forehead.

"I'm fine, really, Doctor," she insisted. "An overnight stay is *not* necessary. Besides, hospitals are so slow about everything, including discharging people."

Dr. Cathy Seymour eyed the determined woman in the hospital bed. The story always went that it was doctors and nurses who made bad patients but in Dr. Seymour's opinion it was anybody who had the twin characteristics of being a caretaker and being used to being in control in most situations. Claire Allen fit the description to a T.

Dr. Seymour hid her smile. "It'll likely only be overnight, Claire, if your tests come back normal. If they do I'll make a point of ensuring that you're out of here first thing when I come in tomorrow morning. You were unconscious for several minutes after your fall."

"But I feel fine."

"You have a concussion at the very least, and the right side of your body will be severely bruised for weeks. Thankfully there were no broken bones. Even so, I think you'll find once you get out of bed and start moving around you're not going to be so wild about the idea of working for several days, at least." Dr. Seymour politely ignored Claire's surly expression. "There's an extremely *fine*-looking man cutting a path in the tile out in the hallway with his pacing. I assume he's yours?"

Claire's defiance ebbed at the doctor's abrupt question regarding Des. "I wouldn't necessarily call him mine."

Doctor Seymour didn't look convinced. "Uh-huh. I saw the way he was looking at you. He's yours, if you want him. And if you ask me, you'd be out of your mind not to," she added under her breath. "He said he'd be taking you home in the morning. Is that right? I have to send you home with someone."

"Er, I guess, if that's what he said," Claire mumbled. She didn't want Des playing nurse to her. He must have already missed an enormous amount of work, all because he'd been watching over her and Kevin Preskill. Her eyes watered, surprising her. God, she must be pretty beat up. She felt so emotionally raw.

A few minutes later, Claire was squirming restlessly on the thin hospital mattress. It crunched every time she moved. She snarled in annoyance. She didn't notice Des standing at the foot of her bed at first. Her mind was busy enumerating the various stupidities inherent to hospital administrations and policies.

Could this damn mattress be any more uncomfortable? Were people actually expected to heal on these things?

"Were you giving that nice doctor a hard time, Claire Allen?" Des murmured in a low, resonant voice that immediately caught Claire's attention.

She glanced at him, definitely admiring the change of the scenery in the drab, institutional room. Damn. He looked just as gorgeous as he had when he picked her up for their date this evening.

She, on the other hand, undoubtedly looked like the battered, clumsy oaf that she was.

"Dr. Seymour just thinks you're hot and she's turning on the charm for you. With me, she could be Hitler's right-hand woman," she muttered.

Des' eyes sparkled with amusement despite the numb, shocked feeling that had pervaded his entire being ever since he'd seen Claire doing a swan dive off the top of the stairs.

He'd mentally chastised himself so many times now that his spirit was feeling raw from the mental flogging. Damn, why hadn't he told her before they left the room to let him go first? The fact that tonight's attack matched no profile associated with this case whatsoever was the obvious answer but that rationalization got him nowhere in the guilt arena.

"Well, well. Kind and compassionate Claire has a few claws, it seems. Amazing what falling down a flight of stairs can teach a man about a woman."

The tension in Claire's shoulders, crossed arms and expression lessened a little at Des' teasing. "I feel like a fool, Des. I don't want to have to stay here overnight because of a diagnosis of 'klutz'."

"I don't know exactly what happened when you fell down those stairs, but trust me, it wasn't just a matter of you tripping. I could maybe buy the idea that you tripped originally, but that's a really big maybe. And that thing that happened after you were flying down the stairs had nothing to do with klutziness and everything to do with the weird stuff that you said has been happening around the house."

"You're saying that you think some kind of ghost or paranormal phenomenon is trying to hurt me?" she asked, surprised. "Look, Des, I know I've told you that I've been sensing Aunt Isabelle's presence in the house, but you honestly don't believe she would try to hurt me, do you?"

He shook his head. "I don't know. I doubt it. But you yourself have been saying that the messages you've been getting are mixed. Who's to say that Isabelle is the only spirit haunting the house?"

"That's ridiculous," she began, but doubt filtered into her mind. She had been getting some really discrepant psychic signals. Sometimes she felt protected by an unseen force in the house, and other times threatened. "Even if that were true, at least one of them has my welfare at heart and is trying to protect me."

He crossed his arms over his wide chest in a gesture of implacability. "You didn't see it, Claire. If that…whatever it was…that force hadn't stopped you, there's no telling how many nights you'd be staying in this hospital or if you would even be alive," he finished starkly, his mouth pulled into a hard, grim line.

Claire finally agreed to go to Des' the next morning only when he insisted that he would return to a semblance of his normal routine. He explained impassively that he needed to go into the office anyway, in order to assess the amount of damage done by Malkovic. He had explained to her that his superiors had forbid him from investigating Kevin, saying there wasn't sufficient evidence for his involvement in the Morningside Murders. Des obviously felt differently, and Claire tended to agree at this point.

She wouldn't have wanted to admit it to Dr. Seymour but by the time she and Des got to his car and began the ride into the city her head, shoulder and hip were pounding with pain. Fatigue assailed her. She was surprised when she woke up twenty minutes later and they were pulling into the underground parking of a rehabbed brick warehouse on the city's west side.

"That was quick," she mumbled when Des and she got out of his car.

"Yeah, it's amazing how time flies when you're sound asleep," he deadpanned.

"Wow, this place is *amazing*, Des," Claire muttered a few minutes later as she entered a foyer that led directly into a spectacular loft great room. The original brick walls remained, their imperfection and bleached reddish-brown color adding texture and character to the room. The roof beams also looked like part of the original structure. The floors were a dark-stained oak. The furniture was mostly done in reds and chocolate browns and had been arranged to create several conversation areas in the large room.

She knew instinctively that the woodwork on the fireplace mantle and the floor-to-ceiling bookcases had been designed and built by Des himself. The wood had been painted to match the warm beige color of the loft beams but the panel on the back wall was painted a toasty brownish-red that matched the hue of the blinds and enhanced the light-colored brick and dark floors. She touched the bookcase with a lingering finger, admiring the fine quality and detailing of his work. Her eyes skimmed his book collection, observing the diversity and quality of his choices.

She recognized several of Des' mother's paintings. A few other fine paintings hung on the walls. It all seemed so strange to her, but vastly exciting, how such a masculine man could have such refined taste. But given Des' background his knowledge of art and literature were far from unusual.

Claire turned around, realizing that she hadn't spoken for the past few moments and neither had Des. He stood several feet away, watching her as she inspected his place. She gave a slow smile.

"Well, it looks like you've done okay for yourself here, Mr. Alvarez."

Des stared. It had struck him more strongly than he had prepared himself for, seeing her here in his home, examining his things, appreciating who he was. Her smile seemed to signify something more than he could grasp, and he was admittedly entranced by its mystery, wanting to explore its meaning with his spirit as much as he wanted to drown in her flesh. The duality of his desires hinted at the reality of Claire's true nature. She was cool elegance and quiet dignity. The strength and kindness of her spirit shone forth in her eyes and smile. Even the pureness of her skin reflected the light and beauty inherent to her soul.

But her physical presence was equally as compelling as her spiritual one was. She was no altar for dry, empty worship, that was for certain. There was a deep carnality to her that amazed him, shocked him at times...gratified him greatly.

Yes, Desi. Take me any way you like.

He closed his eyes briefly to quiet the rush of lust the memory evoked in him.

He caught sight of the white bandage on her head, the purple bruises on the side of her face, and forced himself out of his reverie. She may be sexy as hell but she was still very weak and fatigued from her injury.

"I put your things in here," Des explained as they entered the master suite. "But there is another bedroom suite, Claire, if that's what you want. I wanted to have you here because I was concerned for your safety, not to…keep me entertained."

Claire sat down on his large bed, sinking into the deep, rich bedding. Exhaustion overcame her again at the cool, sensual feel of the fabric. "I think we could probably do all the entertaining of each other that we wanted, as long as we did it lying down."

"Uh-huh, right. You really look up for that," he said wryly. He gently pulled her up from her sitting position and flipped down the comforter. She put her arms up obediently when he signaled and Des pulled off the Northwestern sweatshirt she'd been wearing yesterday when she fell, leaving her in a pair of shorts and a tank top. He removed her sandals and she snuggled into bed. He pulled the sheet and comforter over her.

"Do you want one of your pain pills?"

"No. Just sleep," she murmured.

"All right. I have to go. But listen, if the doorman calls you to say there's a visitor downstairs, don't allow them up. Do you understand? I don't care who it is."

"Yes, Des," she managed to say without rolling her eyes.

He hesitated as he looked down at her. She became aware of his towering concern and raised her brow at him. "I'll be fine, Des. I assure you that I can sleep unassisted. This bed seems pretty klutz-proof. Go on to work. You have some fires to put out, I can imagine. I'll see you tonight, okay?"

He kissed her softly just below her bandage then fully on the lips. Despite her sleepiness Claire moaned at the impact of his mouth on hers. She strained upward and made a sound of protest when he withdrew.

"The doctor's number and my cell phone number are right here. The phone's here, next to the bed. I told my sister Angie that you're here, Claire, and asked her to bring by a late lunch. She has her own key to my place. You hardly ate two bites of that hospital food."

Claire grimaced weakly. Hospital food was disgusting. She knew that Angie Alvarez worked for an accounting firm in the loop. He paused before leaving the room when he heard her soft voice.

"I never thanked you for looking out for me," she whispered. "I know you risked your job to do it."

Des studied her, thinking how small and vulnerable she looked in his king-sized bed, wondering how much it could matter if he said to hell with work and spent the day with her wrapped in his arms. "Don't be dense. You and I both know why I did it."

Claire squirmed a little, avoiding his gaze. She wasn't ready to discuss the explosiveness of their coming together, the fact that it felt so right. It unnerved her.

"I would have never pegged you as such a sybarite, Des. This bed is so comfortable it's downright decadent," she mumbled almost incoherently.

He opened his mouth to respond but realized she was already asleep. He stayed by the door for a minute watching her, feeling primitively gratified at the sight of her in his bed but also deeply concerned for her well-being. The sight of her falling down those stairs, the flash of insight that it was possible that he could lose her so abruptly when he'd finally been united with her, that had slammed it all home.

When he had returned to the Hyde Park mansion, he'd done a thorough investigation of the stairs and the house, looking for any possible signs of why she had fallen so hard. He'd found nothing. No loose boards, no protruding nail, no object left or dropped on the stair over which she could have tripped. Not a god damned thing.

He didn't like it. Apprehension built in him, seemingly by the minute. Someone or something had purposefully caused Claire's fall on those stairs. And Des had a gnawing suspicion that whoever had done it hadn't been intent on mere injury.

Claire awoke several hours later with a start. A woman was calling her name and tapping lightly at the bedroom door. She sat up, disoriented by her strange surroundings. Then the subtle odor of the bed linens entered her awareness—fresh-smelling fabric softener and the unmistakable, masculine, compelling scent of Des. She inhaled and let the sensation ground her, lessening her momentary disorientation.

"Claire?"

"Yes."

"It's me, Angie Alvarez. Can I come in?"

"Yes," Claire answered, sitting up in bed.

"I'm sorry for waking you," Angie said in a stage whisper. "Des told me about your fall. God, look at your head. Does it hurt much?"

Claire had sat up too abruptly. A wave of dizziness swept over her. *Easy does it*, she reminded herself irritably.

"No, only a little." She eyed Angie where she stood at the door. Claire felt decidedly grungy in comparison to Des' sister, who was dressed for work in a well-cut black pantsuit, ivory silk blouse and pearls. She realized she hadn't showered since Saturday evening. She groaned. Had that really been forty-eight hours ago?

"Are you okay, Claire?" Angie asked anxiously.

"I was just realizing how grubby I feel. Do you think we could hold off on eating until after I shower?

"Of course."

"I promise I won't take long. Thank you so much for coming by, although you really shouldn't have worried about it."

Angie was already bustling ahead of her into the bathroom, turning on the light and pulling out clean towels. Claire was touched by her kindness.

"Oh well, you know how it is. Des can be a real worrier once he gets something in his head, and trust me, most of the time it's way out of proportion to the actual situation." Angie studied her face in the bright light of the bathroom. "This time I think he was right on track though, Claire. No offense, but you look really awful."

Claire laughed softly. "No offense taken, Angie, but I really think a hot shower and food will do wonders."

"Right. You have everything you need?" When she assured Angie that she would be fine, Angie left her alone in the large bathroom.

Claire emerged twenty minutes later feeling much better. She'd showered and changed the dressing on her forehead. She'd changed into a lightweight sundress that Des had pulled out of her closet and handed to her when she was packing to come to his place the other night. The cotton material felt soft and sensual against her bare skin, leaving her feeling infinitely comfortable but feminine too…pretty. The blue flowered print enhanced the color of her eyes.

Leave it to Des to pick just the right thing, she thought.

The only jewelry she chose was the omnipresent bracelet and a pair of simple diamond stud earrings. She knew that decorating her bruised body overly much bordered on the absurd.

Her head ached as she walked into the kitchen and she realized she was weak from hunger. Her stomach growled when she saw the delicious-looking Kung Pao chicken that Angie was dishing onto plates.

"Bless you, Angie," she said a few minutes later as she bit into a succulent piece of spicy chicken. "I had no idea how hungry I was."

Claire enjoyed the lunch with Des' animated sister. She described what had happened with the fall on the stairs, leaving out Des' suspicions about her safety with Kevin Preskill in the house and any references to the unusual phenomena occurring in her Hyde Park home. She let Angie assume that she was there in Des' home only because he wanted to watch over here while until she was completely back to normal.

"Which shouldn't be more than a day or two," she assured Angie after they'd cleaned up their lunch things and Angie stood by the door, ready to leave. She hugged Des' sister, thanking her warmly for her kindness and concern. Claire promised to return the favor and take Angie out for dinner sometime soon.

After Angie left Claire occupied herself by choosing a book from Des' large library and curling up on one of the comfortable couches in the great room to read. She jumped, startled, at a loud knock on the front door. She blinked in surprise.

"Angie?" she asked when she neared the door. Claire couldn't hear a response through the thick oak door. She pulled back the deadbolt. Des' loft was in a security building after all. No one could come up to the units without having keys to the locked entryway or permission left with the doorman by the owner. Des' sister had permission from Des and she'd only left a few minutes ago. Maybe she'd forgotten something?

For a few seconds Claire just stared at Kevin Preskill, her mouth slack. An alarm went off in her brain and she began to shut the door. His hand shot out to brace it, easily stopping her.

"What's wrong with you, Claire? What in the hell did that asshole Alvarez tell you that has you slamming the door in my face?"

Chapter Fourteen

Claire's mouth felt as dry as sandpaper. The man in front of her looked both familiar and utterly strange to her at once. The things that Des had told her about Clarisse Myer's murder sprang to her mind in graphic detail. Des! Jeez, he was going to kill her for opening the door to Kevin.

If Kevin didn't kill her first, that is.

She had to resist an urge to scream her head off in blind panic. Something told her that would be a mistake, however. Kevin wasn't acting particularly murderous at the moment. The façade hadn't been smashed yet. If anything, he seemed genuinely surprised by her reaction to him. She tried to smile.

"Kevin...I'm sorry. You just took me by surprise. I'm a little out of it. I thought it was going to be Des' sister." She shook her head as if to clear it. "Pain pills, you know."

Kevin nodded as he studied her soberly. "I've been worried about you, cousin. Alvarez just whisked you away from the hospital. I had to follow him here because he refused to tell me where he was taking you. You should watch that, Claire. They say possessive boyfriends can end up being dangerous, you know. Mind if I come in?"

Yes, Claire thought desperately. "Kevin, it's really not a good time. I'm feeling pretty rotten and I was about to fall asleep when you knocked."

Kevin just shrugged, as if the whole situation was really beneath his notice. He peered rudely into Des' loft.

"Not bad for a neighborhood kid."

Claire frowned at his smugness. Why wouldn't he get the hell out of there? He was giving her the creeps. Her gaze flickered nervously to his hand on the door. He hadn't removed it since she'd opened it. His cool eyes warmed slightly as they ran over her dress-clad figure.

"You make an awfully fetching invalid, cousin."

She tried to ignore his baiting. This was the type of annoyingly familiar remark Kevin had been making for the past fifteen years of her life.

"As you can see I'm fine, just exhausted. I hope you're satisfied."

She saw something dark flash into his brown eyes when they lowered to her breasts. She breathed in slowly. Something in his manner had just changed. His glance was subtly more aggressive than it ever had been in the past.

"I've never been satisfied by you, cousin," he said so quietly that Claire had to question whether she had heard him correctly. Kevin looked amused by her dawning confusion. "I would *like* to feel satisfied by you."

Claire stilled, feeling a deep sense of revulsion. Never, not in all the years that she'd known Kevin, had he dared to speak to her in this way. She had endured his glances, the way his eyes dragged over her body with such agonizing slowness, making her feel chilled and unclean. But never once had he ever officially crossed the line he'd just breached. It was the casualness with which he did it, the obvious enjoyment at sitting back and enjoying her confusion, that struck Claire as much as anything.

"How *dare* you speak to me that way, Kevin?"

His lips stretched into a parody of a smile. Smiles connoted warmth and happiness, while Kevin's expression seemed a brittle façade covering a deep, glittering malice. She began to back away. His hand shot out and grabbed her wrist roughly, stilling her retreat.

"What do you mean?" he asked with feigned misapprehension. "Are you going to pull an innocent routine with me? The ice maiden lives? Only you and I know what a lie that is, right? I heard you the other night. I heard you hot and heavy with your stud Alvarez."

Claire's mouth fell open in disgust. There was a glassy appearance to his eyes that was genuinely alarming. A steady, sharp pain began to pulse behind the bump on her head.

"Get out of here, Kevin. I don't have to listen to this. And I want you to pack up your things and get out of my house as well." She cried out in shocked anger when he abruptly took her captive hand and pressed it to his crotch. She tried to pull herself away from contact with his erection but he pressed down on her hand and gripped her other arm.

"What? Not quite up to par with Alvarez, is that the problem? I remember what the guys used to call him in the locker room. Maybe it's due to his mixed heritage, if you know what I mean. Alanna Hartfield used to be hot for it too, Claire, just like you. What is it with you fair, delicate girls craving the dark meat?" he speculated pleasantly, as though he were discussing the stock market or the weather.

Claire forced herself not to struggle and panic in his hold. She was uncomfortably reminded of his love for hunting animals, and she realized that was how she felt.

Like she was the prey and he was the hunter playing with her.

"Alvarez did tell you about Alanna Hartfield, didn't he?"

"Kevin, get out. You've gone too far."

His eyes looked empty. "I haven't gone nearly far enough, cousin. Now did he tell you about Alanna Hartfield or not?"

"Yes, he told me," she grated out.

His smile looked almost kind. "But did he tell you everything? I would hate to see you making decisions based on incomplete information."

"You're scaring me, Kevin, which is what you were trying to do. So good for you. Mission accomplished," she said scathingly, realizing she didn't sound scared, just pissed off.

He strengthened his hold on her. Claire tried not to flinch when he gripped her bruised arm painfully. She just stared at him, disgust clearly broadcast on her face.

"You're hurting my arm. Let go." Some part of her mind warned her loud and clear that screaming and acting frightened would be her last mistake.

He glanced down to where his hand sank deeply into her flesh, saw the purple bruises that she'd received from the fall beneath his fingers. His eyes flamed with lust. "Little Claire — Isabelle's favorite. So different than I thought you were."

Claire readied herself for battle as she saw his gaze lower over her body, lingering on her breasts. She felt him go still. Her eyes lowered to where he was staring, her heart hammering loudly in her ears. He stared at the bracelet Aunt Isabelle had given her. Claire took advantage of his temporary lack of attention to break free of his hold, twisting from his grasp.

"Excuse me, miss? Is everything all right up here?"

"Oh hello," Claire called out hysterically. She was never so glad to see a complete stranger in her life. The African-American man who stood in the hallway wore a uniform. Claire thought she recognized him from when she came in with Des earlier.

The doorman studied her face for a few seconds. His cool eyes switched to Kevin. "Sir? I'm afraid you'll have to come with me. I'm not sure how you got up here. Mr. Alvarez left explicit instructions before he left that no one was allowed to come up to his unit except for his sister."

Kevin casually ruffled his fingers through his hair. "What is this? Alvarez Prison or something? This woman is part of my family and she's been seriously injured. And for your information it was Angie Alvarez who let me up while you were doing your duty in the john. Ms. Alvarez knows I'm family."

Claire saw the doorman's face stiffen with anger. "Kevin. Just go, okay?" she pleaded softly.

"Fine. I was just leaving anyway. I'm flying out tonight. I'll call you from Boston."

Claire watched warily as the elevator door opened to admit Kevin and the doorman. He glanced down the hallway at her before the doors closed. His eyes were as cold and lifeless as stones as they regarded her steadily.

Claire was shaking badly after she'd locked the front door. She started to make some hot tea and had a better idea. She turned on the tap to the large whirlpool tub in Des' master bath. Maybe if she submerged herself in hot water it would chase away the chills.

And maybe even take away the memory of Kevin's cold eyes.

What had sent him over the edge? Claire wondered as she sat on the edge of the slate surround of the tub, testing the water. She and Des had spoken together last night in the most hushed of tones. While Kevin might have heard some of their sexual activity there was no way in hell that Kevin could have learned from them what Des did for a living or about his suspicions of Kevin. Her cousin had treated her with casual contempt for most of their lives. But never had she expected that he hated her, so thoroughly despised her to the degree that would be necessary to explain his treatment of her just now.

Something about hearing her sexual activity with Des seemed to have sent him over the edge.

The phone began to ring and Claire looked up anxiously. It wasn't Kevin's voice on the answering machine when it clicked on, however. It was Des'.

"Claire? Pick up the phone right now."

"Hi," she answered.

"Are you all right?"

"Everything is fine. I was just running a bath in your lovely big tub," she said with false enthusiasm. "Your sister came by earlier. It was so sweet of her. She brought a really nice lunch and—"

"The doorman just called me, Claire. I know somebody was just up in the loft with you. Why the hell didn't *you* call me? Was that Kevin who was harassing you?"

"Yes," she answered shakily.

"When you recover from your fall I'm going to take a paddle to your butt, Claire Allen. Didn't I explicitly tell you not to let anyone into the loft?"

"No, you didn't!" Claire blustered angrily, stunned by his threat to paddle her. How could he be so sweet and caring and so insufferable all at once? "You said that if the doorman called I should say no one was allowed to come up to the loft."

"You knew exactly what I meant, Claire," he said ominously. "I'm not going to sit here and argue with you about it. Make sure the door is double-locked. I'm on my way. I'll call you on my cell phone when I get there. Look for my number on the caller identification."

"Des, surely the cloak and dagger routine isn't necessary. Kevin said he was flying back to Boston this—"

"If you allow one more patronizing word to leave your mouth, Claire, I'll take a paddle to your bottom when I get home whether you're bruised or not. Do you know how close you came to dying just now? Are you out of your fucking *mind*? Haven't you heard a word I've been saying?"

"I have, Des, but—"

"There's no damn buts about it. Hasn't it struck you that besides the fact that Kevin Preskill sends off some pretty strong sexual vibes around you, you match the physical profile of all the victims of the Morningside Murderer? He may have had enough impulse control to keep his hands off you while Isabelle was alive but his few safety valves have been shut down now that she's dead. Didn't you understand what I was trying to tell you before? I think that the reason he killed Clarisse Myer so brutally and so sloppily, even making the huge mistake of allowing himself to be witnessed with her, is that he's been decompensating psychologically ever since Isabelle's death. You know how close the two of them were. Kevin worshipped his mother."

Claire stared blankly into space. What Des had just said made perfect sense, professionally speaking. Kevin had always been aloof, a loner. The only true human attachment that he'd ever made, at least that Claire knew about, was with Isabelle Preskill. Suddenly the chill that she'd felt ever since Kevin had left threatened to overwhelm her. She began to shiver so hard she was surprised she didn't hear her bones clattering together.

"Claire? Are you there?" Des asked sharply.

"Yes. I'm just cold all of a sudden."

There was another pause on the line. "Just hold tight, baby." All traces of anger had been replaced by concern. "I'll be there in ten minutes."

Claire forced herself out of the hot bath after soaking for only five or six minutes. She knew that she had to let Des in when he came home. She was a little shocked at how difficult it was, due to her soreness and bruising, to lift herself out of the tub. Her head pounded with excruciating pain. Her movements were those of an old woman as she re-dressed herself in the comfortable sundress and changed the bandage on her forehead. The phone rang just as she was leaving the bathroom.

"Stop frowning at me, Desi," Claire mumbled once she'd let him in the front door. Despite her admonishment, her eyes toured him appreciatively as he hung up his suit jacket. He wore a leather shoulder holster for his gun beneath it. Claire guessed that FBI agents were supposed to dress in an understated manner that inspired confidence and a sense of dependability. But what Des' body could do to a plain, well-cut dark gray suit didn't exactly have Claire thinking first and foremost about the quality of *dependability*.

"What are you thinking about?" Des asked as he took her gently into his arms, mindful of her bruising. He inhaled her familiar scent and allowed the sensation of her body to penetrate his awareness, calming his anxiety and unrest. She must have just bathed. Her body felt warm and soft and erotically pliable. He had been sick with worry when Eric, his doorman, had called him at work. Not sick figuratively. Sick literally. He'd almost puked his lunch at the thought of Kevin Preskill in his loft with Claire. Graphic, grotesque memories from the crime scenes of the Morningside Murderer rose in his mind, torturing him. Eric, who only worked part-time as a doorman and whose primary job was that of a Chicago cop, had said that he'd thought he'd seen that sick son of a bitch gripping Claire in a restraining hold.

Des' stomach gave one last heave at the thought.

Claire ran her cheek against his crisp white dress shirt. He saw her small smile. "I was just thinking about how dependable you look in your work clothes. What did you find out about Malkovic, Des?"

He scanned her face. Claire knew by now that his hawk-like eyes were taking in every detail of her fatigued, disheveled appearance. Why did he have to be so damned observant when she looked like hell? She sighed when he abruptly lifted her into his arms and started back toward his bedroom.

He'd noticed, all right.

"Hey, Tarzan? Jane asked you a question," she muttered groggily into his chest. Her pounding head, the events of the afternoon and the hot bath were really getting to her. She sighed with contentment when he lowered her onto his bed.

"Des?"

He smoothed her hair back from her face. "They've put me on paid suspension pending a hearing by the Office of Professional Responsibility. It'll take place next week."

Claire grabbed the hand that was caressing her. "God, Des, I'm so sorry."

He shook his head as if to tell her that her worry was misplaced. "It's not as bad as it sounds. At least everything is out in the open now. Maybe I'll be able to convince someone at the Office of Professional Responsibility about my concerns, even if I haven't been able to convince the SFPD or Special Agent Dawson. I have a good record at the Bureau, Claire. It's not going to be easy for them to get rid of me."

Tears filled her eyes. "Damn it, Des, you did this for me. I'll testify for you at the hearing."

He grinned wryly and wiped away a solitary tear from her cheek. "I think your testimony would hurt me more than help. I doubt they'd give me any brownie points if they heard about how I've lusted after you since I was twenty-three years old, and how we originally met in one of your psychic dreams. And they definitely wouldn't like the part about me handcuffing you to the bed."

"I could just conveniently leave those parts out. They're personal anyway."

Des sighed and stroked her cheek. "Thanks, but I don't think so. It'll be a legal hearing. You'd be committing perjury by doing that. I'm not worried about it right now. And if I'm not worried about it you don't need to be. Go to sleep, baby."

He sat and watched her while she did just that. He studied her, trying to be detached in his assessment, wondering how it was possible that she could have entered his heart so quickly. Of course, it seemed he had been born to be the opposite of detached when it came to Claire, ever since *Abuela* Anita's prediction, ever since he'd first seen those pictures of her at Isabelle Preskill's.

Des pushed an errant piece of reddish-gold hair from her cheek, his fingers brushing against her bruises with a featherlight touch. It brought back the image of her falling, a picture that he'd tried to banish from his mind countless times over the last two days with little success.

He eventually went to his den and logged on to his computer. Kevin Preskill had indeed booked a flight from O'Hare to Logan this afternoon. He made a few phone calls and occupied his time doing some other research using the FBI database.

He breathed a sigh of relief when he saw that Kevin Preskill had checked in for United Flight 457 at four-thirty. He took his first full inhalation all afternoon when he saw that the flight had taken off only ten minutes late, at five forty-five that evening.

As relieved as he was to know that Kevin Preskill had just left the city, part of him wished that he were still here. He'd like to plant his fist in his smug face for having the nerve to come into his home and put his hands on Claire. He knew he was thinking like the caveman that Claire seemed fond of accusing him of being but that didn't have the slightest effect on altering his primitive thoughts or urges.

He wasn't that hungry, but he heated up some soup and made sandwiches. He woke Claire up regrettably. She seemed so exhausted. He was amazed that she was still in the same position she'd been in when he'd put her to bed almost three and a half hours ago.

"Is the pain bad?" he asked her later as he took their bowls to the sink and rinsed them. He saw her hesitate. It was bad all right. Before she could answer, he added, "Why don't you try one of those pain pills the doctor prescribed?" He knew he'd been right about the level of her pain when she nodded her head in reluctant agreement. She went back to sleep almost immediately after swallowing the pill.

Des had turned off a late night talk show at eleven o'clock. Claire still slept. He rechecked the locks on the front door, brushed his teeth, changed into a pair of sweatpants and got into bed with a book. An hour later he closed the book and turned in bed, studying Claire's inert form. She looked so pretty, her face peaceful, her lips full and relaxed enough in sleep that he could see a tiny portion of her teeth. He leaned down and kissed her beautiful mouth gently, breathing in the smell of her, licking at the small indentation between her lips with a restrained but hungry flick of his tongue.

His cock bobbed eagerly.

"Down, boy," he whispered gruffly. "Night, baby. Sweet dreams."

He turned away from her resolutely and shut off the light.

Claire blinked once, twice, three times.

She was still blind. Before panic overcame her she recalled the sensation and recognized she was dreaming. She knew immediately where she was.

She was in a closed closet with a pervert standing above her, not even two feet away.

She tried to breathe slowly to calm her escalating heart and the rising sense of panic. Helplessness gripped at her throat like a strangling rope. She closed her eyes and willed herself out of the dream.

Her concentrated wish to be released from the dream was granted, at least in part, because she found herself in the downstairs hallway of her home. She looked down and saw her bare feet on Isabelle's oriental carpet. Her hands flew across her stomach, her hips, feeling the solidity of her body, touching the soft fabric of the blue dress. It was the dress that Des had brought for her to wear.

She was still in the dream.

Des.

Her feet began moving quickly until she broke into an all-out run. Des needed her. She knew it. She opened the library door and saw him sitting in the armchair, just as she'd known she would. Tonight he was wearing only a pair of sweatpants tied at his lean hips. Sadness and grief seemed to envelop him. Claire's expression tightened with compassion. He was such a big man, typically in control and confident. It tore at her to see him so helpless. Why did he suffer so much in his dreams?

"Desi?" She spoke to him in a hushed voice, her tone pleading. But like the night of the other dream, he didn't respond. He remained locked in grief, his solitude absolute. Determination hardened her. She reached out with trembling fingers. The texture of his hair between her seeking fingers was a treasured, precious sensation.

He went still beneath her. He brought up his hands to cover hers as he leaned back in the chair. His silvery-gray eyes looked at her steadily…so piercing, so soulful. The pad of his thumb began a hypnotizing circling movement on her wrists.

"Claire," he murmured.

"I'm here, Des," she replied. She leaned down and put her hands on his bare shoulders, squeezed the firm, rounded shape of the muscle in her palms. "I'm right here with you."

His hands caressed her as they moved up her sides, lingered on the sides of her breasts. They hung like full, ripe fruit before him. He felt himself grow hard, his erection straining and stretching his skin tautly as he moved his hands over her, seeking out her nipples in the thin fabric of the dress. When he leaned forward she brought herself to him, offering her breasts to his seeking mouth. He tongued her through the soft fabric, letting the moistened cloth drag across her nipple in an erotic sensation that made her moan low in her throat.

He grabbed the dress at the back and pulled the fabric taut over her breasts, continuing his ministrations with his wet tongue and sucking mouth. Claire clung at his hair, lost in the exquisite sensation, feeling herself growing hotter and wetter with every stroke, every suckling bite. After a moment Des leaned back and looked at her, inspecting his handiwork. His eyes gleamed at the sight of the fabric drawn tight and damp against her full breasts and erect nipples. He began to massage the pouting tips with his thumbs. A puzzled look crept into his rapt expression.

"Claire, this is the dress I picked out for you to pack before we left your house."

Claire nodded, finding it hard to remain focused with his fingers plucking such a pleasurable rhythm on her nipples.

He glanced around him with growing unease. "But we're not supposed to be here. We're supposed to be at my house…in my bed."

Claire leaned toward him and placed her mouth close to his ear. Her tongue traced the sensitive folds of flesh. He felt the inevitable tug on his cock when she sucked at the entrance of his ear, creating a vacuum. Her breath caused prickles of aroused sensation on the skin of his chest and nipples when she whispered into his ear, "We are, Desi. Wake up."

"Wait!"

Claire gasped when he clutched at her tightly. She glanced down, amazed, when she realized he was inspecting her right arm.

"We're dreaming together again?" he asked with amazement.

"Yes," Claire whispered. She began to nibble and suckle at his ear again. "Wake up, Des, so that we can make love."

"No, little witch. Stay right where you are."

"Why?"

Des put his hands on either side of her face and kissed her hard. Claire moaned with arousal into his open, hot mouth. He broke the kiss but their moist lips still brushed each other's sensually.

"Because if we both wake up right now we're both going to be very frustrated. I won't make love to you tonight—in the *real* world, anyway. You're too tired and banged up."

"I'll be fine, Desi. Please, just wake up, okay?"

"Uh-uh. No way am I going to pass up this opportunity," Des said as he unzipped her sundress and lowered it below her breasts. "Ah Christ, look at that."

Claire groaned at the sight of his features tightened with arousal, the glow of his silvery eyes as he watched his fingers play with her nipples. Her pussy flooded with liquid heat. After a moment he palmed both of her breasts, pushing them up for his mouth. "Desi," she gasped desperately as he began to lash first one nipple then the other with his long, rough tongue.

"You're not talking me out of it," he said resolutely as he leaned back. He smiled when she closed her eyes and sighed at the sensation of his massaging hands on her breasts. "This is too perfect. Here in the dream world you appear to be completely healthy. Not a bruise in sight. You know what that means, don't you?"

Claire was about to mutter a "no" when she noticed the deviltry in his eyes and recognized the hint of erotic threat inherent in his tone. Her eyes shot open.

"You wouldn't."

"I would. You're lucky to get away with just a little paddling for opening the door to anyone this afternoon, let alone Kevin Preskill."

Claire rolled her eyes and scoffed, despite her vague anxiety, not to mention her rapidly rising lust. Being spanked over the knee by Des had been so hot it had practically melted her perfectly functioning brain. What would happen if that silver-eyed devil had a paddle in his hand? Claire was a good girl growing up. Her ass had never known the feeling of a smack, let alone experienced a paddle, until Des broke her in.

"Give me a break, Des. Are you trying to tell me that you have a paddle stashed away in the library of the Hyde Park mansion?" She studied his calm expression with rising panic.

Christ. He didn't...did he?

"Of course not. Don't be ridiculous. But I do have one in my bedroom. And this is a dream after all, baby. All we have to do is both desire to be in my bedroom so that I can administer a sound paddling and we will be, right?"

"Hah. That's a great theory. Here's the flaw in your argument—I don't want to be paddled."

Claire almost choked when he removed one large hand from her breast and eased it up under her dress. "Oh," she cried out in surprise when he suddenly caressed one bare butt cheek. Hadn't she been wearing underwear when she went to bed? Oh no. What if what he'd said was true and her secret desires could become reality in the dream? Oh, this could be very, very bad.

Almost as if he'd been reading her mind, Des smiled slowly.

"Are you sure you don't want to bend over so that I can paddle your bare ass, Claire? You've been very bad today. You should have listened to me. And don't," Des said abruptly when he saw her open her mouth to argue, "give me some lame excuse about how I said not to let anyone in if the doorman called. You're not a moron, Claire. You know perfectly well that I didn't want anyone entering this loft today except Angie. Didn't you?"

"Well, yes. But at the time I just—"

"I'm not going to belabor it with you. I'm ready to paddle you now. I want you to slip off your dress and bend over my bed. If you don't do what I say quickly I'm going to make you take your paddling with no support while you're bent over holding onto your ankles. That will be much more uncomfortable for you."

Claire snorted in disbelief at his audacity. She did wish he would stop stroking her ass in such a mesmerizing fashion though. And it would certainly help if he stopped describing her paddling in such detail. "We're not in your bedroom, Des," she said in a voice dripping with sarcasm. Her eyes abruptly stopped in their rolling motion when she felt the healthy crack on her ass from Des' palm.

"Think again, little witch. I know you. I know what you want."

"No, I..."

But it was too late. She recognized Des' decadently soft bedding beneath her hands as she leaned over his bed. She dreaded looking over her shoulder but she did anyway as curiosity got the best of her. Des stood behind her. But instead of the smug, satisfied look that she expected to see on his handsome face she saw only tenderness as he caressed the bare skin of her lower back.

"Did you really think I was going to make fun of you?" he asked in a quiet, husky voice.

"You have every right to."

"Wrong, Claire. I have every right to be happy about you admitting to your desires. I have no right to be vindictive toward the part of you that isn't ready to do that yet."

Claire watched him silently as his meaning sank into her consciousness.

"Do you think you'll remember this tomorrow?" Claire asked as he went to his closet and reached up high for something. She swallowed thickly when she saw what it was that he drew down. It was a paddle all right, but not one like Claire was familiar with. It was long and black and only about two inches wide. Oh God, it looked like it was going to hurt. Her pussy began to ache and throb so insistently that she bit her lip over a moan.

Des reached up to grab a handful of lovely, plump ass. Seeing Claire like this, knowing she was patiently waiting for her paddling because it was her true desire, made blood and lust pound into his cock. He reached down and partially freed his raging erection from his boxer briefs and sweats. He saw Claire's beautiful eyes darken as she watched him stroke himself several times before letting go.

"Strangely enough, I think I'm going to remember every detail. I know what you meant now, when you said that our other shared dream had been different for you than it had been for me. I feel completely lucid right now, more awake than I do when I'm awake, if you know what I mean."

Claire just nodded. "You'll remember then." Her eyes were still pinned to his beautiful cock. She was never going to get tired of the sight of it. She jumped when Des tapped her bottom lightly with the paddle. Claire bit her lip in arousal when she saw his cock bob up.

"Face the opposite wall, Claire."

She turned her head away from him and waited with almost unbearable anticipation.

Chapter Fifteen

"Ouch," Claire said when Des landed the first crack.

Des' hand was immediately on her bottom, soothing her. "Too hard? I'm sorry, baby. It's just you have the most beautiful ass in existence. You're so plump and firm."

Claire moaned in arousal. Was it possible to become dehydrated because all the moisture in your body was going straight to your pussy?

"It only hurt a little. I was just surprised. It's different from when you spanked me."

"Are you sure it's okay?"

Claire just nodded, made speechless by Des' rubbing hand on her tingling flesh.

"Hold still then. I'm giving you seven more, Claire. That's how many I would give you if we were awake. Your skin might be able to take more in the dream but remember when I bit you, what happened? I can't take any chances. I want you to count off after each stroke, do you understand?"

She gritted her teeth and nodded. He paddled her again and she obediently called out "one". He did paddle her differently than he spanked her. When he spanked her he liked to grind his hand into her flesh in erotic circular motions after the smack. He also seemed to alternate between one cheek and the other. But with the paddle—she moaned with arousal and muttered "two"—he swatted her entire bottom horizontally, both cheeks at once.

By the time she got to "five" Claire knew Des' favorite stroke. He liked swatting up on the undercurve of her cheeks, just above her thighs. He'd paddled her there three out of the five times. She felt the way her ass leapt up at the stroke, heard the way Des grunted with arousal when he did it. She closed her eyes and imagined the way the long, thin, black paddle must look to him as he swatted her full flesh. He gave her "six" straight across on the fattest part of her cheeks. Claire's fingers were digging into the bedding now from desperation. Her pussy dripped with moisture.

"Desi," she begged when he savored his final stroke, aligning the paddle carefully where he wanted it on the tender undercurve. The little love pats he gave her as he took aim made juice roll down her thighs. Des must have seen, because he suddenly dipped his finger in her moisture and rubbed it where he was about to strike. She moaned and squirmed.

"Hold still, baby, or you'll get more."

He found the spot he wanted and smacked her one final time.

"You okay, baby?" he asked as he fumbled around in his bedside drawer.

"Not really," she mumbled desperately. "I need to come so bad."

"Not yet," Des said sternly as he lubricated his aching cock. "You're still being punished." He pressed his straining cock to her tiny asshole. Claire gasped. "I'm going to fuck your ass and come inside you. You're not allowed to come while I do it, Claire. Do you understand?"

Claire gritted her teeth in frustration. "That's not fair."

"Fair or not, that's the way of it tonight, babe. Maybe next time you'll think before you defy the orders I give you. Now press back on my cock and take me."

Claire held her breath and did what he ordered. She kept pressing, overwhelmed anew by the erotic sensation of him piercing her in such an intimate place. He suddenly smacked her ass.

"Stop there and hold still," Des managed in a strangled voice. He grabbed Claire's hips and began to fuck her slowly, watching his cock as it slid in and out of her ass. It was the delicious sight he'd been deprived of last night and Christ, it was so fucking good.

Des didn't know if it was the dream state that was adding that extra spice to his arousal or what but he didn't think he'd ever been so crazy, so mindless with undiluted lust, than he was for Claire at that moment. He imagined what it would be like to plunge into her to the balls, fuck her long and hard. The vision was so realistic and erotic that he forced himself to pause and shut his eyes. He heard Claire's soft whimpers of arousal, felt her push back on his cock, taking him another inch deeper. He swatted her ass gently in punishment for her action.

He felt her muscles clench tightly around him as she came.

"Little witch, you're going to take it hard for that," he said grimly. She keened as he made good on his threat, slapping his pelvis against her paddled bottom again and again. Finally he couldn't take another second of the sweet torture and he let go. His shout was rough and guttural as what felt like gallons of cum exploded into her.

When he came to full awareness a minute later he was leaning down over Claire and kissing her sweat-dampened neck while she made tiny noises of contentment deep in her throat. Thank God they were still in the dream. He kissed her ear tenderly.

"I specifically recall telling you that you weren't allowed to come, little witch," he murmured even as he teased the sensitive swirls of her ear with his tongue. He felt her shiver and go very still.

"Are you going to paddle me again?"

"No. Since you like to come so much I'm going to make you come again. But this time I'm going to make you come with the paddle. I think it'll do you good to submit to it in yet another way."

Claire gasped and turned to face him. "Des, why—"

"Hush, Claire. No ridiculous accusations about how I'm trying to humiliate you." He stood. Both of them gasped at the feeling of his penis leaving her body.

Claire moaned when he picked up the paddle from the bed. What in the hell did he mean he was going to make her submit to the paddle in another way? She felt him slap both of her thighs gently and she automatically spread her legs wider. Her breath already was coming in short, excited pants.

"Bend down and touch your nipples to the bed. You know how I like it."

She readjusted herself until her erect nipples just brushed the soft comforter on Des' bed. He'd said he was going to make her come. What he planned couldn't be all that bad then, could it? Nevertheless she squawked out in protest when he pressed back her ass cheeks, fully exposing her pussy and lubricated asshole. He put the paddle between her legs and pressed up on her tissues firmly.

"Des, don't do that! Oh…just…oh my. That feels so—"

"What?" he demanded roughly. He grabbed one ass cheek and used it to grind her pussy down on the smooth surface of the paddle. His biceps flexed hard as he steadily pressed the paddle up on her delicate, drenched tissues at the same time.

"Good!" Claire exclaimed as she began to rock wantonly against the paddle. The fact that she was getting off on the instrument of her punishment seemed to make it all that much more exciting.

Des gave a small smile as he watched her gyrate against the paddle. She was such a little hedonist down deep. He didn't stop her when she began to rock her whole body slightly, giving herself the added stimulation of having her nipples scrape across his bedding. "That's right, Claire. Give in to it."

When he sensed that her muscle strain had reached its limit and her moans of arousal were becoming more and more choppy and irregular he asked, "Are you ready to come on the paddle now?"

"Yes, oh God, yes!"

He abruptly lowered the paddle down between her thighs. He had to force himself not to give in to his natural compassion and give her the immediate relief she needed when she screamed out desperately in protest.

Des didn't know why he was pushing her so hard. It was true that he found it exciting to spank and paddle her but their sex play over the past several nights had taken on an intensity that puzzled him. For some strange reason he genuinely wanted Claire to obey when he ordered her to do something. It went way beyond his usual sexual proclivities.

"Tell me why I punished you tonight."

She groaned desperately. She began to clench her thighs together to get relief but Des slanted the paddle between her legs, wedging her thighs apart and preventing her from getting the friction she needed.

"I shouldn't have opened the door to a stranger."

"Why not?"

Claire clenched her jaw in sexual frustration. "Because you made it clear that you didn't want anyone but Angie to come into the loft."

"And was it Angie at the door?"

"No."

Des slowly, seductively moved the paddle back up her thighs. Claire moaned. "I want you to obey me when I give you a serious order, baby. I want you to do everything in your considerable power to do *exactly* what I tell you." He stopped just short of her pussy. "Promise me."

"Don't worry, Desi. I promise."

Her soft reassurance made him pause for a second before he moved the paddle up against her pussy and rubbed her rhythmically. She shouted out and shuddered in orgasm. His paddle was going to be well-seasoned with her juices, he thought with a small grin. But what exactly had she meant in telling him not to worry? Some elusive meaning seemed to hover just outside his conscious understanding.

The severe pain that sluiced through his right calf made him forget his concerns.

"Ah Christ, that hurts."

He tried to focus on Claire, who had turned and was watching him. "It's okay, Desi. Wake up. You're cramping."

"What? I don't want to—"

"Leave you." He heard himself say before he gasped and shifted in bed. He opened his eyes to his dim bedroom. "*Fuck* that hurts."

"Your sleeping body would have normally made the adjustments needed for comfort. But you were holding yourself in the dream. Your body was protesting," Claire explained quietly.

Des flipped on his bedside lamp and saw her regarding him calmly. She looked awake and entirely alert. "Jesus, that was fucking unbelievable!"

She gave a small, anxious smile. "I guess that means you remember it all."

He groaned as he flexed his cramping right calf muscle. "*Remember* it? The memory of that dream is going to be permanently branded on my brain. I feel like I can close my eyes and still perfectly see what your ass looked like when I—"

She cleared her throat loudly. She touched a finger to the bandage on her head and gave him a significant look. "Can you turn out the light, Desi? I'm really tired."

He took one look at the pink tinge on her cheeks, which only partially originated from her dream orgasm, and chuckled. He gently took her into his arms after he turned out the light.

"Des?" Claire mumbled into her pillow.

"Yes, baby?"

"Is there really a paddle in your closet?"

Des grinned into her neck. His cock thumped against her bottom. "Yes. Along with any number of other things I'll be using on you. Disappointed?"

"You know something? I'm really not."

He laughed softly. "Ah *Dios,* I'm a blessed man."

Chapter Sixteen

ಬ

The next morning, Des lingered in bed with Claire while she told him every detail of Kevin's visit. As soon as she told him about Kevin grabbing her he examined her arm. The clear delineation of a handprint on her already bruised, tender skin blinded him temporarily with impotent fury. But after a few concise and descriptive curse words had left his mouth he finally took in the look of sadness on Claire's face. For some reason that he couldn't fathom she was upset over the fact that her relationship with Kevin had irrevocably fractured.

"God, why are you sad? Kevin Preskill is a sick son of a…" He let his heated accusation trail off when he saw her eyes flash to him in anger.

So that was it. Regret softened his features. Even though Claire had never really liked Kevin and even feared him, Isabelle had loved him. Claire's relationship with her cousin had been empty, a sham, but it was still a known structure in Claire's life, something she was used to upholding because of her love for Isabelle. Now Kevin had permanently shattered that fragile structure and Claire was left without even that tenuous reminder of her life-long sacrifice for Isabelle. The fact that the sacrifice was no longer even necessary had left her feeling lonely and missing her beloved aunt.

His head fell back on the headboard. "Isabelle would have hated knowing what Kevin is. But she really would have hated knowing what he did to you yesterday."

"Yes, she would have." She sighed and melted into his arms. "Des? It really bothers me, in those dreams, when you're so sad and alone. You seem lost to me, locked away in grief.

Why? Why do you continue to dream like that night after night?"

"Claire, please. We've had this conversation before. I can handle it."

He saw her sag slightly in sadness and defeat and felt helpless that he had been the one to cause it. He stared into her eyes, seeing all the kindness and gentleness of her soul shine forth. How could she possibly understand that there was a part of him that couldn't be touched by her compassion, that didn't deserve to be touched by it? To bathe in the light of Claire's understanding was an incredibly appealing prospect for him, the promise of a balm to soothe his aching spirit. But to gain her understanding, he would have to forgive himself. He would have to let her see an ugly aspect of who he was.

And there was no way in hell he was going let Claire, of all people, ever do that.

* * * * *

Claire stirred in bed when she heard the muted sound of Des shutting the bathroom door in the hallway. He'd been up for hours. She rose slowly, testing out how she felt, remembering her dizziness when she'd sat up too quickly yesterday. She groaned as she swung her feet over the bed and stood. Her body had stiffened overnight and protested her movements with a bone-deep pain. As if her head didn't want to be left out of the chorus of bodily complaints, it too began to throb in unison with the rest of her symphony of physical discomfort.

She changed the dressing and washed her face. She looked pale in Des' bathroom mirror, probably a result of the pain that continued to rack her head and right side. Dr. Seymour had been right. The pain was more problematic than Claire had first imagined it would be. She gave in and took another pain pill. She forced herself to eat some toast so the medication wouldn't make her nauseated. The book she'd been reading last night was still on the floor next to the loveseat in Des' great room. She cuddled up there to read while Des worked in his den.

The next thing that she was aware of was Des' voice next to her ear. "Wake up, sleeping beauty."

Claire's eyes opened but Des could tell from the heaviness of her eyelids that she wanted to do nothing more but close them again. "There's a delivery man here with groceries. I didn't want to let him in until I checked to see if you're decent. I'm going to carry you back to the bedroom so he won't disturb you."

Claire made a sound of protest but Des was already lifting her off the loveseat. "I can walk. I'm not that much of an invalid," she muttered into his neck, taking the opportunity to breathe in the scent that was uniquely Des. She sighed with relief when he put her down on his soft bed. It really was the most decadently comfortable bed she'd ever been in.

"I know you can walk. I just like to make up excuses to have my hands on you. I'll be right back, okay?"

She nodded sleepily as she listened through the open door to the sounds of him letting in the deliveryman and the subsequent noises of groceries being unloaded in the kitchen. The next thing she knew it was one in the afternoon. She had a burst of energy and used it to call work and check in with a few of her more needy patients. Afterward she straightened Des' bedroom and bathroom. By that time the pill she'd taken had worn off and she was beginning to feel fatigued from fighting the increasing pain. He took one look at her strained expression and recommended that she eat dinner and go back to bed. She agreed to a bowl of soup, saying she wasn't hungry. She was curled up on her left side in his bed, fast asleep, by seven p.m.

When Des got into bed with her that night she didn't stir. Her breathing was deep and regular and much of the strain he'd seen on her face earlier had diminished. The room plunged into darkness when he switched off the bedside light. He brought himself closer to her and breathed deep.

He fell asleep with the scent of Claire pervading every cell of his being

Claire came into awareness with a jolt. Her gaze skittered around her surroundings in confusion and anxiety. She recognized the room. It was the game room in her house. But she didn't know any of the people who were in it. She started when she realized she was wrong. *Kevin.* Not Kevin as he was now but Kevin as he had been when he first came to Chicago with Isabelle, as an aloof, handsome, edgy teenager.

Her eyes went wide in amazement. She had never seen the past in a dream. *But that's clearly what this is,* she thought. At the same time she realized that she wasn't "there" within the dream corporally, as she felt like she was sometimes with Des. She was nothing more than a specter, a pair of eyes.

There were fifteen or twenty teenagers scattered across the room, playing pool, listening to music and chatting. Some of the girls were wearing red and black cheerleading uniforms.

She moved closer to Kevin. He was talking to a husky brown-haired boy wearing a letter jacket with the same colors as the girls' cheerleading outfits. They were both holding beers in their hands and Kevin had a lit cigarette that he dangled negligently between two fingers. Kevin and the other boy were intently watching an interaction that was taking place over across the game room.

"Alvarez isn't going to like it."

Kevin's eyebrow rose slightly in disgust. "Why *wouldn't* he like it? She's tipsy from those beers you gave her and she looks like she's begging for it. He doesn't even have to lift a finger to get laid tonight. Unlike you and McMillan. I saw the way you guys were trying to scare Alanna and her little cheerleader friends when they got here, showing them the dumbwaiter and the attic, making up stories about hearing moans and thumping noises when you guys spend the night here. Is that your plan for getting fucked? Try to scare the girl to death and then she'll spread her legs for you? You're pitiful, Ripoli."

Claire glanced to where Kevin's and Ripoli's attention was focused. She swallowed heavily. A strawberry blonde, petite girl in a cheerleader uniform was standing in the middle of several people in the seating area. There were tears in her eyes. Her tone was pleading as she spoke to a tall, dark-haired young man on the couch. Claire's heart leapt in her chest. It was Des at seventeen years old.

He looked close to his adult height even then, although the muscles of his chest and shoulders hadn't attained the bulk that they would in adulthood. He wore jeans and a dark green shirt. Claire could only see him in profile but she could make out the youthfulness of his features, the serious, troubled look on his face as he gazed up at the girl in front of him.

Her attention flickered back to Kevin and Ripoli.

"Well we weren't just planning on scaring them. We gave them beer too," Ripoli assured a disgusted-looking Kevin.

"Ten to one he goes with her. Look at her body. Who would turn that invitation down?"

Ripoli shook his head. "Nah. Des isn't like that. They've broken up before but I think he's done with her for good this time. He thinks she's fun and nice and all but he says she's really moody. Alanna starts crying and yelling at him and it takes him days to know what she's even upset about, or if it was even anything at all. Vanessa Rivers told me that Alanna tried to commit suicide by taking a bottle of Tylenol back when we were freshmen but it just made her really sick to her stomach. She's not normal, that girl."

"And I suppose you would have been worried about that if she'd gone along with your stupid plan for fucking her brains out tonight." Kevin took a deep drag on his cigarette.

Ripoli shrugged, grinning. "Come on, Preskill, you think she's just as good-looking as every guy in this room does. *Somebody's* gotta console her after Des broke up with her."

"Well, it looks like the big man will be the one to do the consoling himself." Kevin's brown eyes kindled with real interest for the first time.

Claire watched, emotion building in her as the seventeen-year-old Des stood up and followed Alanna Hartfield up the stairs.

The dream shifted and Claire found herself in a sterile-looking room with no window, cold tile flooring and a battered wooden table. Her heart seemed to rise into her throat when she saw a young Des sitting at the table alone. The need to comfort him almost overwhelmed her. He looked so young and miserable and alone. But once again, she had no corporeal body. She was just a watcher, a helpless observer. She recognized the exhausted, defeated posture of his body, striking in one so young.

He barely looked up when the door opened and closed again. A heavy-set balding man in his fifties grabbed a chair and sat down at the table with Des. For a moment they just inspected each other, Des looking at the bald man with resignation. The man studied Des with interest and not a little compassion.

"You're just here for questioning, son. You're not in any trouble, you realize that, don't you?"

Des nodded.

"Your mother and father wanted to come in here with you but I told them you might be more comfortable talking to me about what happened alone. Am I right about that?"

No, I don't want them in here," he said, quietly but forcefully. For a second Claire caught a glimpse of the confident, powerful man that Des would become.

The man held up his hands in a pacifying gesture. "Okay, son, that's why I asked."

He sat back in his chair and casually pulled out a cigarette. "Did you know that your girlfriend had tried to commit suicide before?" When Des just stared at him blankly he continued, "Mrs. Hartfield said she's made two previous attempts, once when she was fourteen and again when she was fifteen. None of them were as serious as this time, obviously. The first time around she took a bottle of Tylenol. The next time she swallowed some Tylenol and a few of her mom's sleeping pills. The first time she got scared and told her mother but she'd already thrown up most of the Tylenol by that time. The second time she wrote a note and her father found it. They were able to get her to the emergency room in time. I guess this time she must have realized the combination of Tylenol and sleeping pills wasn't good enough on its own because she hanged herself on top of it. You really didn't know about any of this?"

"No, I didn't know. And just so you know, she wasn't really my girlfriend anymore. We broke up a few days ago."

The police officer sat quietly for a moment and studied Des. "We had some preliminary exams done on the body. Miss Hartfield left a note, and there is little doubt that she committed suicide. Her parents wouldn't agree to an autopsy, even though it was recommended by the medical examiner because of some inconsistencies of the bruising on her throat, but even he had to admit that her struggle after she hanged herself very likely was the cause." He began to toy with his unlit cigarette, placing one end down and sliding his fingers along the length until he turned it over and began again. Des watched the movement mutely. He looked tense, miserable.

"The examiner put in his report that Alanna Hartfield had sexual intercourse before she committed suicide. Not just any kind of sex. The examiner said it must have been rough sex," the cop said matter-of-factly. "Did you have sex with her that night, son?"

"What…what do you mean, rough sex?" Des asked hoarsely, looking confused.

The cop shrugged. "Look, I'm not saying that there was any sign that she was forced or anything. The medical examiner just said she looked like she'd engaged in particularly...forceful sex."

Des still looked shocked and perplexed. "You mean like—"

"There was some slight bleeding and discoloration of her vaginal tissues. You never did answer me, son. Did you have sex with Alanna Hartfield last night before she committed suicide?"

Claire hated seeing the way Des' skin seemed drained of blood, the haunted look in his soulful eyes, the vulnerability in a face that was so similar to that of the man whom she'd come to love but that still contained some of the vestiges of childhood.

"Yeah, I did."

Claire thought she saw the last traces of his innocence leave Des' face forever in that moment.

Chapter Seventeen

෨

When she opened her eyes again she was staring down at her own bare feet on top of Isabelle's oriental carpet in the downstairs hallway of her own home.

God, no wonder Des suffered. He truly *did* believe he was responsible for Alanna Hartfield's death. She could fill in the blanks. Both of them had been drinking. He had broken up with her and she'd wanted him back. She'd likely seduced him, hoping that sex would bind them together again. And Des had made the mistake of complying with her wishes.

As for the rest, nature hadn't made Des a small man and Alanna Hartfield was very petite. Claire supposed if they'd gotten carried away that could explain the state of Alanna's genitals when she died. She felt a little confused by that detail though. She knew firsthand how sex with Des could get so hot it surpassed boiling, but Des was always so careful of her well-being.

Stupid, she admonished herself. Now she knew exactly why he always worried so much about losing control during sexual activity.

Sadness constricted her throat. It had been a wrong decision on his part and she knew it. But how many teenage boys had engaged in sexual intercourse for the wrong reasons—peer pressure, the inherent fascination with sex that was fueled by hormones that would never flow so strongly in their life as they would during those years. Add to that the fact that Des had obviously cared for Alanna and hadn't been entirely clear on his feelings for her. How many of those misguided teenage boys who had sex for the wrong reasons had to be forced to consider the possibility that one of the consequences of their actions might have been the death of their lover? Hardly none. But Des had been forced to face the consequences of what he'd done.

Obviously Alanna's attempt to get him back had failed and, even following sex, Des had refused to begin seeing her again. That was why Des felt so guilty about her death. He believed his refusal to get back together with Alanna had fueled her suicide.

She didn't know if she had all the details exactly right but Claire thought she had the main idea. Something else seemed important but—

The thought disappeared from her mind as she became acutely aware that Des was here again, in his own dream, guilt and sadness locking him irrevocably into the pattern of returning to this house. She hurried down the hallway and opened the library doors.

He was there, sitting in the armchair by the fireplace, his head in his hands. Why was he always drawn here, to this place? Claire wondered. Perhaps because he had come here after he left Alanna Hartfield that night? Had he sat here in this same spot, filled with regret, even before he'd known what Alanna had done?

He was shirtless again, wearing only a pair of thigh-length shorts. She knew that he was probably wearing the same thing as he lay beside her asleep at the loft. Claire approached him cautiously, everything she'd seen filling her awareness. The compassion that she experienced in the face of his suffering increased until it filled every space in her being.

Des had suffered enough for the choice he had made. He had grown into an admirable, conscientious man. Instead of ignoring whatever responsibility he'd had for that night he had accepted it, used it to forge himself into a more principled human being.

But he'd taken on too much of the blame and Claire suspected his shame had caused him to suffer in silence about that night. She recalled the look on the seventeen-year-old Des in the dream when the police officer had mentioned that Carl and Ellen Alvarez had wanted to sit with him during the questioning. She thought about the deep love and respect that his father had for his mother, the principles that Carl and Ellen had likely taught their children. He had felt guilt-ridden about having sexual intercourse with Alanna that night, and Claire believed that much of his self-blame came from believing that he had acted against the principles that were ingrained in him by his parents' everyday words and deeds. She suspected that Des had never revealed what had happened that night to anyone. Keeping it locked away inside was part of the reason that he'd never healed.

She stared down at him where he sat in the chair, his misery a palpable force. She reached out to touch him, as she had before, to bring him into contact with her. But tonight Des eluded her seeking fingers by leaning away.

His eyes shone like silvery shards of ice when they looked directly into hers. His mouth was set in a grim, hard line.

"Don't touch me, Claire."

Claire awoke with a gasp, the sensation of his gaze and words the equivalent of being thrown in icy water. She glanced around, seeing him immediately, a dark shadow lying on his side of the bed. She could tell by the rigidity of his body that he was awake.

"Des?" Her voice trembled.

For a moment he didn't move. His head rested on his bent arm. Suddenly he sat up and turned on the bedside lamp. When he twisted around and looked at her Claire cringed. Fury poured from his eyes. Oh no. Somehow he knew what she'd seen in the dream. He must feel terribly exposed. He hadn't wanted to tell her about that night and now she knew, despite his wishes to the contrary.

"I'm sorry. I wasn't trying to see it. You have to believe me. I didn't ask to see it. I just did."

He continued to stare at her. Claire realized that he was so filled with emotion that he couldn't speak.

"I didn't ask you in, Claire," he finally gritted out between teeth clenched in anger. "You can't just force yourself into other people's minds."

Tears fell down her cheek as she shook her head. His fury was the obvious emotion that she could sense but Claire knew that it was the result of his pain at being seen so vulnerable, at knowing that she had witnessed something that he found so shameful about himself.

"No, Des, you're wrong. I didn't force myself on you at all. I don't know how it happened but I don't think it could have occurred if some part of you hadn't wanted to let me in."

"That's bullshit, Claire," he shouted so sharply that she flinched back. Claire had rarely heard him speak in anything but his typical resonant, quiet voice. "I *know* that's bullshit because you are the last person on the face of the Earth that I would have wanted to know about any of that. I told you to let it go last night. But you just couldn't, could you?" His eyes pierced into her accusingly.

"I'm not disgusted by anything I saw in the dream. You were a kid and you made a bad choice but you didn't kill anyone. You were right to feel remorse but you've built it up too big in your mind because you haven't let it out for all these years. And another thing, there was nothing that I saw in that dream that I hadn't already suspected either from you or from Kevin or from my own intuition. A part of me already knew, Des, and it didn't stop me from falling in love with you. Do you think that seeing the specifics could really make a difference?"

For a full twenty seconds he just stared at her in disbelief.

"Just keep your damned psychic ability out of my brain."

She watched him helplessly as he grabbed his pillow and stalked out of the room, slamming the bedroom door behind him.

Chapter Eighteen

She heard him the following morning, moving around the loft. She wanted to call out his name when he entered the room briefly a while later to retrieve some clothes. But her courage failed her. He was still angry with her. She could tell by the way he pointedly avoided looking at the bed.

Claire couldn't really blame him for it. As a psychiatrist she knew a person should never be pushed to reveal anything until they were ready. The consequence of pushing someone too hard in many cases was exactly what Des was experiencing right now— feelings of vulnerability, anger and betrayal. Claire squeezed back the tears in her eyes as she listened to Des shut the door behind him.

That was how he'd looked last night. Betrayed.

She was a little shaky when she got out of bed. She hadn't really slept last night after Des had left. Instead she'd lain there going over and over it in her mind, trying to determine if there was some point in the dream when she could have chosen to turn away. By the time morning came Claire still didn't have any answers and she was only feeling worse about the whole thing. She was culpable, whether she had been conscious of what she was doing or not.

Des deserved the privacy of his own mind.

Her sleepless night had left her feeling sore both emotionally and physically. Her muscles, joints and head throbbed with pain but Claire hardly noticed them in her emotional misery. It didn't take her long to get her things together.

She inspected her appearance briefly before she turned out the light in Des' bathroom. Her skin was too pale next to the purple bruises on her cheek. Her eyes looked too big and deep-set in her skull. She was dressed in a pair of jeans and a tight three-quarter-length-sleeve t-shirt. Well, she wasn't going to win any beauty contests but it would have to do.

She quickly made Des' bed and straightened up, then called a cab company she had preprogrammed into her cell phone. She opened the bedroom door and craned her head into the hallway, listening. A sigh of relief passed her lips when she heard the treadmill in the extra bedroom start.

Good. She wouldn't have to face him on her way out the door.

By the time the cab dropped Claire off at her house she was feeling terrible. Her body aches had receded into minor pulses of pain but her head pounded so severely that she actually removed her bandage when she got home to make sure that the stitches were in place and that they hadn't become infected.

A quick flip through her schedule reminded her that Cindy Everly, a good friend from college, was supposed to stop by that evening for dinner. At first she thought of canceling. Then she decided the distraction might do her good. Maybe a nice nap would get her in the mood for entertaining. She lay down on her bed and almost immediately fell into a deep sleep.

She dreamed that Aunt Isabelle sat at the end of her bed. The pink scarf that Claire had found around the book was tied artfully around Isabelle's neck. Claire watched her aunt casually flip her pump on and off her heel as they talked, one of Isabelle's characteristic gestures.

Such a little detail—yet so real, so human.

And they did talk. Didn't they? Later Claire couldn't recall many of the details. She only knew the effect was the same as a long heart-to-heart conversation. She felt like she'd never known Isabelle so completely, never comprehended every twist and turn of her personality so well...never loved her so much.

"No one should have to make the decision," Aunt Isabelle said. "It's a terrible thing to have to choose."

"Yes, I can imagine."

"You understand, Claire? You don't think poorly of me?" Isabelle asked uncertainly.

Claire nodded. She understood completely but exactly what she couldn't wrap language around. The expression in Isabelle's dark blue eyes, so similar to Claire's own, lightened. She inhaled deeply and breathed out as though she had just finished a task. Her face turned toward the bedroom door.

"Now—what are you going to do about Desi?" Isabelle asked, her familiar imperious tone laced with unheard laughter. And then she was fading, only her expression of amusement and love lingering in Claire's dream-befuddled mind.

"Claire?"

"Isabelle?" Claire murmured drowsily. But it wasn't Isabelle she saw when she opened her eyes. It was Des. He was standing next to her bed looking down at her. Claire foggily registered his appearance, his faded jeans and the soft, button-down dark blue shirt, the crisp white t-shirt beneath it. Her gaze transferred to his handsome face, the neatly trimmed dark goatee and his beautifully shaped lips.

She smiled contentedly. Then she registered that his mouth was pulled into a hard, irritated line.

The recollection of last night crashed down on her all at once.

"Des?" She sat up in the bed. Her eyes immediately went to the bottom of the bed where Isabelle had just been sitting. *Hadn't she?*

Confusion swamped her. "Des, what are you doing here?"

"I'm the one who should be asking you that, Claire."

Claire paused at the icy edge to his voice. "How did you get in?"

She cried out in surprise when he scooped her off the bed. Despite the suddenness of his movements, Claire noticed that he was very careful of her bruising.

"What are you doing?"

He didn't answer or even look at her until he was halfway down the grand staircase. "What the hell did you think you were doing by sneaking out of my place like that?"

"I didn't *sneak*. This is my home. Why wouldn't I come here? Surely you're not suggesting that you wanted me to stay at your place after last night?"

Once again he refused to answer her or to look into her eyes while he strode rapidly down the hallway. He paused at the front door and nodded. "You asked me how I got in just now. There's your answer. You left the *god damned* door hanging wide open!"

"What?" She was still in the process of waking up and befuddled by the abrupt jump from conversing with a dead woman to being carried by a very angry hunk of a man. She clearly recalled shutting and locking the front door but she also clearly recalled talking to her Aunt Isabelle. Maybe her memories weren't something to be trusted at this point. Despite her sympathy for Des being upset, her own temper flared.

"Well, excuse me for that unforgivable crime. Put me down this second, Des."

Much to her surprise, he did. They stared at each other for several moments, emotional sparks seeming to pop and snap in the space between them. She found that her emotions and intentions were slowly morphing from irritation to lust, from desiring distance from Des' overbearing attitude to wanting to soften it with passion. She didn't know if her thoughts were becoming obvious on her face but she knew Des was beginning to have similar ones when his eyes lowered to her body. They gleamed with new awareness and kindled interest at the sight of her standing there in only a tight t-shirt and underwear.

Des took a deep, steadying breath. He'd be a damn liar if he just hadn't been considering hauling Claire straight to bed and planting himself deeply between her thighs with no further ado, despite the fact that he was furious at her. He still couldn't believe she'd just waltzed out of his loft!

"I have to assume that I'm just not making myself clear on this. I don't want you to stay in this house alone," he bellowed.

After a moment he became aware that her eyes were wide in shock at his concentrated fury. He cursed under his breath. The incongruity of his emotions—anger, shame, anxiety, lust—made him feel like he had a whirlwind in his brain.

"Des, we need to talk about this."

"I don't want to talk about it, Claire. I want you to get your things and come with me back to the loft."

Her mouth fell open. "Have I actually done something that gave you the monumentally wrong assumption that you're my boss, Des Alvarez? For your information I have a friend from college coming by tonight for dinner. And I have every intention of being right here."

Des wondered if he was going to grind his molars down to the roots. It suddenly struck him that he'd grabbed a completely helpless, vulnerable woman out of her bed and carried her against her will down the stairs. Not just any woman either. Claire. Christ, what the hell was wrong with him?

He exhaled slowly, trying to chase away the remnants of his anger. He wasn't mad at her exactly…or was he? God, he wasn't sure. He knew it was wrong to lash out at her like this but the knowledge of what she knew about him scalded his consciousness, made him feel jittery and uncomfortable, as though he wasn't at home in his own body. At times he wanted to shout himself hoarse at Claire, to punish her, humiliate her in return for his own humiliation. Mostly he was filled with a desire to make love to her, to force her to admit that what she'd said about loving him was true even though he knew it must be impossible.

But always, steady through it all, he felt a need to protect her and a genuine anxiety for what he perceived as a vague, rising threat.

"Fine," he said eventually. He saw Claire blink in surprise. "If you want to stay I'll stay as well. After your friend goes we'll go back to my loft. Agreed?"

"But, Des, we should at least talk about—"

He put up his hand. "We will but not now. I'm not ready yet." He crossed his arms over his chest. "You still look tired. Why don't you go back to bed for a while? I'll wake you later."

Claire bit her lip with indecision. "What are you going to do while I sleep?"

He put his hand on her shoulder and urged her toward the stairs. "Don't worry about it. I'll find something to do."

Claire had a pleasant visit with Cindy despite the fact that Des refused to join them, mumbling something about taking his meal to the recreation room so that they could enjoy their time together.

"Who the heck is that guy, Claire?" Cindy whispered after Des stalked out of the kitchen. "He's gorgeous and he can't keep his eyes off you. But talk about a stone face. Doesn't he ever smile?"

Claire frowned as she checked on the salmon she had broiling. "I think I might have seen the phenomenon once or twice." When Cindy gave her a doubtful look, Claire added, "You'd never believe it if I told you. Suffice it to say that he's an FBI agent. He's appointed himself to be my bodyguard and he thinks he's more effective when he's as surly and rude as possible."

"Bodyguard, huh? Jeez, I want one. Where do I sign up?"

Claire had thrown her oven mitt at her friend. They'd been laughing together when Des entered the kitchen again. She'd had to resist an urge to stick out her tongue at him when he gave her a hard look, like she was in trouble for having fun or something. How long was he going to punish her with his scowling and surliness anyway?

He'd avoided them for the rest of the evening. She glanced behind her in surprise after Cindy had left when she heard him enter the kitchen.

"Did you get enough to eat?"

He merely nodded his head, distracted by the sight of her. He loved when she wore skirts and heels. The skirt she wore tonight was narrow and formfitting, highlighting the shape of her hips and ass. The image of her moving around the kitchen and bumping closed the refrigerator door with her hip had his cock doing a throbbing, jerky dance in his suddenly too-tight briefs.

"How long have you known Cindy?" he asked as he sat at the kitchen island.

"Since college." She paused while she wrapped plastic around a plate of food. "She lived across the hall from me. Her mother died our freshman year, from cancer."

"And you were there for her?"

"Well, yes. I suppose I was. Why did you ask me that?"

"Because you're good at what you do. I'd have to be blind not to notice it."

"What do you mean?"

He just shrugged, avoiding her eyes. "You're good at helping people."

"Why doesn't it apply to you then?"

The motor in the refrigerator kicked on, creating the only noise in the prolonged silence that followed. Des didn't know exactly how long their gazes held but he became aware that at some point he'd stood. His muscles were tight, as though he were preparing to pounce.

"It's not the same and you know it," he growled.

"Why not?" Claire asked. She squared her shoulders as she faced him.

"I'm not one of your *projects*," he bit out. "I'm not looking for your pity. You can play Mother Theresa with someone else."

He hadn't made a conscious decision to move toward her but he was. Her words maddened him, made him want to strike out at something, made him want to hold her so tightly that he could absorb her, make her reside somewhere inside him for always.

Claire felt a little alarmed as he stalked slowly toward her, reminding her of an unpredictable, sinuous, wild animal. His eyes were shiny, silvery crescents between the slits of his eyelids.

"I don't think you're a *project*. If what you think I do is pity people you're sorely mistaken. You don't believe it either. You're just trying to insult me."

Des gritted his teeth in anger, mostly because he recognized she was right. He reached behind her and pushed. The refrigerator door slammed, making Claire jump.

"I don't want to fight about this right now." His eyes skimmed hotly over her body before they returned to meet her gaze. "I want to fuck you."

Claire felt a pulse begin to throb heavily at the injury on her head but it wasn't the only place on her body that was starting ache.

"Well, why didn't you just say so?" she snapped.

Chapter Nineteen

୧୨

Claire could have guessed precisely where Des stared as he followed her up the stairs. Her ass tingled. Though her awareness of him was always great, tonight it swelled and surged beyond its usual bounds. She felt wary, worked up...excited. The thought struck her that his powerful, pent energy was affecting her. She was picking up on his emotional unrest, sharing it.

Well, so be it, she thought grimly. If he could survive the tumult then so could she. There was little doubt that they both needed an outlet for the electricity popping between them.

When she bent to turn on her bedside lamp he was already behind her, wrapping her in his arms, pressing her against him. She groaned when he lifted her hair from her neck and buried his hot mouth there. His big hands splayed across her stomach, pushing her bottom tightly against him.

He couldn't get enough of her. She smelled so good, like subtle spring flowers and clean skin. He liked the feel of her silk blouse under his wandering fingers. She was so feminine, so perfectly curved for his palms, so intoxicating in the way her body fit his. The thought struck him that he hadn't made love to her in days, since before her fall—at least not in a waking state anyway.

Claire stretched her throat and laid her head against his shoulder in order to give his hungry mouth more skin to devour. She was vaguely surprised that she hadn't the faintest interest in withholding herself from him, punishing him for his anger at her. Her only interest was in meeting him on whatever territory he thought he could handle. If that territory was sex Claire would accept that. At least he wasn't running away from her.

He murmured her name into her throat when his hands slid over the silky blouse and onto her breasts. His thumbs moved over the nipples, causing them to peak through her bra and blouse. Claire moaned. The sensation of his stroking fingers felt overwhelmingly erotic through the satin of her bra and the silk of the blouse. Des continued to mouth her neck sporadically but Claire sensed he was watching his fingers as they pulled her blouse out of her waistband and began unbuttoning it. He removed her blouse but didn't bother to remove her bra, merely plunged his hands into the cups and lifted her breasts, freeing them from their confinement. Claire experienced a wave of dizziness when he lightly skimmed and pinched her stiff nipples. She whimpered.

Des felt her sway and caught her with one hand. "Are you okay, Claire?" he asked roughly into her neck.

Claire nodded quickly, knowing that she was a good deal better than "okay". Des barely acknowledged her affirmation before utilizing the hand that had been steadying her to unbutton and unzip her skirt.

"It was driving me crazy seeing you in this skirt."

Claire's eyes blinked open dazedly. "Why?"

"Because you have beautiful legs and a sexy walk and a sinful ass."

"Oh," Claire breathed. She helped him push her skirt and panties down her hips and legs but when she tried to break their embrace just for a moment to push them off her lower legs, ankles and feet, Des wouldn't let her go.

"Des, let me take off my things. I'm going to trip," Claire murmured in amusement as she tried to bend over to reach her feet.

"Let me do it," Des said hoarsely. But Claire couldn't help but notice that he didn't seem like he was in any hurry to release her naked hips from his firm grasp. Claire had to agree that it was incredibly erotic for her bare bottom to be pressed so solidly against his full erection, and the fact that he was still fully clothed and that she was almost completely naked added another arousing aspect to the whole thing. She moaned in desperation at the feeling of his cock throbbing against her lower buttock and thigh.

He placed one hand below the base of her spine and slid it slowly up the length of her backbone. It came back down, brushing against the side of her full breast, gliding over the curve that led from her waist to her buttock. She shivered in pleasure.

"You're so beautiful. Your skin is so white, so flawless."

"Des," Claire groaned in rising need. He knelt and tenderly kissed her hip where it curved into her bottom, her buttock, the sensitive place beneath where her butt curved down to become her thigh.

"Over," he ordered in a hard whisper.

She whimpered as she obeyed, bending over and placing her hands on her thighs. She scrunched her eyes shut at the feeling of him pressing back her ass cheeks and lightly tonguing the tender skin at the crevice of her ass. Thick cream surged out of her pussy onto her thighs. Her pussy felt achy, wet and swollen. She experienced such a strong desire at that moment for Des to put his mouth directly on her pussy it made her feel faint.

"Please. Oh please, make me come."

But Des seemed to have other things in mind—primarily torture. She cried out when he masterfully, but far too quickly, lashed at her labia and erect clit with his hot, long tongue.

"More," was all Claire could manage to get out as she panted in excitement. But he had already moved down to her thighs. He kissed, nibbled and licked at the sensitive skin. Her sex quivered in pleasure when he thrust his tongue down into the tops of her thigh highs in a fucking, in and out motion. He praised her inner thighs until she thought she would scream from the elusive erotic movements of his lips and tongue.

"Desi," she moaned.

But his voracious, talented mouth moved down her legs. She gasped as he worshiped the surprisingly sensitive skin at the back of her knees. With one hand he dragged her clothes over her feet while the other supported her firmly at her hip. Just when Claire thought she couldn't take any more of his teasing mouth he started the trip back up again. The feeling of his hot, moist mouth through her stockings was beyond erotic. She groaned in frustration when his mouth came so close to her pussy. Claire was glad for Des' steadying hands at her hips when he ordered her to spread her legs wider.

She shook in anticipation.

He began eating her with a potent mixture of gentleness and greed. A desperate, beseeching wail entered Claire's awareness and it took her a moment to realize that the sound was emanating from her own throat. God, she burned. He held her to him, not allowing her to move or alleviate the pressure. Claire cried out, begging him, and her pleas finally broke through his focused concentration.

"Do you want to come, baby?"

"Yes, oh *please*."

Des glanced up at her. Her lovely face was tight and frantic with need. She was hanging on the precipice of desire, fighting for control. He realized with abrupt amazement that he also was grasping for a measure of control. It must be his chaotic emotions that had him so piqued, so excited, so ready to blow.

He stood and unfastened his jeans. All the while he watched her intently, as though he wanted to assure himself she wasn't going to disappear.

"Stand up, baby."

She stood and removed her bra. Her hands and legs were trembling, weak with desire. She stared at his engorged penis when he shoved his jeans and briefs down his thighs.

"Go and bend over the bed," Des said huskily.

"You aren't…aren't going to take off the rest of your clothes?" she asked, vaguely confused as she walked toward the bed. He just shook his head. She bent over the bed, hyperaware of him behind her. The need for relief felt like it would envelop her, swallow all rational thought.

She cried out at his first powerful stroke into her soaking pussy. He held her tightly to him, both of them gasping for breath, trying to ride the crest of powerful sex energy without crashing too quickly. When Des became aware of Claire's tiny moans of unbearable pressure he reached around her and found her swollen flesh. Claire shouted out when he massaged her with a tight, circular motion.

"Come for me."

He palmed one of her breasts, using it to bring her back against him. Claire's vision temporarily darkened and she was only aware of the immensity of the wave that was about to crash over her. All the while she heard Des' voice next to her ear muttering words of encouragement and, afterward, his erotic, breathless description of what it felt like to be buried in the midst of her orgasm.

After she'd quieted, Des ran his hand longingly over the long, smooth expanse from her neck to where he joined with her. His face clenched in pleasure when he began to fuck her, marveling at the perfection of her slick flesh, the way it squeezed him, milked him. He'd planned to go slower, to savor the moment, but Claire—even so soon after her own release—thrust him into her tight pussy with a surprising strength. He sank his fingers into the rounded plumpness of her bottom and brought her against him even harder, faster. Their flesh slapped together time and again, blending with their gasps and moans of pleasure.

He threw his head back and clamped his eyes shut. Watching himself fuck her so forcefully was sufficient for him to climax, and he wanted to make it last. He shook the sweat from his eyes, tried to concentrate on anything but how gorgeous Claire looked and what he was doing to her beautiful body. It worked for a minute but when he felt Claire start to shudder around him again he gave up all semblance of control. He held her tightly to him, slamming her against his thighs mercilessly. He couldn't recall ever taking a woman so hard but she met every stroke eagerly.

The feelings he'd been having for Claire for the last day had brewed, boiled, reached the point of explosion. His hands moved to her breasts, holding the weight of her upper body and pushing her down and back onto his straining cock. He sank his teeth gently into the soft skin at her neck.

"Tell me, Claire," he ordered hoarsely, his climax looming. "Tell me."

Claire turned her face to him, glimpsed the tension of incipient release on his features and heard the raw emotion in his voice.

"I love you, Desi. I love you."

He shouted out as he came in her endlessly, powerfully, riding out his orgasm by bringing her against him with short, forceful thrusts.

"God, Claire," Des groaned into the hollow of her throat and shoulder. They held each other tightly. Their harsh breathing was the only noise in the otherwise quiet room.

After a few moments Claire became aware that Des was still trying to catch his breath. She realized how much energy he must have been expending in those final moments. She regretfully separated their bodies and took his hand, encouraging him to lie on the bed with her. Des stretched out beside her. His breathing finally calmed as Claire twined her fingers through his silky hair.

Several minutes passed. Neither spoke, both feeling drained and scored. At some point Claire became aware that Des was watching her steadily. When he spoke he did so in such a hushed voice.

"I came inside of you."

"I know."

For almost a minute, their gazes held as messages flew back and forth between them in the silence. Des touched her cheek softly.

"I'm sorry. I'm not angry with you. I've been angry with myself. I shouldn't have taken it out on you."

"I didn't feel like it was angry sex, Des."

"It may have begun that way but that's not how it finished. That's not what I meant though," he said quietly.

When her brow creased in question he sat up slowly. Claire tried to keep her expression neutral as he stood and recovered his clothing from the floor. She silently watched him dress. Her mind raced with uncomfortable questions. Des must have seen the anxiety on her face. He looked regretful as he pulled the sheets and comforter over her naked body.

"It'll be okay, baby. I just need a few minutes to myself and then we'll talk. Maybe you should sleep a little first," he suggested as his eyes skimmed over her bandage and bruises.

The ache in her chest felt like a weight as she watched him walk out the door. The door latch clicked quietly shut after him but to Claire it sounded ominous in its potential meaning.

She grabbed one of her pillows and curled her body around it. Tears gathered in her eyes. Des had been processing a lot of difficult memories and emotional stimuli in the past day and night. Was it at all surprising that he requested some time alone? At least the edge of anger had been absent from his eyes.

She stifled a sob and rose from the bed.

Some things just needed to be worked through in solitude, she reminded herself as she pulled some panties and a t-shirt out of her drawer and donned them. Claire started over to her bathroom, deep in thought. She turned on the tap water and reached down to retrieve a clean towel from the cabinet below.

Her eyes widened in shock when she looked in the bathroom mirror and saw Kevin standing directly behind her.

Chapter Twenty

☙

"Wha—"

Her words were cut off by a gloved hand across her mouth and a hard forearm pressed into her throat. Her eyes watched him in the mirror with growing disbelief and horror.

"Surprised, cousin? Did you think we weren't going to finish the friendly conversation we started the other day?" Kevin asked with a slashing grin.

When she began to struggle and make strangled screaming noises he restrained her by pressing more forcefully on her throat. "Stop it, Claire. I have a gun with me. I would have preferred a more subtle way of killing that son of a bitch Alvarez. Why couldn't he have been the one to trip on that fishing line I stretched across the stairs like I'd intended? But if he comes in this room I'll do it. If you scream he'll come racing in here and I'll shoot him. You wouldn't want that, would you, Claire?"

She stilled. Her eyes, on him, were wide and wary.

"That's what I thought."

For a moment they inspected each other in the mirror. Claire thought he looked ghastly. His cheeks were hollow, his facial muscles pulled tight, his skin slick and waxy. It was like he was wearing a horrific mask. She fought for air, all the while realizing that the other Kevin she knew—the handsome, aloof sophisticate—was the actual façade. This man…this monster, was the true Kevin Preskill.

He liked having Claire like this in his arms, vulnerable and ready to be bent to his will. His fantasies about her had begun when she was a mere teenager. Kevin felt inordinately proud of himself in his restraint when it came to Claire.

Isabelle's precious Claire.

Rage pricked in his gut when he thought of how much Isabelle had loved her. She had loved Claire like a daughter. Isabelle's love should have been reserved only for him. *He* was her child, not Claire.

But no, as much as he worshipped his mother, her love had never been solely for him like it should have been. There had been his father and Claire and that son of a bitch that Isabelle had allowed to fuck her once while Kevin observed from his newly discovered peep hole.

Once he'd discovered his mother was no more than a rutting slut, just like every other woman on the face of the Earth, Kevin had begun to suspect all women were worthless creatures. He'd held out hope for Claire to be worthy of him. But of course he'd found out that she was just as bad.

Worse.

He'd never seen a woman so greedy for a cock as Claire was for Alvarez's. He studied his beautiful cousin in the mirror. The smell of sex that rose off her both enraged and aroused him.

"No Isabelle to save you now, is there, Claire? You shouldn't have worn the bracelet. That was very stupid. You were always such a goddamned pest when you were little, Claire, following me around all the time. I have to admit, though, I'm surprised that you actually found my stash. Didn't I tell you what would happen to you if you didn't stay away from my place?"

Her face froze with fear when she saw his ghastly smile.

"You must have scissors in one of these drawers. Get them right now. If you make a fuss I'm going to shoot Alvarez point-blank the second he walks into the room."

Tears flowed down her face as she slowly opened one of her cabinet drawers. He stopped her with a bruising grip on her wrist when she reached for the scissors. "I don't think so, cousin. Now be a good girl and braid your hair."

He laughed tauntingly while he watched her in the bathroom mirror as she did what he said with shaking fingers.

"Too bad Alvarez just treated you like a piece of meat, huh, Claire? I tried to warn you that you shouldn't trust him. How does it make you feel that he walked away from you after he made you beg for that huge cock, huh?"

Kevin saw her anger. He laughed mockingly but it was more for show than genuine. Why hadn't he ever noticed how much Claire's eyes resembled Isabelle's before? The thought made him uneasy. The erection that had taunted him relentlessly while he listened to Alvarez fuck Claire diminished some at the thought, making him feel temporarily powerless.

She whimpered when he cut off one braid then the other, only partially completed, one. He grinned when he saw the blank look of horror on Claire's face.

He pressed her to him tightly, his arousal returning at the sight of her helpless, pale face and the two reddish-gold braids lying on the bathroom floor. They would be his tokens—along with the bracelet of course. He started to pull her with him out of the bathroom.

"I have the gun right here in my pocket. The minute I hear Alvarez on the stairs I'm going to be ready to shoot him. I've never killed a person that way, you know. I usually like a more…personal touch," he said conversationally as he pushed her out of the bathroom and into her closet.

Claire's legs dragged in noncompliance but Kevin just lifted her body against him and carried her.

"I always reserve bullets for animals. Guns are such a crude way to kill, don't you think? I prefer a more hands-on approach."

Claire began struggling in earnest, fear blinding her just as the darkness did when he closed the closet door. Her mind felt numb at the impact of his casually spoken words but her body struggled, her instinct for survival triggered into high gear.

"Don't worry, Claire, I'm not going to kill you in the closet. I want to be able to have the same eyeful Alvarez was gifted with a few minutes ago when I do that."

Claire became aware of his hand reaching behind some clothes at the back of her closet. Then she heard it, the click and the sliding noise, the sound from her dreams. Kevin shoved her forward into another space. Terror swamped her. Even without seeing Claire immediately knew she was in the space from her nightmares.

"Interesting, isn't it, cousin? I discovered it soon after we moved here. There's another one between my room's closet and the guest bedroom's. Someone who lived here long ago must have shared my proclivities for watching."

Kevin reached around her and opened the door that entered into Isabelle's room.

The image from her dream of the man listening and watching at the rectangular opening came to her oxygen-deprived brain. Of course. The location in her dreams had been *right here*, in this very house.

And what followed... Claire began to struggle again in his hold as she realized what Kevin planned. Every cell in her being seemed to cry out in protest and denial at the looming prospect of her own death.

Kevin reacted to her frantic movements by increasing the pressure on her throat. When he briefly let go Claire inhaled choppily, filling her lungs with air. Too quickly the pressure was back though.

And this time it was far worse.

Her eyes opened wide in panic when she realized that instead of his arm, a rope bit into her neck. He pulled up and back tightly with both hands. She fought with all of her strength, kicking back at him desperately, flailing with her trapped arms and slapping backward at his body with her hands.

After a moment though, her movements slowed and black dots began to appear before her eyes. Just as she began to lose consciousness Kevin decreased the pressure enough for her to take in a tiny gasp of oxygen, keeping the pressure steady with just one hand, up and away from her neck. It wasn't enough. Claire fought for more but Kevin skillfully manipulated the flow of oxygen into her trachea in order to keep her under his control.

"I think you begin to see it, don't you, Claire?" he breathed softly into her ear in a terrible parody of warmth and intimacy. "Isn't it funny? It makes me laugh, it really does. Do you know Alanna Hartfield was my first? Not sexually. I lost my virginity when I was thirteen. Sex was all right but it got boring really quickly. Not enough thrill to get me to the finish," he whispered softly as he allowed her a small burst of precious air before his chokehold on her resumed. He continued to do that as he talked, watching her face for signs of unconsciousness, giving her air just when it appeared that the last struggle had left her.

"That night I watched and listened while Alvarez fucked Alanna. I'd done it before. You know how Mom used to travel all the time, leaving me to my own devices. I found I had a taste for watching. I used to have parties here, and if it looked like one of my friends was going to get lucky I directed them to use one of these four rooms." He laughed at the memory. "Most of them were pitiful, the lies they would come up with, the way they would beg and whine. A lot of the time it didn't even get me that excited. But that night with Alanna Hartfield and Alvarez, that was different. That was really inspiring. You've been with him, Claire, you should know. I could have pounded wood with my hard-on when I listened to you taking every last inch of him just now. Little Claire, you turned out to be such a surprise."

He tightened his hold on the rope around her neck when Claire regained enough strength to fight him with slow, sluggish movements.

"Go ahead, Claire, fight it some. Alanna Hartfield did that night too. Just enough that she was still alive, if barely, when I tied her up in that dumbwaiter and let her drop."

Claire closed her eyes and screamed silently. God help her, she was going to die. For a moment everything went utterly black and she cried out in agony for Des, wishing with all of her being that she could see him one last time, let him know that nothing had been his fault.

Please God, don't let him suffer, she prayed.

She coughed and gasped for air. She groggily became aware of Kevin's hand squeezing her breast, his erection pressing into her ass. "Of course, that night was even more perfect than this. Not because Alanna Hartfield was more desirable than you, cousin. No, if anything, she was pretty pitiful, the pills that she'd taken already took a lot of the fight out of her. But the fact that she'd written that note...how *perfect*. I laughed when I saw it. The reason why that stands out as the most perfect of nights for me was because Alanna's own stupidity in writing that note and the fact that Alvarez had sex with her allowed me to...plunge into the same waters, shall I say, that Alvarez had just dipped into. Yeah, little Alanna liked it rough. And just at the sweet end, well... She wanted to die anyway. Reasonable people would say I was just doing her a favor.

"Now in this day and age of forensic science, and with no suicide note, I'm sorry to have to tell you that I won't be able to pleasure you in that way, Claire."

He maneuvered her over toward the wall, pressing her into it so that he could increase the pressure of his erection against her ass. He shoved his left hand under her t-shirt and grabbed at her breast so roughly that even in her weakened state Claire struggled in pain and revulsion. He continued his dry thrusting, his breathing quickening with excitement.

"That kind of evidence would be an obvious mistake to leave behind but I'd love nothing more than to come inside you, cousin. It would be such a pleasurable way for you to die. Alvarez is such a Boy Scout. In a fit of guilt he'll probably admit that he fucked you and left you. Perhaps his rejection of you sent you over the edge? It's a possibility anyway. And even if it's proved otherwise there's nothing to show that I was here. Alvarez would be a much more likely suspect for murder than me anyway. I mean, it does look pretty incriminating for him to have been involved with two different women who died in the exact same way, doesn't it?"

The fact that she had indeed foreseen her own death made Claire experience a wave of hopelessness. But that realization was nowhere near as terrible as the recognition that history would repeat itself in such a tragic fashion. Des would suffer, just as she'd seen that he would, likely feeling just as responsible for her death as Alanna Hartfield's, whether the police labeled it as suicide or murder. And what if Kevin was right and he became the suspect in her murder?

Her mind screamed silently at the unfairness of it.

But then there was no room even for her anger at the irrevocable quality of fate. There was only darkness.

Chapter Twenty-One

Des sat in the library with his long legs sprawled in front of him as he leaned back on in the armchair by the fireplace. He pressed his forehead to his hands, deep in thought.

He had never told anyone except for the cop about sleeping with Alanna the night that she died. He'd kept it locked inside. His parents and friends had never blamed him. If Alanna's parents knew they never said anything to him and had only been polite and concerned at the funeral.

He'd never had the perspective, until Claire, to really know how much he'd always blamed himself.

The conversations about responsible sexual behavior that Carl Alvarez used to subject him to when he was a teenager came to his mind. His father assured him that it was natural to have sexual desires but that a man had to be responsible for his actions, and that the motivation for having sex couldn't merely involve self-gratification for it to be right. Des used to get so embarrassed during those talks. As a teenager he'd wanted nothing more than to escape those infrequent lectures. After the night of Alanna's death it was as if every single word and expression that his father had uttered during those lectures were indelibly printed in his memory.

I finally understood what he was trying to tell me but it was too late, he thought dismally.

He'd known Alanna since the sixth grade. They'd had some fun times together. When they'd reached adolescence he'd become sexually preoccupied with her. God, when he was seventeen it had been like he was switched into the "go" position constantly. He remembered becoming hard as a rock at the most innocuous stimuli and in the most inconvenient places. It was no excuse for his behavior, but now that he was an adult he realized the incredible strength of his sex drive as a teenager.

They'd lost their virginity together. They'd been sexually active for a year before she'd died. At first Des had been ecstatic with their relationship. After dating her for a while though, he began to realize how moody she was.

She drank too much and picked fights with him. She never thought she was pretty enough. Des remembered the way she used to cry and yell at him if she caught him in the most innocent conversations with another girl. He laughed sadly at the memory. In his naïve sixteen- and seventeen-year-old brain Alanna Hartfield was the most beautiful girl on the face of the earth.

He'd never been able to convince her of that though.

Des was beginning to realize that there hadn't been any shortcomings in his feelings for her. Claire was more than likely correct when she said that Alanna must have been sick in a way that tragically went unnoticed and untreated. Alanna had been unable to hear him when he told her how beautiful she was, how much she meant to him.

She'd come to the party at the Preskills' that night with the pills in her purse. In hindsight Des recognized that it was possible she could have taken them whether he'd messed up and slept with her or not.

But the fact that she *hanged* herself. He winced, the impact of the memory still strong. God, why would she have done it? It somehow seemed so out of her character, so aggressive and angry. Part of him still couldn't believe that she had done something so deliberately violent.

And what the police officer had said about it being obvious that she'd been involved in rough sex that night. God. The memory still had the power to make him cringe with regret.

The train of his thoughts reminded him of what Claire had said Kevin had insinuated about his involvement with Alanna the night she'd died.

How could Kevin have known about his culpability? No one else he'd known had ever suggested such a thing. The thought nagged at him, bothered him deeply. He gradually realized it was behind his increasing concern for Claire's safety.

Kevin would have had to be somewhere nearby, even in the room with Alanna and him, to have known what had taken place that night.

You need to see through the black veil! I can't reach you.

Des sat up straighter in the chair at the abrupt memory of Claire's voice as she awoke from her dream. *The black veil.* It was a good description of the thick, impenetrable guilt he'd experienced for almost two decades in regard to Alanna's death.

He became instantly alert. His gaze swept the room warily. He could have sworn that Claire had just touched him, just as she had done before in their dreams. But there was no sign of her.

Suddenly it was her absence that seemed meaningful.

Claire needed him. *Now.* He could almost hear her calling out to him in his mind. Although he would have thought nothing in the world could have made him hesitate in running up the stairs toward Claire, the cold touch on his neck of icy fingertips did stop him, if only briefly.

When he turned to look behind him his eyes widened in shock.

A few moments later he was climbing the stairs with all the rapidity and stealth he could muster. He entered Claire's room directly, already knowing that he wouldn't find her there.

Des didn't allow himself to think when he silently entered Isabelle's room. If he'd thought about what Kevin Preskill was doing to Claire he might have growled out in animalistic rage and blown his one chance to help her. Instead he distanced himself from everything but what he knew he had to do. He was a silent-flying arrow and Kevin was his only target.

It happened quickly, done in the moment it takes to breathe in and breathe out. He knew it was Claire's breath he was fighting for, and no span of time was too brief to be considered inconsequential.

He came behind Kevin silently, took his head in both his hands and snapped it quickly and with extreme force against the wood paneling of the wall.

His muscles surged and pulsed with blood and adrenaline, ready for Kevin to resist. But following the sickening thwack of sound when his skull hit the wall Kevin's limbs lost their rigidity. He crumpled to the floor.

Des caught him only to rip the rope that he still gripped out of his hand, instantly relieving the pressure on Claire's trachea. He shoved Kevin's body aside roughly, not sparing him another thought. He reached out to catch Claire gently as she began to fall.

A low moan issued from his mouth when he noted her death-like pallor, her utter stillness. She wasn't breathing. He lowered her to the floor and came down beside her. She had a pulse, thready and barely perceptible but still there.

Des pinched her nose, tilted her head back carefully and gave her his own breath, once, then twice. He watched her face intently.

"Come back to me, baby." He issued the order in hard, relentless voice. "You're not allowed to leave, Claire. Do you hear me? I want you to breathe!"

He bent to give her his breath again. She gagged and coughed. Her chin came down as if to protect her throat. She turned her head and breathed raggedly. Des was acutely aware of the first small rise and fall of her chest...then the miraculous second and third. Thank God. She was breathing now on her own but she still was partially unconscious. He heard sirens. He considered the form of her trauma and thought he could risk moving her if he was careful. As he reached the downstairs hallway with his precious cargo in his arms Claire suddenly moved her head slightly and her eyelids fluttered.

"It's okay, honey. Everything's going to be all right," he murmured reassuringly.

Claire moved her face into his chest and took a long, deep breath.

He opened the front door to two emergency medical technicians. He saw two police cars pulling up on the street in front of Claire's house. The EMTs asked him several brisk questions as they took Claire from him, placing her on a stretcher on the porch and examining her.

He waited until the first two police officers came up the front steps to explain, flashing his badge as he did so.

"He's upstairs. He was unconscious when I left him. He has a gun." He guided them into the house with his own gun drawn.

A loud popping noise rent the air. The newel post at the end of the grand staircase directly in front of him flew up. He shoved the police officer in front of him down for cover beneath the stairs and dove toward the wall. Another shot rang out and one of the cops cursed as blood splattered on his shoulder. A tall, beefy officer who stood farther down the hallway aimed his gun up the stairs and fired off several shots, covering his fellow officers in their momentary vulnerability. Des was exposed against the wall but the angle would have been too awkward for Kevin to get off a good shot.

But apparently Des' death was the sole purpose for Kevin's suicidal behavior. Kevin stood abruptly from his protected position in order to lean over the railing and shoot at Des where he lay next to the wall. Des saw and rolled quickly away into more exposed space. He took careful aim and squeezed. He saw Kevin staring down at him, the side of his face dripping blood.

Des had a weird flashback to the expression in Kevin Preskill's eyes in the moments after Des had hit him in the locker room when they were teenagers. The same expression of pure hate was on Kevin's face when he slumped, as if in slow motion, over the banister at the top of the stairs.

Chapter Twenty-Two

ೞ

Claire cuddled comfortably on what she'd already decided was her favorite loveseat in the great room of Des' loft. She could hear the reassuring rumble of Des' deep voice as he showed her parents out.

Learning about what had happened to Claire, and at the hands of their own nephew, had been hard on both her parents but she thought it had struck Randall Allen the hardest. Claire had seen the pallor under his tan, the look of shock when Des and Claire both had told them most of the details of what had happened. She sadly recalled what her father had said just minutes ago.

"I just can't help but going back to the fact that we should have known about Kevin. I should have *known*. How can I have missed such a glaring lack of basic humanity in my own nephew?"

Claire inhaled and slowly let out her breath. It was the same thought she'd had again and again for the last several days as she'd endured the questions during the police investigation, the frightening memories and then yesterday the interview with Special Agent Dawson while Des stood sentinel next to her in the hospital room.

"Dad, please don't. I'm the one who is trained in human behavior and I didn't recognize anything until it was too late. Kevin thrived on creating a charming public image. There was nothing wrong with our basic sensors. We all knew that we didn't care for him. But that's one of the consequences of not being a psychopath yourself. You just don't make the assumption that other people would act without even an inkling of conscience. We didn't recognize what he was because we're not like him."

Claire didn't add that there were a few times when she was with Kevin that night that she wondered if he was even human. Something so elementally human seemed missing in him, making him feel frighteningly alien.

"But what about Isabelle? Surely she must have suspected something?"

Claire sighed. She and Des had talked over this topic as much as her sore throat would allow for the past several days. Claire hadn't felt comfortable telling her parents about the paranormal events that had occurred in her Hyde Park home leading up to Kevin's attack. She knew that they would try to be sympathetic and understanding but the world of the supernatural was just not where they functioned.

Des and she had wondered at one point whether two separate spirits caused the conflicting messages Claire had received in the house. Claire now knew that was true but only in a manner of speaking. Two sides of Isabelle's spirit had haunted Claire—one the wrathful mother who would protect her child at all costs and the other the aunt and responsible human being who knew that Kevin Preskill needed to be stopped. Isabelle must have been only dimly aware of her conflict during life, but with death it began to batter at her spirit.

Des had been furious at the possibility that Isabelle had suspected the dangerousness of her son. But Claire was only accepting. She had been with peace with Isabelle since their strange dream conversation the day that Kevin attacked her.

But Claire didn't think it was necessary to lay that all on her father.

"Dad, Isabelle loved Kevin as all mothers love their children. I don't know how much Kevin was actually capable of feeling love but whatever he could feel he reserved for his mother. Of course she never suspected something so heinous about her son."

Her father sighed. "At least Isabelle wasn't here to see it. She would never have recovered from that if she were still alive."

Des' phone rang and Claire started to get up to answer it. Des waved her back after he'd said a final goodbye to Randall and Cecilia Allen. She heard him speaking in a low voice in the kitchen.

"What is it?" she asked quietly when he entered the great room. Their emotional connection had grown so deep she knew immediately something was bothering him.

"That was Dawson. They found the box buried beneath the oak tree in the backyard, just like you'd said they would. They found that woman's—Clarisse Myers—earrings inside it. He must have put them in there some time when he was staying at the house with you."

"Oh," Claire murmured huskily. Her ears seemed to roar with sound but she tried to keep her face impassive for Des' sake. After she'd awakened in the hospital she'd known what they would find when they dug beneath the oak tree in the backyard. Still, hearing Des say it had struck her more powerfully than she'd expected.

She swallowed painfully, her throat still sore from Kevin's attack. "And...and the others?"

She felt the tension emanating from Des. Still, he kept eye contact with her as he spoke. "There were nine other pieces of jewelry buried under the oak tree."

"*Nine?*" Claire asked, panicked. "But I thought the Morningside Murderer..."

Des just shook his head. "It happens sometimes, baby. We make the connections that we can but a few murders occasionally miss our radar. Locals attribute the cause to something else and we don't get called in. Or he might have killed in other countries, ones not linked to our database. Dawson is going to have his hands full trying to figure it out."

Her hand went automatically to her wrist to touch the bracelet Ellen Alvarez had made, the bracelet that Alanna Hartfield had been wearing on the night that she died.

Kevin's first token.

No wonder he had been so filled with anger when he saw it on her wrist. Isabelle must have located Kevin's gruesome collection at some point and taken the bracelet. Claire's mind resisted the clear evidence before her but her denial couldn't persist for long. From the moment that Isabelle had wrapped the bracelet around Claire's wrist she had been setting her only son on the path of his inevitable downfall. *That* was why Isabelle had been asking for forgiveness in the dream. She had chosen Claire to be the instrument of Kevin's destruction because she hadn't been strong enough herself to see it through herself.

When she looked up Des was staring at her hand on the bracelet. She knew they were thinking the same thing.

He came and sat down next to her. For a moment neither of them spoke but Des took her hand in his, caressed it softly.

"This is so hard for my parents," Claire said hoarsely.

Des had to force his gaze to stay steady on her when his eyes moved to her neck, and then to her short hair. She still wore gauze bandaging around her throat from Kevin's attempt to strangle her with the rope. Purplish bruises could be seen around the edges of the white dressing. The hairdresser who normally cut her hair had come to his loft last evening and stylishly cut the hair that remained when Kevin had hacked off her braids. Every time Des saw it, his rage and fear surged anew. He felt so helpless at the sight of her vulnerability. He thought she looked more luminescent and indescribably beautiful than he'd ever seen her.

Claire saw the flash of pain in Des' soulful light eyes when his gaze dropped to her neck. Kevin had left so many types of wounds, only a few of which were the physical kind. Des had been so attentive to her since she'd regained full consciousness in the hospital. She would have had to be utterly blind not to see the caring in his eyes. But she was worried about the inherent sadness when he looked at her, the careful, cautious way he was treating her. She was starting to feel like he felt sorry for her, an emotion that she wouldn't accept from him.

"Stop looking at me that way."

He looked surprised at the edge in her voice. His gaze leapt to hers. "What do you mean?"

"Stop looking at me like I'm a leper or something. Don't pity me. I'm the same person that I was before, just a little banged up that's all."

"I don't know what you mean," he said coolly.

Claire sat up straighter as anger flashed through her. "Oh you don't? What about last night when I was in the bath and you came in to make sure I was okay? You looked at me while I was naked and you looked like you were going to be sick. You couldn't have gotten out of there fast enough."

"Christ, Claire. You know very well the sight of you doesn't make me sick. I love everything about you," he said forcefully.

"You do?" Claire managed to ask after a moment.

"Of course I do. What did you think?"

Claire gave a little shrug at the interesting turn of the conversation. "Oh, I knew you loved me. I was just wondering how long it would take you to tell me."

He raked his fingers through his hair. "I just didn't think you'd be interested in sex right now, that's all."

"Well, you were wrong if that's what you thought. How are we supposed to get through this if not for our love for each other?"

Des sat back on the couch, frustration still on his face. He was clearly at a loss. "Claire, what do want from me, honey? Whatever it is, you know I'll try."

Claire reached out and touched his face gently. She caressed the creases of tension around his mouth and then pressed her thumb into his warm lower lip. She'd felt deprived of the masculine heat that she had always been able to stir in him in the past. It was still there but Des was running from it, afraid.

"I don't want you to see Kevin's potential victim when you look at me. I want you to acknowledge the rest of me. The part that needs you to make love to me."

Des looked uncomfortable. "Surely you don't want to make love so soon after…" He paused, looking away.

"Don't stop. Say it, Des."

"After what he did to you!" Des shouted abruptly. "I know you say you can't remember it that well. For that, I'm only grateful. But I saw what he was doing, the way he was pawing you…pushing himself against you and trying to kill you at the same time," Des grated out slowly, as though the words themselves were volatile material that needed to be handled with caution.

As if the words had the power to explode in both of their faces.

She waited, filled with compassion. His breathing escalated, his eyes looked haunted by the memory. Des' eyes flickered to her face and she felt his pain and conflict as if it were her own.

"Claire, I don't find you pitiful or disgusting. You're more beautiful to me than you ever were. It just reminds me of what he did to you. It makes me so sick that I couldn't have stopped him sooner," Des finally said. He looked so lost. Claire moved closer to him, enclosed him in her arms. He continued in a voice gravelly with emotion.

"Yesterday, when you were in the bath, my first reaction to seeing you naked was how much I wanted you. And then I saw the bruises on your breasts and it made me sick. But not in the way you're thinking. It made me disgusted with myself that I had been thinking about making love to you when the evidence of what Kevin had done to you was still fresh on your body."

"Desi," she murmured feelingly. "What you and I do together can't be compared to what Kevin did to me that night. His idea of sex is an aberration, a sickness. Your desire for me is clean and beautiful."

"You're so fearless, you know that?" he finally said gruffly.

Claire shook her head. "I'm selfish when it comes to our relationship, that's all."

He reached for her and they kissed for the first time since she'd been attacked. Claire melted into him, cherishing the slight rasp of his rougher texture on her softer skin. Their mouths clung together languidly, patiently, fully satisfied with the taste and sensation of the other. They held each other's faces, their entire beings focused on the sensual movements of their tongues and mouths. It was as if they were the creators of a new language and every caress of the lips, every slide of the tongue and every new foray into the warmth of the other's mouth held infinite numbers of revealed secrets and new meaning.

It was the most gratifying and erotic kiss that Claire had ever experienced.

"Claire, I never got to tell you about why I left you that night, after we made love," he murmured next to her lips awhile later. "I don't know if I made you understand that I was sorry for being so angry with you. God, I've thought so many times about how much I would have regretted not telling you that I wasn't really angry with you if Kevin had..."

Claire nodded. "I understood that you just needed time to think, to process everything. You'd kept that night with Alanna so locked away. It was such a private wound. I'm sorry for having pushed you to reveal it against your will."

"No, you were right. I don't think you could have forced yourself on me in the way that I accused you of doing. I think part of me wanted, no, *needed* for you to know what I had done that night."

"You wanted to forgive yourself. You're not a cruel man. Maybe a part of you was sick of punishing yourself after all these years. Letting me in was your way of beginning to accept the past and move on. Besides, if you hadn't finally forgiven yourself I don't think you would have ever had the intuition, unformed as it was, to know what was really happening in that house."

"Maybe you're right."

Claire was thoughtful too as she considered him. "Des? You never did explain about that. How did you know how to get to me through that secret room?"

He lowered his head and sighed. "I was in the library, thinking about Alanna Hartfield and the night she'd died. It suddenly occurred to me that Kevin was the only person who had ever insinuated that I had played a part in her death by sleeping with her and still refusing to get back together with her. Of course, I had personally blamed myself for it but no one else did. It made me realize that Kevin must have somehow known about what happened with Alanna that night, and the only way he could have was by spying on us. And if had spied on us having sex, the chances are that he had known about Alanna's actions afterward, when she was alone.

"I'd been reliving in my mind how awful it was finding her, thinking about how out of character it was for Alanna to have killed herself in such a bizarre way. Just as I was starting to add it all up I got the impression that you were there with me. I couldn't see you or hear you but I felt like my thoughts had been touched by you. The only thing that I knew with surety was that you needed me and that you were in danger. I felt desperate and started to run like crazy out of the library."

Claire nodded, remembering how her thoughts were of Des before she'd lost consciousness. "But you called the police first. And during the investigation you said that you saw the closet door open in my room and that was how you figured out about the hidden entrance. But I remember Kevin closing the closet door after us, because I felt afraid in the darkness, not knowing what he was planning to do with me in there."

"What I didn't tell you was that I had a little help about the details of what was happening upstairs. Isabelle told me."

Claire's eyes widened in surprise. "*Isabelle?*"

He nodded. "Or maybe I shouldn't say she told me exactly. But just as I was about to run upstairs, and likely get myself shot and you killed by trying to enter the room in the way Kevin would have expected me to come, I felt something behind me in the library and I hesitated. I saw her, Claire. She was standing over by the fireplace, just as real as she ever was. When our eyes met it was like...the information just transferred from her into me. It was really weird but I didn't doubt it for a second."

"I'm glad you didn't," Claire murmured, still amazed. For a moment neither one of them spoke, lost in their private thoughts.

"She was so torn about Kevin, so sad."

Des' expression was less sympathetic. "I'm glad that she warned me, Claire. But it all came a little too last minute for my taste. You could have easily been dead by the time I got there, and then what would all of Isabelle's lame warnings have accomplished? And she was way too late for Clarisse Myers."

Claire shook her head. Des had a right to be angry. They would have to agree to disagree on their feelings about Isabelle. For a few minutes they sat quietly, taking reassurance from the nearness and warmth of the other. Slowly Claire became aware of the tension that was rising between them, a tension that had nothing to do with their disagreement about Isabelle Preskill.

"Claire? Let's go to bed," he said gruffly.

She nodded. She rose and took his hand, leading him back to the bedroom. When they eventually stood by the bed neither spoke nor moved for a moment. Her eyes dropped to his hands when he began unbuttoning and removing his own clothing. His eyes were a banked fire as he watched her.

"Take off your clothes."

She nodded, hooking her fingers into her sweatpants and underwear and pulling them down her legs. She hesitated before she removed her t-shirt. The memory of what Des said about the sight of the bruises on her breasts made her uncertain. Maybe it would be better to hide the sight that caused him so much discomfort?

His mouth pulled in regret when he saw Claire's self-consciousness. He held her gaze as he pulled the t-shirt off her himself. His eyes lowered but he didn't flinch when he saw the fading bruises on her right shoulder and hip. Nor did he falter when he visually caressed her breasts.

"*Desi*," she whispered hoarsely.

They made love tenderly, deliberately, practicing with their bodies what they had accomplished with their earlier kiss. They created the bonfire of passion slowly, controlling the flames, knowing that they would be consumed by them soon enough. They stoked the fire into brilliance time and time again, only to let it calm itself temporarily before they fueled it once again into an eager white-hot flame. When they finally gave themselves to the conflagration that enveloped them they were left cleansed and transformed by the power of their feelings.

Neither of them spoke for a while afterward, clinging to each other like the survivors of a great storm. Claire may have dropped into sleep, she couldn't be sure. When she came fully to awareness Des was nuzzling her ear and murmuring in the quiet, sexy way that she had come to love.

"You're mine, Claire. I'm never gonna let you go."

Claire smiled at his familiar words. "Heaven forbid I should argue with you. You're so fond of telling me what to do that you wouldn't even let me die."

He examined her in the growing darkness of the room. "You actually remember that?"

"No. I don't remember it, not exactly. I just *know* it. I know that you ordered me to come back to you at some point. And I did."

"I was wondering why I was so insistent with you when we made love, so controlling, so bent on forcing you to my will. It's like some part of me knew that I was preparing you..." He paused with his eyes far away in thought.

"Des?"

"Yeah, baby?"

"I hope that doesn't mean that the paddle is going to gather dust in the closet."

"I don't know. How do you know I really like that kind of sex outside of all the paranormal circumstances?"

Claire grinned and kissed him soundly. "Duh. I'm a psychic, remember."

He responded by devouring every last giggle that she gave him.

"There's one thing that I can't understand," Des said after a long pause. "Why would Isabelle have tried to keep us apart? Why did she say that we weren't for each other? She couldn't have been any more off-base than with that prediction."

"She didn't say it, Des. Not really."

"What? I *know* what she said, Claire. I was the one she said it to."

"I don't know if Isabelle could actually see all the details of what was to come in the future. But I think that somehow she understood that when you and I came together it would signal Kevin's end. I can't remember everything Isabelle and I talked about in my dream but I do feel that she knew we were together and that she was happy for me. For us."

"But she said—"

"No, Des. You misunderstood. She was saying that I wasn't for you *then*. 'She isn't for you now'. That's what she said, Des. Not that I would *never* be for you."

Des' brow wrinkled in confusion but then he comprehended what Claire meant. Isabelle's same words with a slightly different emphasis had an entirely different meaning.

She isn't for you now. *I know it seems odd, Desi — that I would say it with such confidence — but you'll have to take my word on it.*

Des made a scoffing noise. "She just said that for her own purposes. I have a feeling that you were as much for me when Isabelle said that as you will be when I'm eighty-two."

She didn't respond, waiting for his frustration with Isabelle to calm. Eventually the tension did leave his body. When he spoke again his voice sounded amused, even playful. "As far as predictions from our relatives go I'll bet on *Abuela* Anita over Isabelle anytime."

Claire leaned back so that she could see his face. Her heart warmed when she saw his mischievous grin. "What predictions has *Abuela* Anita been making that you like so much?"

"She and the ghost relatives have already picked out our son's name," he mumbled, clearly embarrassed.

"*What?*" Claire asked in amazement.

Des nodded. "It's true. You wouldn't believe what it has cost me with Angie for her to keep the secret. I've had to bribe her with everything from promising to never be anything but sweet and polite to her boyfriends to swearing that I would feed her cats every single time she leaves town for the next five years. Now that I've told you, though, all bets are off. She can't keep blackmailing me anymore by saying she's going to tell you." Laughter rumbled out of his chest.

"What are you *talking* about?"

"*Abuela* Anita predicted you and I would be together when I visited Columbia as a young man. She even knew your last name."

Claire shook her head in amazement, remembering the way Angie had looked at Claire and laughed while she spoke to Anita, obviously highly entertained by the conversation.

Des pulled her closer in his arms. His voice became low and husky. "*Abuela* Anita said that everyone but *Tia* Maria had agreed on the name. *Tia* Maria is under the firm belief that her great-grand-nephew will actually be a great-grand-niece, and so obviously was putting up a fuss about the name."

Claire laughed. "Well? Don't leave me in suspense."

He brushed his finger over her cheek. "It's just *Abuela* Anita's silliness. You don't have to take it seriously if you don't want to."

"I'll decide if I take it seriously or not, thanks. What's the name the ancestors picked?" she demanded.

"Do you really want to know?" he asked quietly, all traces of laughter gone from his handsome mouth.

"Of course! Are you crazy? Look how perfectly they named you, Desi."

"Vicente. Vicente Allen Alvarez." He watched as she mouthed the name silently. "Too Hispanic for you?" he asked cautiously.

"If you ever have a son…" There was a dreamy quality to her dark eyes when she trailed off. "He should definitely be Vicente. No doubt about it."

Des gave a slow smile that caused a thrilling fluttering sensation in her lower belly. He nuzzled her nose with his own. "The ghost ancestors are never wrong, you know."

The End

Also by Beth Kery
୭

eBooks:
Come To Me Freely
Exorcising Sean's Ghost
Fire Angel
Fleet Blade
Flirting in Traffic
Groom's Gift
Subtle Lovers: Subtle Voyage
Subtle Lovers 1: Subtle Magic
Subtle Lovers 2: Subtle Touch
Subtle Lovers 3: Subtle Release
Subtle Lovers 4: Subtle Destiny
Through Her Eyes

Print Books:
Come To Me Freely
Exorcising Sean's Ghost
Fleet Blade
Naughty Nuptials *(anthology)*
Subtle Lovers 1: Subtle Magic
Subtle Lovers 2: Subtle Touch
Subtle Lovers 3: Subtle Release
Subtle Lovers 4: Subtle Destiny

About the Author

ಐ

Beth Kery grew up in a huge house built in the nineteenth century, where she cultivated her love of mystery and the paranormal. When she wasn't hunting for secret passageways and ghosts with her friends, she was gobbling up fantasy novels and any other books she could get her hands on. As an adult she learned about the vast mysteries of romance and sex and started to investigate that phenomenon thoroughly, as well. Her writing today reflects her passion for all of the above.

ಐ

The author welcomes comments from readers. You can find her website and email address on her author bio page at www.ellorascave.com.

Tell Us What You Think

We appreciate hearing reader opinions about our books. You can email us at Comments@EllorasCave.com.

Why an electronic book?

We live in the Information Age—an exciting time in the history of human civilization, in which technology rules supreme and continues to progress in leaps and bounds every minute of every day. For a multitude of reasons, more and more avid literary fans are opting to purchase e-books instead of paper books. The question from those not yet initiated into the world of electronic reading is simply: *Why?*

1. ***Price.*** An electronic title at Ellora's Cave Publishing runs anywhere from 40% to 75% less than the cover price of the exact same title in paperback format. Why? Basic mathematics and cost. It is less expensive to publish an e-book (no paper and printing, no warehousing and shipping) than it is to publish a paperback, so the savings are passed along to the consumer.

2. ***Space.*** Running out of room in your house for your books? That is one worry you will never have with electronic books. For a low one-time cost, you can purchase a handheld device specifically designed for e-reading. Many e-readers have large, convenient screens for viewing. Better yet, hundreds of titles can be stored within your new library—on a single microchip. There are a variety of e-readers from different manufacturers. You can also read e-books on your PC or laptop computer. (Please note that Ellora's Cave does not endorse any specific brands.

You can check our website at www.ellorascave.com for information we make available to new consumers.)
3. *Mobility.* Because your new e-library consists of only a microchip within a small, easily transportable e-reader, your entire cache of books can be taken with you wherever you go.
4. *Personal Viewing Preferences.* Are the words you are currently reading too small? Too large? Too... ANNOYING? Paperback books cannot be modified according to personal preferences, but e-books can.
5. *Instant Gratification.* Is it the middle of the night and all the bookstores near you are closed? Are you tired of waiting days, sometimes weeks, for bookstores to ship the novels you bought? Ellora's Cave Publishing sells instantaneous downloads twenty-four hours a day, seven days a week, every day of the year. Our webstore is never closed. Our e-book delivery system is 100% automated, meaning your order is filled as soon as you pay for it.

Those are a few of the top reasons why electronic books are replacing paperbacks for many avid readers.

As always, Ellora's Cave welcomes your questions and comments. We invite you to email us at Comments@ellorascave.com or write to us directly at Ellora's Cave Publishing Inc., 1056 Home Avenue, Akron, OH 44310-3502.

MAKE EACH DAY MORE EXCITING WITH OUR

Ellora's Cavemen Calendar

✝ www.EllorasCave.com ✝

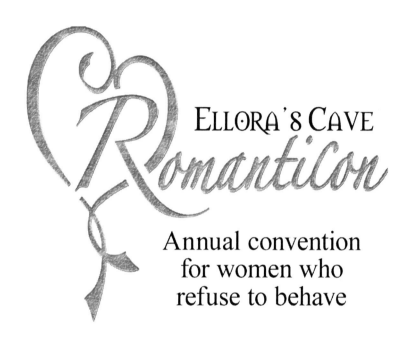

Discover for yourself why readers can't get enough of the multiple award-winning publisher Ellora's Cave.

Whether you prefer e-books or paperbacks, be sure to visit EC on the web at www.ellorascave.com for an erotic reading experience that will leave you breathless.

CPSIA information can be obtained at www.ICGtesting.com
Printed in the USA
LVOW121948051012

301688LV00001B/83/P